A TASTE

of forever

THE SAINTS OF SERENITY FALLS

USA TODAY BESTSELLING AUTHOR

LILY WILDHART

To those struggling just to get out of bed every day.

I see you.

I am you.

We got this

CONTENT WARNING

This book is a dark, college, why choose romance with some aspects of bullying.

It contains scenes and references of drug use (off page), abuse/ sexual assault to a minor and sexual assault that some readers may find triggering, along with graphic sex scenes, cursing and violence.

ONE

BRIAR

I feel lost.

When I look at the girl I am right now, my reflection in the window of the cop car as I'm taken through the city, my wrists cuffed, I don't recognize her.

Old me, the girl who got off the plane from California… yeah, she'd be horrified at the person I've become. It's not like I haven't been around bad shit before. Hell, I hate myself for some of the things I've done, that I've experienced, but this—killing Crawford, covering it up, hiding from it, hoping someone else would take the fall.

This isn't who I am at all.

The problem is that the guys tried to protect me, and if I

confess, I take them down with me.

My soul screams in the torn ribbons of its existence for me to tell the truth. To stop hiding. From myself as well as everyone else. It yearns for healing, for the salvation that comes with being held accountable.

But I can't do that to them.

I should probably have already been in prison. The things I've done... to survive, and sometimes not—well, there's a reason I'm more than just broken. Shattered? Maybe.

This is the second time in my life other people have cleared up a mess of my making and I've stood by and done nothing. Said nothing.

Except this time, karma is coming for me.

I've never really believed in much in the way of deities, but karma? That bitch I believe in. I've seen it come to pass too often to ignore it. Even if it doesn't get everyone who deserves it, most people come to pay their penance, and it feels like my time is up.

I know that wallowing isn't going to get me anywhere, that it's very likely the guys are already trying to figure out how to fix this, because that's what they do. For me at least.

I can't help but feel like this might be it for me.

Defeated.

That's how I feel.

Lost and defeated.

I've never been this girl, but then, there isn't much about

me now that resembles anything close to the me I thought I was.

Resilient, that's who I was. Even though I'd rather have been whole, safe, lived at ease; that isn't what life gave me. So I was resilient. I was strong. A survivor.

Me from before summer would kick my fucking ass right now. Scream at me to stop wallowing in the potential of maybe, to fight, just like I always have, but I don't know if I have much more left.

All I've done my entire life is fight and it isn't getting me anywhere. Well, anywhere except the back of this cop car.

Fuck knows how this is going to go.

The lights of the city are beautiful, but I know the truth of this place. Its beauty hides the truth of all the despair beneath the surface.

I guess I'm more like this city than I ever realized.

We pass the buildings slower than I'd have thought. There's a lot of traffic considering the time, but I guess that's New York for you. I've obviously gotten too used to Serenity Falls already.

I slump back against the hard plastic seat, closing my eyes and leaning my head against the headrest, trying to shut out the overwhelming silence in the car.

Only when the car stops and the officers start speaking do I open my eyes. The door beside me opens and I'm pulled out of the car and into the building.

As they drag me through the hall and start talking to the officer behind the booking desk, it sinks in where I am and why.

I need to pull myself the fuck together.

I've learned quite a bit about this process since the last time I was in here. Cole drilled it into me to keep my mouth shut—apparently him being a law student is a good thing when I keep having run-ins with the police.

Who would've thought?

So I do what he told me. I'm compliant enough, but I keep my mouth shut other than to answer my name and repeat one word.

Lawyer.

The detective who questioned me the first time I was here—Thompson, I think his name is—arrives, a grin on his round, red face.

"Hello again, Miss Moore. I told you I'd see you soon."

"What's wrong, Briar?" Iris asks, her big eyes gazing up at me from where she's sitting at the counter waiting for her breakfast.

I wrap an arm around my gurgling stomach and fake a smile. "Nothing, Princess Pea, everything is bright and sunshiny."

"But I heard you crying." Her statement is so matter of fact that I nearly start crying again, but I refuse to put that sort of burden on her. So I swallow around the lump in my throat, ignore the aches of my body, and continue to smile. The pretending makes my throat feel like it's going to close up, but it has nothing

on the shame that coats me like a layer of oil that's impossible to wash off. Even in the hottest of showers, I don't think I'd be able to fully scrub myself clean, let alone the icy cold one I tried in this morning.

I blink, pulling myself from my thoughts to find her still waiting for me to answer. "Maybe you were having a nightmare. No crying here."

The gaze she aims at me is full of suspicion, so I smile even wider before turning my attention back to pouring her cereal. I sniff-check the last of the milk before adding it to her bowl.

"You wanna share?" Her question is so naïve and innocent that my heart hurts.

"No, Princess. You eat up. You need to get big and strong."

"Big and strong, just like you." Her smile is wide, her gappy teeth on display, and some of the ache in my body lifts. I wish I was even half as big and strong as she thinks I am.

"Yeah, Bug. Just like me. Now eat up." I ruffle her hair and hand her a spoon, and she stays on the counter, counting out the mini marshmallows in her cereal, clapping with glee every time she gets a rainbow—because magic lives at the end of a rainbow.

I stare up at the dingy, browning ceiling and hope to God she never has to live through what I do. My entire body hurts from trying to fight him last night. Sometimes I wonder why I bother. Fighting never gets me anywhere, he just hurts me more for not giving in to him straight away, but there isn't one bone in my body that would ever not *fight him.*

Just thinking about the mottled bruises on my flesh that are hidden beneath my clothes makes me want to cry again. I so rarely cry, but he's been here every night this weekend. Every single night he's stumbled into my room once my mom has passed out.

He tells me I should be grateful that the power is on, that we have heat and food. That he provides those things. That I should thank him rather than fighting him and making him work even harder for what he wants in return.

I tried to tell my mom once, but she just laughed in my face and called me a liar.

If my own mother doesn't believe me, who the hell is going to?

As long as I can keep him from Iris, I'll endure what I have to. Because that's what he threatens each time he finally pins me so that I don't scream or fight anymore. It's enough to scare me into submission and I hate it, but I won't ever allow this to happen to her. I'll be old enough to get us out of here soon, and the minute that happens, we're running.

I make a promise to myself that once we're free, no man will ever take advantage of me ever again. Even if I have to kill them to survive.

I will endure this once, but never again.

"Is it time for school?" Iris asks sweetly, tapping my shoulder. I check the clock and grimace.

"Yes, Bug, it is. Come on, let's get going." I lift her from the counter, my ribs screaming, but I don't make a sound. She runs to grab her bag and I double check that she has everything she needs for the day before we leave the house.

She takes my hand and begs me to skip with her, so I do, because keeping the smile on her face is my every reason for being.

I jolt upward. It takes a second for me to realize that I'm still in the interrogation room. I swipe the drool from the corner of my mouth as my nightmare replays in my mind.

Maybe if I'd known that morning was our last one together, I'd have smiled a little wider. Laughed a little louder. Or just run the hell away with her right then.

But I didn't, and nothing in my life will ever be a bigger regret than that.

Including the events that led me to sitting in this chair. Because I did what I swore I would always do. I didn't let him win.

It seems fitting that the worst morning of my life should haunt me when I'm being held under suspicion of the second worst moment of my life: killing Crawford.

My sperm donor.

I still haven't managed to process that one fully, or work out why he was trying to kill me, but now I need to work out how the fuck I'm going to convince the police of my innocence. Not that I hold much hope. Why would they believe someone like me?

Travis repeated what Cole had already said and told me not to answer any questions until someone arrived for me, which is what I've done, beyond giving them my name. Doesn't seem to have won me any points though.

I've lost count of how long I've been in here. Partially because I don't have my belongings, partially because there's no clock, but it has to have been a while if I actually fell asleep waiting for them.

The boning of my dress is digging into me and I'm tempted to discard it like I did my shoes when I was thrown in here.

This gown is not exactly warm or comfortable, and the heat is definitely shut off in this room. I swear I can see my breath as I rub the chilled skin of my arms.

"Hello?" I call out, and I'm met with nothing but silence.

I guess if this is going to be what my future holds, I should probably get used to it.

TWO

TRAVIS

"What do you mean, you won't do anything?" My raised voice echoes in the hall as I try to keep a lid on my shit.

Chase just smiles at me in that smug, arrogant bastard way he has. "I said what I said. She didn't want to help the family; she caused issues. If she's gotten herself into a mess, she can clean it up. Thomas already helped her once. I won't cover the bill again. Maybe then she'll reconsider her position in this family."

Without another word, he turns and walks away, practically with a skip in his step, like he orchestrated this.

It's only now, in this moment, that I consider that to be

a possibility. It wouldn't be the first time my father has had information on me that no one else had, that he couldn't possibly have had… yet, he didn't even question *why* Briar was arrested.

Son of a bitch.

He knows.

I don't know how he knows, but he must. It's too clean and he's not worried enough about the backlash. The only reason he wouldn't be worried is if he already knows what's coming and has a story to control the narrative should the media catch wind of it.

I grip my hair, trying to think of another way to help Briar since, obviously, our parents aren't going to, when a thought occurs to me.

Marco Mancini.

I head back outside to where the guys have been talking with their own parents, and the second the icy air hits my face and I see them, I accept their parents are as useful as Chase.

Not even a little.

I stride toward them, shoving my hands in my pockets as Sawyer yells at his father about being a coward. On the inside I wince, but on the surface, you wouldn't even know I'd heard it.

"I see your folks are as willing to help as mine." My words are met with grumbles and vitriol about stupid, rich, heads-stuck-up-their-ass humans.

"We need a plan," Asher states, and I nod.

"I think I have one," I tell him, and the three of them turn to look at me. "I'm not saying it's a good one, but it's an idea."

Nothing like building suspense. Usually, I wouldn't consider dealing with someone like Mancini, especially since my father seems so interested in him, but I'm desperate right now and there isn't much I wouldn't do for Briar.

"Well, what is it?" Cole asks impatiently. He's wound up tighter than usual, so I'm assuming the conversation with his dad went about as well as mine did.

"Marco Mancini. He offered Briar a favor. Pretty sure he didn't expect it to ever be cashed in, let alone this quickly, but a guy like that can make shit happen."

"Or he can make it disappear," Sawyer adds, nodding. "I support this decision. Marco is ruthless enough that he could probably make this entire situation disappear without even breaking a sweat."

"Do we really want to get involved with the guy who is essentially the boss of the underbelly of New York?" Asher asks, and I can tell Cole was thinking the same thing. I quirk a brow at him and he raises his hands in surrender. "I'm not saying I wouldn't do anything for her, I'm just saying once we make this bed, we have to lie in it. He might owe Briar a favor, but this might be more than he was thinking."

"It's a possibility, but do you have another option? 'Cause I'm open to ideas."

I'm met with silence from them, nothing but the sounds of New York City in the dark of night filling the space between us.

"Who has her bag?" I ask, and Sawyer hands me her purse. I search for the card from Marco but can't find it. It must still be tucked in her dress.

Shit.

Next option, I guess. I pull her phone from her purse, glad we still have it. "Anyone know her passcode?"

"0-7-1-6." I glance at Asher, who reeled off the numbers, and he shrugs. "It's Iris's birthday."

Probably should have known that.

I tap the numbers on the screen, unlocking her phone, and head straight for her contacts. I just hope she saved River's number in here. I scroll through her contacts, trying not to read into the very limited numbers she has, and tap River's name.

It rings out until I get a voicemail option.

Fuck.

I try again and get the voicemail again. "River, it's Travis Kensington. Briar is in trouble and I think she's going to need Marco's help. Can you please call me as soon as you get this?"

Rattling off my number at the end of the message before I hang up, I try not to let my frustration show.

"We need a lawyer," Cole says once I put Briar's phone back in her bag. "Someone needs to be talking with Briar until we can get this shit cleared up."

"You got anyone in mind?" I ask, and he nods.

"Carter owes me a favor. He has Denton on his payroll."

"Why the fuck does Carter owe you a favor?" Asher lets

out a hiss. Carter Davenport is almost as bad as Marco, but he doesn't run on the East Coast anymore... And I can say that, because he's my cousin. I might not know the worst of what he's done, but I know enough to know that he's not someone who tends to give out favors.

"Does it really matter?" Cole responds.

"He's down south now. Is he really going to be up for sending Denton to us?" I ask. I should probably be the one calling Carter, but I'm not the one he owes. Even if he is family, business is business.

"I can ask."

"Do it. The quicker we know, the better. I'd rather not leave her alone for too long. Especially since we can't get any fucking information without having someone in there with her."

Cole nods, pulling his phone from his pocket and strolling away to make the call.

"Can someone explain to me how the fuck all this happened?" Sawyer asks, tugging at his hair.

I grimace and pinch the bridge of my nose. "I don't have any proof, but I think it was Chase."

"Your dad?" he balks.

I nod in response. "Yeah, I think we need to check the car and house for bugs. He looked too smug, like he knew just what shit Briar was in, and there's no way he could know unless he was spying on us."

"Would Bentley—" Asher starts, and I shake my head.

"No, my uncle wouldn't sell us out like that." I might not know much about my uncle, but I do know that.

"Okay," he says with a nod. "Then I guess we better get to work."

Cole heads back over with a grimace. "Denton is on the way…"

"But?" I ask, a sinking feeling in my stomach.

Cole scrubs a hand down his face.

"But it's going to cost us."

It took a few hours for River to call me back, but she arranged a meeting with Marco for me first thing this morning. Cole headed to the station last night, but no one would tell him anything about what is happening with Briar.

Apparently, my dad's sway there is greater than any loyalty Cole has built up with people at the station.

He's staying put until Denton arrives. He should touch down in the next hour and the twins are on standby to take him straight to Briar, leaving me to deal with Mancini myself.

It's not a problem, I've interacted with people like him my entire life, but the stories about Marco make even me wary.

Especially since we're asking for his help.

I key the address River gave me for a warehouse over in Queens into my phone and pour another cup of coffee before heading out to the car. Could I be more prepared for this meeting? Absolutely, but lack of sleep will make anyone a little edgy.

I called Bentley last night and he's coming to the house to do a sweep tomorrow, but right now, my priority is getting Briar home.

Avenged Sevenfold blasts through the speakers as I make the drive to the location I was given, the loud music helping me keep my shit in check. I tap my hands on the steering wheel, the only sign of the anxiousness that I feel.

Traffic means that it takes longer than I expected to get here, but when I pull up, the building looks derelict, as if no one has been here for years. I check the address that River sent again and confirm I'm in the right place. The four-story building is seriously worn down. With all the shutters down, it gives me the fucking creeps.

Happy that I'm here first, I lock the car and scope out the building, surprised to find literally not a soul around.

I complete a full loop of the area and decide to try the door. Surprisingly, I find it unlocked. Heading inside, my footsteps echo around the cavernous space.

"You didn't think you were really alone here, did you, Mr. Kensington?"

My head whips up, and I spot Marco and two other men flanking him as they walk toward me. They pause and let me close the distance, so I keep my shoulders back and my head high as I approach them. I might be a nobody in their world, but

I know better than to show weakness to people like this.

Power is all about perception.

"Thank you for agreeing to meet with me so quickly." He waves to a table with a few chairs around it to his left before taking a seat.

I follow suit, trying not to think of what the cost of Marco's help is going to be, because I don't want that tainting this conversation. A small part of me is hoping that saving his wife will have been enough for Marco to help Briar out of her current situation.

"So, how can I help you, Mr. Kensington?"

I take a deep breath and clear my throat as I lean forward on the table. "After the event last night, Briar was arrested on suspicion of murder."

"Did she do it?" he asks, brow quirked. "Yes, it matters."

"It was self-defense," I tell him, knowing that lying isn't an option here. "But we disposed of the body because of who it was."

He waits, silent, so I tell him everything. From Crawford's penchant for young girls, to his behavior toward Briar, him attacking her, and all of the surrounding murders linked to everything that's happened.

He's seemingly patient until I'm finished. "So, what would you like me to do?"

"We need help getting her out of this situation. I'm pretty certain my father is the reason she was arrested, but if they have any sort of evidence…" I trail off, and he nods.

"I understand. We can help with this. You have a lawyer for her?"

"We do," I respond, and he nods once more.

"Good, better that I'm not involved that way. Enzo, see to it that anything linking our friends to this is handled." The man standing behind him grunts what I'm assuming is a yes before he turns and walks away. "And what about these other murders? Do you have any insight into that?"

I shake my head. "Not one, and anyone I've had look into it comes up empty too."

"Mhmmm." He pulls his phone from his pocket and shoots off a message before looking back at me. "I can't make any promises, but I'll have someone get in touch to see if they can help. Your girl saved River's life, the least I can do is save hers. But I think you and I need to talk further. Your father… he wants my support, which is a fucking joke, but I think I'd rather have you on my side than him."

"Me?"

He smiles and a shiver runs down my spine. "Yes, you."

THREE

BRIAR

I groan with my forehead resting on my forearms as I lean down on the interrogation table. The two detectives have been in here with me for what feels like an eternity. I've been allowed to pee exactly once since I got here and all I've had is water, despite asking for food and coffee. My stomach is growling and I feel like I might pass out soon. The quick nap, plagued by nightmares, wasn't exactly enough to sustain me.

I know it's the next morning now because when they came in, the bright lights from the windows in the hall made my eyes sting and the smell of their coffee made my mouth water. Plus, the stiffness in my bones from sleeping in this chair makes me feel like I'm basically a glow stick.

I didn't think I was old enough to feel like a glow stick cracking every time I move, but here we are.

"Miss Moore, if you would just answer our questions," the younger detective says, exasperated. He's been trying to play good cop since they came in here this morning, so I raise my head and rest the bottom of my chin on my wrists, repeating the same word that I've said since I got here. "Law-yer."

Yes, it's exaggerated. Yes, it's brattish. But also, I am so past caring.

The older detective slams his hand down on the table and basically growls at me. "If you're not guilty of anything, why would you need a lawyer?"

I open my mouth and repeat the word again. "Lawyer."

His face turns a mottled kind of purple, and while it probably shouldn't bring me the amount of joy that it does to see him become so frustrated, it does.

They've presented me with zero evidence as to why they hauled me in here from the gala and arrested me.

They keep telling me that I'm not under arrest, that I'm just here for questioning, but they're also refusing to let me go.

I'm not exactly sure how I'm not arrested, considering they mirandized me and threw me in the back of a police car, but hey, I never claimed to be a lawyer. I'm fairly certain that they're also not allowed to keep me here under these circumstances, especially when I've asked for a lawyer, but a corrupt police station isn't exactly a surprise in New York City.

When you grow up the way I did, you learn not to trust the police, which is the entire reason I didn't report anything that happened to me when I was a kid. Or the things that have happened to me since I came to Serenity Falls.

Most of the time, the good guy isn't a good guy and it's the villain of the story who will usually be the one to save the day. Because he doesn't care about the world. He just cares about you.

I sigh, wishing that I was home, lost in one of my more morally corrupt fiction stories, instead of here. Hell, at this point, I'd rather be walking over hot burning coals.

They haven't processed me, they haven't taken a mugshot, they haven't taken my fingerprints. None of the standard things that they should have done when I was arrested have been done, yet, here I am, stuck in this room, starving and really needing to pee again.

I let out a squeak when the door slams open and a man I don't recognize storms into the room. He looks and smells like a million dollars as he strides toward me, glaring at the two officers. "I'd like to speak to my client now, gentlemen."

He doesn't say another word, but the two of them stand and leave, one of them grumbling about Denton Callaway and how him being here must mean that I'm guilty.

Outside of the relief at the potential that whoever this man is will say he's my lawyer, the fact that the police seem to think that him being here makes me guilty doesn't really fill me with

29

joy.

Once the door closes behind the detectives, the guy turns to face me, the frown on his face deep and troubled. "Your boyfriends sent me in here to get you out. So that's what I'm going to do. You'll have to excuse me if my bedside manner isn't exactly great, but I've been on a plane since the early hours and I haven't had coffee."

"Yeah." I roll my eyes at him. "Get in line for being bitchy, buddy. I've been here since last night, peed once and had a small cup of water. If someone doesn't give me coffee soon, I really am going to kill people."

He smirks at me. "I think I like you already."

"Get me out of here and maybe I'll like you too," I tell him.

He asks me for a rundown of what's happened. So I tell him the basics and he barks out a laugh once I explain everything to him. "Okay, Sweetheart, give me a minute. We'll be out here in two shakes of a lamb's tail."

With that, he strides back to the door, yanks it open, and bellows down the hall as he starts walking. Something about his southern drawl mixed with the whole mafia boss look that he has going on with his slicked back hair makes me smile.

Totally didn't picture anybody like him ever existing, but I'm really not sad about it. Plus, the man smells like a freaking dream. I can't even put my finger on what the smell is, but he smells like safety and warmth and protection.

That could be delirious me talking, but who knows? It's

only a few moments later when he swaggers back into the room with a smile on his face. "Come on, Sweetheart. Let's rock this joint."

He holds the door open for me and I scramble from the seat, grabbing my shoes before I make my way out of the room.

It's almost unbelievable that this guy's here for less than two fucking minutes and I'm being released, when I've been asking for a lawyer for hours, and been asking to leave for hours, and gotten absolutely nowhere.

It's almost funny how they treat a girl who comes from nothing compared to what this guy who absolutely screams *money can make happen.*

"We'll be seeing you soon, Miss Moore," the older detective calls out as Denton walks me down the hall. He turns his wolfish grin on the detective.

"If I so much as hear that you've looked at my client, Thompson, I'll have you filed for harassment and I'll sue you with a lawsuit so big you'll beg me, on your fucking knees, to leave you alone. Do I make myself clear? This is the second time you've had her in now with zero cause and zero evidence and refused to release her. You better believe that if you even so much as breathe in her direction again that you will regret it for the rest of your life."

The mottled purple deepens on the detective's face and neck, and what I can see of his chest turns the same shade as he clenches his fists, glaring at me while we leave.

"Any idea why that detective has such a hard on for you?" Denton asks, and I bark out a laugh as he opens the door. Fresh air hits me and I suck in a lungful as a delirious kind of joy fills me.

"I wish I knew what his problem was," I tell him once I've soaked up some of the early morning sunshine. "But I don't have a clue and, right now, my brain won't function enough to think on it too hard."

"Come on, Sweetheart. Let's go get coffee. And then I can run down what I've worked out so far."

A black town car idles on the street and I follow him as he strides toward it with purpose. I take in my surroundings and startle when I see two police officers walking toward me, realizing I know one of them.

"Jamie?" His name falls from my lips in little more than a shocked whisper, but he must hear because he looks over at me. I haven't seen him in… well, in forever. He used to make up the third part of the unholy trinity that was me, him, and Emerson, even though he was a few years older than us. His dad moved him away just before everything with Iris, but before that, we were tight. Well, as tight as I was with anyone, which wasn't all that much, really, considering everything else I had going on.

"Briar Moore? Is that you?" he asks with a wide grin on his face. "Holy shit, it is!" He bounds over to me and lifts me from the ground, spinning me around in a bear hug.

"You're a cop?" I murmur.

He laughs as he puts me down. "What gave me away?"

His smile is just as bright as I remember and there's a lightness around him I'd forgotten about. Or maybe it didn't exist before.

"What are you doing here?" he asks, his smile turning to a frown when he glances over my shoulder. I follow his line of sight and find Denton leaning against the car, watching us intently.

"Jailbreak," I eventually answer him with a grimace.

"They hauled you in? What did you get yourself mixed up in this time? Emerson again?" His frown deepens as he asks. He never did like her.

"No. I don't really talk to her anymore," I tell him, trying to avoid the question of why I'm really here.

"Briar," Denton calls out, tapping his watch as I turn to look back at him.

I nod at him before turning back to Jamie. "I should go, I need to shower."

His grin reappears and he wraps me in a hug again. "Well, now I know you're here, don't be a stranger, you hear?"

"I'll try," I say honestly with a small smile as he releases me. He hands me his card, since I very obviously don't have my phone, before heading into the station, and I make my way over to Denton.

"A friend of yours?" he questions, and I shrug.

"Not really."

He opens the door for me, waving me in, and I slide across the back seat. He follows and closes the door.

"Coffee. I don't care where we get it from, just get me coffee," is what he calls to the driver once the door closes.

I sink into the plush, comfortable seat and murmur, "You're a man after my own heart."

"Ha, coffee is a staple of life. Without it, many would die," he says back with a smile as he closes his eyes and leans his head back on the headrest.

It's not long before we're pulling into a coffee shop on the outskirts of the city. It's glaringly evident that we're heading back toward Serenity Falls, and somehow I find comfort in that. Not long ago, I wanted to be anywhere but there.

I can't help but wonder where the guys are, but since they sent Denton, I have to assume more happened after I was taken.

We climb out and head into the coffee shop, and I can't help but giggle at the stares we get with him in the slickness of his pinstripe suit and me with my harried look of last night's hair and dress.

God only knows what these people think. But on the other hand, I really can't give less of a fuck right now.

I order my standard peppermint mocha with oat milk and extra whip, and Denton looks at me like I have three heads before turning to the barista and ordering the same. "This coffee better be good, girlie. I'm usually a black coffee kind of guy, but I like to be adventurous every now and then." He winks at me, and I swear if I was more coherent, my panties would turn to dust. "You go take a seat and I'll bring the drinks over."

I make my way over to one of the giant sofas, curling into it while I wait for him. He stands, watching the barista while the drinks are being made, with one hand in his pocket and the other tapping away on his phone, and I can't help but wonder exactly who my supposed savior is. I know he said that he was sent to help me, but that doesn't really clear anything up. Maybe it's the exhaustion, maybe it's the lack of caffeine, but there's something about this guy that just screams antihero. Hell, I don't even really know who he is. He could be anyone, and I went right along with him, because he has this energy that just screams, 'I'll burn the world for you'.

With coffee in hand, he makes his way over and hands me mine with a mountain of whipped cream on top. "I knew I liked you," I parrot back at him with a giant grin as I take the mocha and basically fall face first into the sweet treat. I groan as the coffee hits my lips and I swear to all that is holy and precious, a full body shiver runs through me as my body responds to the caffeine finally being reintroduced into my system.

"Do you want to wait for your boyfriends to get here or do you want the low down?" he asks after watching me closely while I basically orgasm over the drink in my hands.

"Tell me everything now," I respond, not wanting to be left in the dark anymore. Plus, knowing Travis, he'll try to spirit me away without giving me all the details anyway. "We can tell the guys once I'm back home, but right now, I want coffee and I want to know what the fuck is going on with my life. Then I need to go home and shower and sleep."

He lets out this weird sort of laugh-grunt thing before taking a sip of his coffee and pulling a face at me. "Something that requires a degree in decoding language shouldn't taste this good."

I laugh at him, shaking my head. "It shouldn't, but it's amazing. Wait until it's summer and I've got my cold brew vibes on. It'll blow your mind."

"I'm not even sure what you just said," he murmurs, his southern drawl making me smile. "Anyway, what I managed to learn on my way here is that your detective friends are very confused because the dates don't line up with the evidence they have. Since they already hauled you in once, they wanted to again. Though, from what I understand, your delightful stepfather had a role to play in that this time, but I'll let Travis explain that part to you."

He pauses and I nod, but I don't respond. I think he expects me to be shocked, but at this point, nothing really shocks me when it comes to Chase Kensington. Even Lucifer himself would be outdone by that asshat.

"Okay, well, they have no firm evidence against you, or even information that directly ties you to anything, other than some photographs of you with some of the victims, though half of those could be thrown out purely due to circumstance. Just because you happen to be in the vicinity of a human doesn't mean anything without motive. They're under pressure to provide answers from the brass up top, and with your stepfather's input, they decided to give it a crack because they have no idea what the fuck is going on in the city and they're chasing their fucking tails."

I nod, taking another sip of the coffee. I wish I was surprised about the whole Chase thing, but I'm not. He hasn't exactly been my biggest fan since Thanksgiving. Though, I don't understand how he would know about any of this and I say as much to Denton. He shrugs. "That much I don't know, Sweetheart. I was just asked to get you out and that's what I've done. I know the Beckett boy was at the station for most of the night and the twins met me at the airport, but I sent the three of them home once I got there because teenagers weren't going to help anything in that place. They tried to put up a fight, but well, darlin', I'm hard to argue with."

He grins at me and I roll my eyes while trying not to laugh. I can just imagine how well that went down.

"At least they tried," I say with a shrug. "It's more than most people would do."

Instead of heading home like I thought we would, I realize that Denton is taking us to the McMansion. I glance over at him and he shrugs without even looking at me as he taps away on his phone

"Don't look at me, Sweetheart. I'm just following instructions. I was told to bring you to the Death Star, so to the Death Star we go."

I can't help but laugh at the nerdy references coming from the mouth of this man.

"You're a Star Wars fan?" I ask skeptically and he finally glances over, turning that wolfish grin on me.

"Don't judge a book by its cover, Sweetheart. You never get to know the real story inside if you do that."

He winks at me and I bark out a laugh, the coffee and pastry that he got me finally starting to put a little bit of pep back in my step. "You're really just a big nerd underneath this fancy suit, aren't you, Denton?"

His grin widens at my question. "Maybe I am, but it's not something you'll ever find out."

He winks at me again as the gates to the McMansion open and we drive through. It's weird pulling up to the main doors rather than heading into the garage, but I guess Denton's not sticking around for long.

"Your boyfriends have my number, but take my card anyway. You never know when you'll need a friend. And if you ever want to escape all of this," he says, motioning to the tomb of a house. "Well, you have my number."

His grin turns wicked before he opens the door of the

stopped car. I follow him out and give him a quick hug, which is completely out of character, but he did just pull me from a potential hell.

"Thank you, Denton."

He gives me a squeeze back before releasing me.

"Anytime, Sweetheart. Just try not to get yourself arrested again. But if you do... well, call me." He mock-tips a hat that isn't on his head and climbs back into the car, closing the door behind him, and I watch him leave, almost wishing that I could climb in with him and run away.

Running away from my problems isn't going to get me anywhere though. I mean, it might, but I've never run from a problem in my life and I'm not about to start now. Instead, I take a deep breath, trying to steel myself against whatever the hell is waiting for me on the other side of this door.

I head inside, discarding my shoes by the door, giving zero fucks right now because I have nothing left to give to Chase that he hasn't already tried to take.

Rather than running the gauntlet of walking around the house, I go straight to the kitchen, my feet slapping against the cold, hard floors, knowing that I'll find Tobias in there. He is the wizard weaver of the household. He knows everything that happens here, so I know he'll be able to tell me where the others are.

I find him making a round of coffees and he lets out a sigh of relief when he sees me. "Oh, there you are, Briar. Thank goodness. I've been so worried. Are you okay?"

"Morning, Tobias. Thank you, I'm okay, just tired. I'd love nothing more than a shower and bed," I say when he rushes over and hugs me. Apparently, today is going to be a hugging kind of day. Awesome. "Where is everyone?"

"Travis and his friends are in the study with Mr. Kensington. I've made you a coffee. Why don't you go grab a shower and get changed? Once you're ready, you can go find them. I'll let Travis know that you're here."

A shower sounds like heaven, so I nod my head in response. He taps around on the machine and moments later, the smell of coffee fills the air as it hisses. He hands me over a mug of darkness and bliss that tastes just as good as the one that I had earlier.

I head upstairs to my 'bare to the bones' bedroom that isn't really mine, but fuck it. I don't care about that right now because the shower in here, if I remember right, is literal heaven and that is all I want in life right now.

I finish my coffee by the time I reach the top of the staircase in this mausoleum of a house and head straight for my room and into the bathroom.

Pulling down the zipper on my dress as I stride across the space, it glides to the ground and I step out of it before turning the heat for the shower on. I move to the mirror, pulling out all the pins that are left in my hair without even really looking at myself, scattering them across the countertop before stepping out of my underwear and under the hot spray.

I let out a hiss as the hot water stings when it hits my body, but it hurts so good. Feeling the grime of the last twelve hours wash off of me is a new kind of bliss I didn't know existed. It's hard to believe that it's only been sixteen hours since I was leaving the gala last night. With everything that's happened since then, it feels like it's been at least a week. I scrub my body down and do the same with my hair, trying to wash the smell of police station off of me, all while attempting not to let thoughts of Crawford sink me.

I know what I did was wrong, but he was trying to kill me.

Maybe what I did could have been handled differently, but at the time… well, it's not like I was *trying* to kill him. I just wanted him to stop.

Pulling myself from that train of thought, I rinse my hair and shut the water off. Grabbing a fluffy towel, I step out of the shower and wipe the condensation from the mirror, taking in my reflection.

The girl looking back at me looks nothing like the girl who stood here six months ago, fresh off a plane from California wondering what the point of her life was. I mean, my thought pattern still hasn't changed. I'm still wondering how the hell this is my life, but there's something about me that is fundamentally different now.

So much has changed since then.

It's amazing how much can change in two seasons. The fact

that spring is looming already is kind of terrifying.

I feel like I'm going to blink and my entire life is going to pass me by, especially if I keep living like this, carrying these secrets and trying to run from my past.

Maybe it really is time to find a shrink and do the work on healing myself.

But first I need to make sure that the past isn't going to come back and bite me in the ass.

So I guess that means it's time to face my demons in the form of my own version of Lucifer.

I pull on a pair of leggings and a soft as hell hoodie I find in the back of the closet, then roughly dry my hair before putting it up in a messy bun.

I take a deep breath and give myself the ultimate pep talk.

It's time to face the music. I just wonder if this will be my final curtain call.

FOUR

BRIAR

I walk into the study where the guys are congregated, along with Chase, Senator Beckett, and Thomas St. Vincent, and pause at the threshold.

They all look over at me, and the disdain on the senior men's faces when they take in my appearance is impossible to miss.

"Oh, good. The wrecking ball decided to join us. Why couldn't you just be a good little whore and do what you were told?" The sneer from the senator shocks me stupid for a moment. I open my mouth but no words fall out.

Cole jumps to his feet, bellowing at his dad, "You don't get to talk to her like that when all of this was *your* fucking doing."

"You better sit down and shut the fuck up, boy," the senator growls back, facing off with his son.

Shit.

This isn't exactly what I expected to happen when I came in here. Not that I really had a clue *what* to expect, but it definitely wasn't this.

"Take the trash out," Chase sneers, and Travis stands to face his dad, but I can't hear what he says over the Becketts' posturing.

Sawyer bounces over to me with all of the Golden Retriever energy that he embodies and wraps me up in a hug. "I'm so glad you're okay," he murmurs quietly. *Understatement of the year, Sawyer.* "This is really not the place for you to be right now."

I'm not even sure what that means, or what it is I've stepped into, but I squeeze back and take comfort in the smell of him. The warmth coming off of him is almost enough to take away the chill that's been seeping into my bones since the moment I stepped out of the shower.

"Let's get you out of here," he says, and I glance over at Chase. He's still staring daggers at me but I don't understand why.

Denton said something about my arrest being because of Chase, so surely I'm the one who gets to be angry here. All these assholes have done is try to play God and pull the strings of my life. The only thing I've been doing is trying to keep control of my own freaking path.

I contemplate saying as much but decide against it. The

tension in the room is thick enough to be cut with a rusty freaking knife.

This might have been the moment of reckoning that I had built up for myself but, apparently, that's gonna have to wait. I have no idea what's happening in this room, but it's more than apparent that I'm not wanted here. Why they asked Denton to bring me here confuses me, but now really isn't the time for questions. Especially since the shouting is just getting louder.

Instead, I let Sawyer lead me from the room, his fingers intertwined with mine as we pad down to the basement where his ridiculous sports car is waiting for us. He opens the door for me, leaning forward to make sure that I'm buckled in properly, before rounding the car to climb in the driver's side.

I close my eyes and lean my head back on the head rest, and he seems to take the hint and doesn't say a word. I cross my legs on the seat, sitting on my bare feet as he starts the engine. While there's so much that I want to say and so much that I don't understand, I'm not sure I have the energy for the manipulative and calculating ways of his world right now.

Of the world that I've been thrust into against my will. Even my meager doggy paddle isn't keeping me afloat right now and I'm just here, trying not to drown.

Who would have thought that living this life would be the thing I'd end up surviving instead of thriving in?

Sometimes I think that I would have been better off just being left on the streets of the city to fend for myself. I mean, at least I know how to fight in that world. This one is completely out of my wheelhouse and more often than not, I feel like I'm going to drown rather than keep my head afloat.

We arrive back at the house and I can hear the dogs barking as soon as we pull into the driveway. I'm fairly certain Travis will be pissed at Sawyer for parking here, considering this is where his car normally goes, but that's not my problem right now.

All I want is a puppy pile in my bed and to sleep for about seven days.

I kind of wish I could be that blissfully ignorant girl that just let the men handle the problems, the one who just lived and floated through life, not caring about what was happening around her. But that's not who I am, no matter how exhausted I am.

I open the front door to be met by the not-so-little-anymore puppies and crouch down to say hello. I let out a laugh when they end up pushing me onto my back on the porch. Sawyer just steps around us, laughing and shaking his head as he goes into the house, knowing that there's no point in trying to get the four Rottweilers off of me because one: I'm enjoying it too much, and two: moving them is not as easy as it sounds.

Once I finish playing with the puppies, and they finally let me back up, I head inside with Shadow who, unsurprisingly, doesn't leave my side. He might be called Shadow, but he's my little ray of sunshine, really.

"I'm gonna go up to bed," I say to Sawyer, who smiles sadly at me.

"Okay, Sunshine. Do you want company or do you want to be alone?"

I think on it a minute and shrug. "Company might be nice, but I'm gonna sleep like the dead and I probably have some stuff to work through, so being alone is probably the better idea."

The light in his eyes dims a little as he nods. "I get that entirely. We'll talk once you're awake. Head on up and I'll make sure that nobody disturbs you when they get back."

I go up the stairs into my room and once I'm inside with the door shut, I drop face first onto my bed. Shadow jumps up beside me, the mattress bouncing around as I replay all the things in my head that I wanted to say to Chase. About how it was his decision to pull me into this world, how he was the one who tried to marry me off and if he hadn't done any of these things, I probably wouldn't be in this situation right now. But fuck knows what was happening in that room.

As much as I want to know, that inkling to run away with Denton screams through my mind again, even though I know it's not really an option. But the part of me that is primed for survival tells me to run as fast and as far away from here as I physically can. Because nothing good can come from this.

Instead, I groan as I roll off the bed, stripping down and putting on a pair of shorts and a cami before crawling under the comforter. I curl up and Shadow lies along my back, facing the door like my very own protector.

I might have a lot of stuff I need to deal with outside of this room and, I mean, I *could* deal with it all, or I could just sleep. So I'm going to sleep and future me can handle the rest.

I stir awake as the bed dips and I hear Shadow grumble as he moves around beside me. "Get out, you big mutt. Your dinner is downstairs."

I smile at Asher's chastising of my favorite monster and turn over to see him.

"Shit. Sorry, I didn't mean to wake you." He runs a hand through his hair, an apologetic smile on his face.

"Come, climb in," I say sleepily, yawning as I lift the cover. He pauses for a second, like he's debating if he should, and I see on his face the instant he decides to ignore whatever he was doing to get in bed with me.

He closes the door softly, pulling his phone from his pocket and tapping at his screen before he strips down to his boxers and scoots into the bed behind me. He pulls me toward him, my back flush to his chest, and I get all fuzzy on the inside being his little spoon.

One hand splays across my stomach while the other traces up and down my thigh. He presses his lips against the sensitive skin of my neck and a shiver runs down my body as I suck in a breath.

"Come here." Asher pulls me even closer to him, his cock nestling between my ass cheeks and poking at the small of my back as he does.

"If I come any closer, you'll be inside me." I shimmy just enough to hear him groan behind me, his dick pressing even harder into my flesh.

"Exactly."

Resting in the safety of his arms, I sigh as Asher peppers kisses along the crook of my neck, his warm breath caressing every inch he passes. It should be relaxing and comforting, but his heat mixed with his hard length twitching between my ass cheeks just accelerates my heartbeat, and my entire body comes alive under his shiver-inducing touch.

"This is supposed to be soothing," he whispers between kisses like he's almost annoyed, but amused that I'm getting all worked up.

"Well, all it's doing is making me horny."

"I can work with horny."

He works my shorts down my legs, frustratingly slowly, while I tear off my cami. His body shakes as he laughs at me but his hands trail back up my body, so I can totally deal with the laughing.

Suddenly, I'm on my back, my wrists pinned above my head and Asher's magnificent body hovers just above mine, his cock nudging at the entrance of my pussy.

His dark blond hair falls into one eye just as he winks and grins down at me. With one thrust of his hips, he's fully seated inside me, our bodies totally connected.

"I have zero doubts about that," I finally respond as I lift my hips, needing him to move a little, give me more than just filling me, but as soon as I demand it, he squeezes my wrists and tuts at me like a naughty kid.

"I'll fuck you when I decide to fuck you, Briar." My entire body freezes as he speaks, like a switch going off inside of me at the tone of his voice. He always seems so carefree and fun, but when it comes to sex, he loves taking control and has no issue stopping every fucking thing just to make a point.

Clamping my mouth shut so I don't say something that'll make him stop what he's doing, I relax onto the mattress and hand him the reins.

"See? Such a good girl."

Sliding—oh so fucking slowly—out of me, he leans in and kisses me, his tongue swiping left then right before breaching my lips and making me dizzy with his attention. I'm so invested in our mouth fucking that I forget I'm waiting on him to actually fuck my pussy. Right up until he plunges back inside me, my breath suddenly vacating my lungs.

"You're so fucking tight, all wet and needy for me." His words are whispered across my lips, his tongue licking the top, then the bottom, before he traps it between his teeth and pulls enough to drag a groan from my mouth.

"I could do anything I want to you and you'd let me. Wouldn't you?"

"Yes." God I'm such a slut for Asher and I am totally okay with that.

"Good. Now, I want to hear you come nice and loud." He braces himself on his elbows and it's all the warning I get before he's driving into me like he's fucking possessed. We're staring at each other, our eyes focused and clear, our bodies fitting like perfect gloves as he pulls out and quickly pushes right back inside. Every time he fills me to the hilt, he hits that perfect spot inside me that makes me lose my fucking mind.

"You're fucking perfect, Briar. Do you know that?" He adjusts the position of his knees so he pulls one of my legs up and above his shoulder, allowing him to sink impossibly deeper. I moan at the feel of him and he grins like a fucking Cheshire cat that's just drunk the entire bowl of milk.

"Proud of yourself, huh?" I can barely get the words out, my breaths are so shallow.

"Not yet. I'll be proud when your cum is coating the entire length of my dick." Another grin crosses his face, except this one is a dare, and this asshole knows I can't pass up a good challenge.

Using his hold on me as leverage, I wait for him to thrust hard before pushing my hips up off the bed and slamming into him, rubbing my aching clit against his pelvis.

"That's it, Sunshine, take what you need from me."

Still staring at each other, we fuck slow and hard. There's nothing frantic about this but it's fucking intense, like he's goading me into an orgasm. Lifting my head off the pillow, I reach up for him. Instead of giving me what I'm clearly seeking, he only grins.

"Use your words, Briar. Tell me what you need."

"Your fucking mouth." I don't have time to realize that my answer was way off key before his teeth are sinking into the meaty flesh at the base of my neck and I have no fucking clue why, instead of screaming from pain, my natural reaction is to moan like a fucking banshee. Now, with his body closer, my clit is skin to skin with his pelvis and my entire bottom half is rubbing shamelessly against his body.

"Fuck, you're so fucking feral. That's it, Baby, show me what a good girl you are."

That's when I lose my fucking mind. My heel digs into his shoulder and my thighs burn from the position he has me in, so I circle my free leg around his waist and pull him closer to me so I can get what I want.

And, fuck, do I ever.

It starts with a burst of light on the back of my lids as Asher fucks me with abandon, his cock plunging in and out of me in the most perfect rhythm. I feel the orgasm travel along every nerve ending until it reaches the bundle of nerves that turns a good sensation into fucking fireworks.

I come loud and I come hard, all over his cock, as he

continues to fuck me, coating himself in my release with every thrust inside me.

"Yes, fuck yes. God, Asher!" I have no more rhythm. I'm just jerking my way through all of this until my orgasm subsides and Asher pulls right out of me. The emptiness inside me is instantaneous, but it's all forgotten as he takes my other leg and brings it over his other shoulder to join its mate, his palms over each of my ass cheeks and his mouth at my entrance, lapping up every fucking drop that I have to give him.

I hear him slurping and licking and moaning like he's drinking some kind of million-year-old bourbon that only he's discovered. It's like he can't get enough and his tongue searches out every single inch of me before he's remotely satisfied.

"Never tasted anything better than you." He latches onto my clit and I explode all fucking over again.

It takes me by surprise, the second orgasm, and before I know what the fuck is happening, Asher plunges back inside me, deep and hard, and fucks that climax right out of me.

He stills and I try in vain to catch my breath when his cock begins to swell. I know he's finally coming because his mouth is at my ear, his words like a balm to my soul.

"Fuck yes, feels so good with you, Briar. Only you." It's his turn to coat me with his cum and because I can't help myself, I reach down and scoop up anything I can get and bring it to my mouth, sucking on my fingers and groaning.

"You're my new favorite flavor."

Asher grins down at me and we both sigh. He doesn't pull out, we just lie back down, his cock nestled inside me, right where he belongs.

"Think you can sleep now?" he asks, his voice both sleepy and teasing. I murmur my agreement and nod.

I feel myself starting to drift when I hear his words and my heart bursts. "You are just too easy to love, Sunshine. It's no surprise I fell for you so quickly."

A TASTE OF FOREVER

FIVE

SAWYER

The sound of smashing glass, followed by the barking of six dogs, has me up and out of bed in a fucking instant. I climbed in with her and my brother last night, jealous of the puppy pile. How dare I not be included right?

"Stay here," I say to Briar, not giving her a chance to argue as I hop out of bed, noticing Asher has already left, and slide on my boxers before I make my way out of the bedroom as quietly as I can.

Of course the other two stayed out last night. For fuck's sake.

I dive past my room, grabbing the bat before moving down the stairs to where the Rottweilers are losing their fucking minds.

I let out a high whistle and they all instantly shut up and move toward me. The glass from the broken window at the front of the house covers the floor and a brick sits in the middle of it.

Awesome.

I scope out the downstairs quickly, even though I know no one would have made it past the dogs. Once I've reassured myself, I head to the front door and make sure whoever was out there is gone.

After I've rounded the house, checked every nook and fucking cranny I can see, I head back inside and find Briar with a broom in the living room, cleaning up the broken glass.

"You were supposed to stay put," I grumble, and she shrugs at me.

Fucking shrugs.

Sometimes I question her ability to survive, despite what I know about her.

"I heard you go outside and figured the house was safe. I got dressed, came down, saw the mess and decided the dogs were too close to the broken glass so I figured I'd get it sorted."

She's so nonchalant, like someone didn't just break our window. It's only a little emasculating when I'm standing here, my heart racing as adrenaline floods my system.

"I put the brick and note on the table," she tells me as she bends down and finishes scooping up the last of the glass before taking it to the trash can.

"Note?" I ask as a shiver runs over my body. Fuck, it's cold in here with that window gone. I spot the offending projectile where she said she put it and nod. "Ah, note. I'm going to put some clothes on, call the others, and we should probably call the police too. Or at least Bentley."

"Okay," she responds, almost like she's shut down and removed herself from the situation as she curls up on the sofa with the dogs. "Should probably think about how to cover the window too."

"Probably," I say with a nod, watching her closely. When I'm sure she's not going to freak out or have a panic attack, I dash upstairs, throw on some clothes, grab my phone, and jump into the group chat.

Me:

You all need to get home. Now.

I pocket the phone, assuming most of them are sleeping, considering the time on my phone says three in the morning.

Fuck me, it's early.

I guess I'll be drinking coffee with my girl to survive this day, 'cause there's no way in hell we're going back to sleep now.

My phone buzzes as I hit the stairs and once I reach the bottom, finding Briar still curled up with the dogs, all except for Hel, who moves to my side, I check it.

Travis:

What happened?

Asher:

Sawyer? Answer the question.

Cole:

On my way.

I let out a sigh, not surprised that Cole is the only one heading back. I love my brother, but he overthinks everything.

Me:

Someone launched a brick through a downstairs window. Briar is safe, but there's a note.

Travis:

Won't be long

Asher:

Jumping in the car now

Running a hand down my face, I take a deep breath and wonder what it might be like to live a normal life.

I mean, I've lived a normal life, or *did,* for a bit. Before we moved here. Sometimes I miss it, but I wouldn't change it. Not really.

Since Briar came into our world, stuff definitely got less normal. I didn't think it was possible, but here we are, and I sure as hell wouldn't ever give her up for a chance at normal.

"Coffee?" I ask, startling her a little. "You okay?"

"Fine, just half asleep still, lost in my head. Did you say coffee?" She pastes on a grin, but I know it's just for show. I'm not going to push her if she's not ready to talk though. Fuck knows I know how much that sucks.

"I did."

"Yes, please. You want a hand?"

I laugh softly and shake my head. "I can make coffee, you stay put."

I'm sure she's incapable of letting other people take care of her, and I can see on her face just how much she hates that she's not the one doing such a simple task. I know she's spent her entire life looking after everyone around her, but it pisses me off that even something so simple as me making her coffee makes her uncomfortable. Like her needs aren't important.

I try to hide my clenched jaw as I head into the kitchen to make her coffee. "Syrup?" I call out when the machine starts to whir.

"Peppermint, please," she answers, but even in that, I can hear the hesitation at asking for what she wants.

I grab the milk frother, add a few scoops of chocolate powder before adding the milk, and wait for the espresso to brew. One thing I will say about her coming into my life… I sure as hell never knew how to make coffee before.

By the time the milk has heated, car lights illuminate the dim room. Moments later, the engine shuts off and Cole is strolling into the house.

"Everyone okay?" he asks before the door even closes behind him.

"Yeah, good," I reply as I grab the drinks. When I turn back around, he's lifting Briar from the couch, tucking her against his chest before sitting in the spot she was in with her curled in his arms.

I put her drink on the table and sit on the couch opposite them, letting some of the tension evaporate from my body now that I'm not the only one here protecting her. While I know I can, I also know that the others, namely Cole and Travis, are far more physically able to protect her than I am. I keep in shape and I can throw a punch, but I'm way better at lifting her up emotionally.

I know my strengths and I play to them.

Tonight? Definitely not my strength.

My phone pings with a news alert, and when I see that it has to do with the local police station, I open it.

LOCAL STATION GOES UP IN FLAMES, EVIDENCE LOST BUT NO LOSS OF LIFE.

I take a screenshot and send it over to Travis.

Me:

Was this your deal with Marco?

Travis:

Yes.

The succinct answer is all I need. I know I should tell Briar about it, but she's on edge enough right now. I make a mental note to tell her later if someone else doesn't bring it up tonight.

Asher arrives a few minutes later, followed swiftly by Travis, who does what he does best and takes charge of the situation. Without even asking Briar how she is, he looks at me and asks, "Where's the note?"

I point to the coffee table, where it very obviously sits. "Haven't touched it since Briar moved it to the table. Didn't know if we should call the police, or at least Bentley."

He pauses a second and pulls his phone from his pocket, tapping on the screen before returning it. "I've asked Bentley to swing by in the morning. I'll grab some gloves."

And just like that, I feel more at peace again, happy to play the sidekick rather than the superhero.

Once Travis has the note in a ziplock bag, he lays it back on the table. "What does it say?"

He glances up at me, before looking over at her.

"It's fine. I'd rather know than live life in ignorant bliss," she tells him with a nod as Cole tightens his grip on her.

Travis lifts the bag from the table and lets out a sigh as Asher perches on the arm of my chair. He glances at us all, then all emotion drops from his face as he reads the note aloud.

Little Miss Perfect thinks she's free of me.

You'll see, you can never escape.

You're mine, and you always will be.

Everything I do is for you, and one day you'll have to thank me for it.

I wince at the implications of it, but I swear Briar doesn't even flinch.

"Awesome," is all that she says before resting her head on Cole's shoulder. I glance over at Briar, who smiles softly at me despite everything. I strengthen my resolve once more and promise her silently we'll fix this. I'll happily destroy the world for her, but I'll need these three at my side to do it and I'm not ashamed to admit it.

A TASTE OF FOREVER

SIX

BRIAR

I wake up on the sofa, still wrapped in Cole with the puppies by our feet. Sawyer is asleep in the chair opposite us while Asher and Travis talk in the kitchen. I'm not sure exactly what woke me up, it could be the insane amount of cold in the room despite the fact that the guys covered the window last night with some plywood they had in the garage.

Who would have thought that these four guys actually had practical things in this house?

Not me, that's who.

After reading the note, the guys started throwing around ideas of who they think could be sending them. At least I think that's what happened. I was on the cusp of falling asleep by the time they got here, and after hearing what the note said, it's like my body just said one big nope. Who knows what happened once I passed out?

I try not to move because Cole is asleep beneath me, but the urge to pee is overwhelming, so I try to get off of him as gently as possible so as not to disturb him. But when I go to move, his arms tighten around me and a grumble rumbles through his chest.

"Where do you think you're going?" he asks, snuggling his face into the crook of my neck.

"Bathroom," I say quietly, trying not to smile. "Please don't squeeze too hard."

He snuggles against my skin and squeezes me gently, just for a moment, before releasing me. "I suppose I'll let you go then."

I turn and kiss his cheek before running up the stairs, hearing him laugh behind me as I go.

Once my bladder has been dealt with, I get dressed for the day, putting on a pair of thick fuzzy socks and a T-shirt, along with my jeans and a warm hoodie before heading back downstairs. I'm more surprised that the dogs, especially Shadow, didn't follow me upstairs, but I guess after last night they're still on high alert.

Even if they were asleep when I woke up.

By the time I've made it back downstairs, everybody's awake and congregating in the kitchen. Cole hands me a mug of coffee once I reach him and pulls me back into his side; apparently someone's feeling a little protective after last night, but I'm not gonna complain because he radiates about as much heat as the werewolves in my books do. I snuggle up against him, taking a sip of my coffee before looking over at Travis, because the one thing I've come to realize is that he is the man with the plan.

"So, what's happening?" I ask, and he looks over at me, but I can't read the expression on his face. Sometimes I swear that boy is half in love with me, then other times, like now, I feel like the biggest inconvenience ever to exist because he just has this look of utter nothingness. I'm not even sure that he knows he's doing it.

"Bentley is on his way over. He texted me about half an hour ago to say that he was leaving so he should be here soon."

"Breakfast, anyone?" Sawyer asks as he stretches out beside me, the hem of his T-shirt riding up as he lifts his arms above his head. I definitely shouldn't be thinking about how good that V of his looks right now, but that is where my brain goes. *You* try being around these guys and not constantly being distracted by things that you shouldn't be.

"My eyes are up here, Sunshine," he says with a laugh.

I pretend to wipe drool from my mouth before taking another sip of my coffee, wagging my eyebrows at him. "I could eat."

His eyes narrow as a smile spreads across his face. "Oh, I bet you could, but I asked if you wanted breakfast."

I laugh in response and Cole shakes beside me as he chuckles. I can always count on Sawyer to lift the mood.

It's not long before he has food made and plated up for everybody. It's nothing fancy, just some simple bacon and eggs, but my mouth waters at the smell. Just as we're sitting down to eat, Bentley walks through the door.

"Uncle B!" Sawyer calls out. I can't help but smile at how his unwavering positivity always shines through.

"I made you breakfast," Sawyer says, putting a plate for him on the counter.

Bentley saunters over, smiling at Sawyer as he takes the offered seat.

"Thanks, kid. Sounds like you guys had an eventful night."

"You could say that," Travis says, glaring at the brick on the coffee table. "We need to go through everything. And then I was hoping that you'd install a security system for us. We never really needed anything but the base model, but I'm starting to think that we're going to need more than that."

Bentley nods as he digs into his breakfast while I keep my trap shut, because I'm very aware that I am the reason that they require high security. Which is the most ridiculous thing I've ever heard. I survived with no security in some of the worst suburbs of New York City, yet here I am in Serenity Falls needing full-on protection. It seems unfathomable and beyond ridiculous.

The scope of my reality has definitely changed in the last six months and sometimes I wish for a simpler life again, even if it was a much harder life. Because while life before was hard, I knew how to navigate that kind of hard. This hard… this hard I have no idea how to work through and not drown, or to keep the people around me alive.

Bentley and Travis talk between themselves as we eat breakfast and once we're done, I offer to clear the plates and tidy up since I got a decent night's sleep last night and nobody else really seems to have.

Knowing that the four of them were here made me feel much safer, so I passed out once Cole had me in his arms on the sofa.

Asher and Sawyer make their way upstairs once they confirm that Travis has the situation handled, heading to their respective beds. Cole, who did sleep with me, is apparently going to practice, even though it is the ass crack of dawn, because he still has a team to show up for, leaving me with Travis and Bentley.

"I'm gonna go try and catch a few hours of sleep. You good here?" Travis asks Bentley, who nods, before coming over to me and giving me a hug, kissing me on the forehead.

"If you need anything, come and get me," he says, staring at me intently. "I mean it, Briar. Anything," he reiterates before moving upstairs, leaving me alone with his uncle.

I sit quietly on the sofa, trying to stay out of the way while Bentley gets to work, dusting the brick and the note before lifting prints from them. It's a fascinating thing to watch. It's the sort of thing I've seen on TV, but never thought was actually real.

Bentley chuckles and looks up at me. "Oh, it's real."

Apparently, I said that out loud. Awesome.

"Sorry," I say to him, my cheeks reddening at the fact that I actually spoke aloud.

"It's fine, don't sweat it. You'd be amazed at the amount of people that have no idea what really happens behind the scenes. Though, I hear that you might have more knowledge than most, considering the events of everything the last couple of months."

The heat on my cheeks rises and spreads across my chest. "You could say that."

I assume Travis has told him everything he knows, but there is just something about him that makes me want to confide in him.

"Yeah, I know most of it. Travis needed to tell me so that I could start looking into the emails in your professor's account after everything at Thanksgiving."

"None of this makes any sense to me," I confess, and he nods at my confusion.

"People become obsessed with things. It doesn't always make sense. Trying to make heads or tails of it will likely drive you insane."

Somehow, at his words, I find myself spilling my guts, telling him every little thing that's happened since I got here. Some stuff that I haven't even talked to the guys about yet. Not because I was withholding it from them, I just haven't deemed it significant enough to tell them. Every single detail spills from my lips as I tell him about the last few months. From the note I found after Serena's death, to being attacked on campus, right up to seeing Jamie at the police station the other day. I don't know what is significant and what isn't, but since this is what he does, I figure knowing all the details can't hurt. Even if they don't seem important to me.

He sits quietly while I word-vomit all over him and smiles at me when I finally finish. "Sorry, that was a lot."

He shakes his head. "It's always good to know the details," he responds. "Sometimes you don't see something and fresh eyes can help, especially in situations like this."

I can't help but wonder exactly what it is that Bentley has done to make him the guy for this, but I also know that asking people questions like that, especially when he obviously has certain skill sets, is pretty rude, so I keep my mouth shut and tell myself I'll ask Sawyer later.

He is definitely the gossip of the group.

"All of these details could help you, but I'm trying to work out exactly what it is that's going on, so don't worry about thinking you overshared." He claps his hands on his knees before pushing back to his feet. "I'm gonna go ahead and get started installing the security system. I brought one with me because I know my nephew well enough to assume he'd want something after last night. You should probably try and get some more sleep too. It's still super early and I have a feeling that this is going to get worse before it gets better."

He strides away from me, leaving me with those foreboding words. I let out a deep sigh and hang my head. *Worse before it gets better...*

Isn't that just the story of my life?

After Bentley installed all of the security yesterday, the guys and I spent the day chilling out at home and relaxing. Despite the fact that Travis spent most of the day trying to teach me how to use the security system, I'm still not sure I know exactly how it works, but I do know that it's hooked up to my phone.

And that if the alarm goes off, it will call all of us as well as the police.

So I at least feel a little safer, which is one of the strangest things to say because who would have thought that home would actually be a safe place?

I finish getting dressed, because I need to head to the library and actually catch up on my course load, when my phone pings.

The notification tells me I have an email from the dean's office and something in my stomach drops when I see it. I already know this isn't going to be good, especially with a title like, *Please read - urgent.*

A sense of foreboding washes over me as I click on the email.

Dear Miss Moore,

I would like to request your presence in a meeting with the dean first thing this morning. The dean has stressed the urgency of the meeting and requests that you meet promptly.

To ensure the safety of all, please respond at your soonest convenience.

Emma Whittaker
PA to the Dean.

I hit respond, letting her know that I'll see him shortly. The guys have already left for the day because they went to train with Cole this morning and on to class from there.

Since this security system is as insane as it is, apparently they all feel that I'm okay being in the house on my own. Which is weirdly freeing because it doesn't happen very often and I almost feel like I can breathe again.

It's the strangest sensation. I've never really been looked after or watched, so having people around me all the time hasn't ever really been a thing until recently. I hadn't even realized how suffocating it was becoming until it wasn't there, and I'm surprised at how comforting the suffocation has become. Like a security blanket wrapped around me.

Picking up my phone, I let the guys know that I have a meeting with the dean in our group chat and pocket my phone again, knowing the questions that I don't have answers to will undoubtedly start coming in soon.

I grab my bag and head down the stairs with Shadow at my feet like always. He's getting so big now that he is less of a tripping hazard and more of a fall hazard because I'm not sure that he's quite worked out how big he is. He definitely still seems to think that he's the size of my arm rather than almost the same size as me.

After I sort out food for all of the dogs, I pour myself a cup of coffee and set the security system. I head out, grimacing when I see the plywood on the window—it's still ugly as shit but, apparently, somebody's coming to solve that today, so by the time I get home from class, we should have a window again.

Which should also mean that there's less of a chill in the house. The plywood is great and all, and I'm sure it's better than nothing, but there is definitely still a breeze coming through that thing.

I jump in the Batmobile and head to campus, my stomach twisting the entire way, dreading this meeting.

I haven't met the dean yet, but I don't get the feeling that this is going to be a good first meeting.

I head straight for the office when I arrive, coming face-to-face with the woman who still, to this day, reminds me of Fiona from *A Cinderella Story*. The space hasn't changed at all, which

I suppose isn't that shocking considering I haven't even been here two full semesters.

It still screams old money.

"Ah, Miss Moore. The dean said you'd be popping by. I'll let him know you're here. Please, take a seat." Her smile is as fake as it was last time, but I find myself, once again, sitting on the very plush sofa, taking in the wood paneling, thick carpets, and earthy tones of the space.

Maybe it's intended to make you feel at peace, but for me, it just pushes my anxiety up a notch.

My foot bounces while I sit and wait, my bag in my lap as I try to stop my leg from doing its little anxiety dance, and failing miserably.

It feels like I've been waiting an age, watching the clock tick, when the phone on her desk finally rings. She lifts the receiver and makes weird noises before hanging up, smiling fakely at me.

"The dean will see you now," she says. "His office is next door, knock once and his assistant will let you in."

I raise my brows, because well, I thought she was his assistant, hence me waiting in here. This shit is so confusing, but I don't say a word, because rich people and their bullshit, instead I just grab my bag and stand, thanking her on my way out.

I knock on the door to the dean's office, and when it opens, a bright and sparkly type of human answers it with such flourish,

I'm momentarily stumped.

"Briar! So lovely of you to come by. The dean will see you now." Even her voice freaking twinkles.

She motions to a door behind her in the small space, so I move to that, knocking once before opening the door.

"Ah, Miss Moore. Thank you for making the time to come and see me," the dean says as he stands. "Please sit."

He motions to the single chair on the opposite side of his huge, dark wooden desk before sitting again. The room is so dark, from the wood of his desk and bookshelves to the dark thick carpet and the dark blinds on the windows.

Huh, maybe the dean is a vampire.

I press my lips together so I don't giggle-snort in the middle of his office, looking at the ground as I move to take the seat he offered while I try to school my face.

He waits for me to sit before leaning back in his chair, studying me. I notice the plaque on his desk, finally discovering his name. Well, kind of. Dean Kinsey.

Different.

"I'm sure you're curious as to why I asked you here," he starts, leaning forward, steepling his fingers beneath his chin as he leans on the desk.

"A little," I respond, not sure what else to say.

"Well," he resumes, clearing his throat. "It has been brought to my attention the recent... difficulties you've been experiencing. From the loss of your friend, to the recent run-ins with the police—"

"Run-ins?" I say, interrupting him. "You mean, the false arrests I suffered that were so out of line that my lawyer threatened to sue the police department?"

He startles backward, his mouth opening and closing twice before he gathers himself.

"Yes, well, as I'm sure you're aware, the media has started taking an interest in the stories, and therefore you. We do not want to have the University tied to this… scandal, any more than necessary."

"Is that so?" I retort, raising a brow as I fold my arms across my chest.

"Yes," he states, trying to regain the power he had at the start of the conversation. "So, it is with that in mind that I am going to ask you to finish your semester with online classes and exams. It isn't something we would usually offer, but considering the circumstances, we feel it would be best for all involved."

"And who is *we*?" I ask, the sass rolling from me in waves. The audacity of this man! If this isn't victim blaming at its finest…

I mean, sure, I'm not exactly squeaky clean, but I'd put money on Chase being behind part of this.

"Your parents and I," he stammers. Obviously, he wasn't expecting a fight from me. "With everything going on at home on top of all of this, your mother said that this would likely be the best option for you."

And just like that, the wind leaves my sails.

Of course my mom is in on this. Isn't she always?

"Fine," I respond dejectedly. "I obviously don't have any say in this anyway. You could have just put it in an email. Though, I suppose that would just be more fodder for the media, wouldn't it?"

He pales at the veiled threat, but he doesn't know I'd never actually trash him or the school, even when he's being a dick. Really, he's just a puppet in this show too.

"Thank you, Miss Moore. I'll ensure the administration emails you over details of how we'll proceed from here."

I stand, my bag still clutched in my hands. "Was there anything else?"

He shakes his head, and I leave the office without another word. I pull my phone from my pocket and open the group text.

Me:

Heading home. Not allowed back to school. Will explain later.

I send something similar to Penn, letting her know I'll meet her for dinner later, before climbing back in the Batmobile.

Fuck this entire day, and it's not even ten in the morning yet.

A TASTE OF FOREVER

LILY WILDHART

SEVEN

BRIAR

After spending most of the day wondering about what happened this morning and explaining it all to the guys, I'm really not in the mood to go through it all again with Penn, but I told her we'd go out for dinner tonight, so I'm sucking it up.

She's picking me up in twenty minutes and I really need to get my shit together. We're not going anywhere fancy, so I've swapped out my hoodie, T-shirt, and jeans for a sweater dress and a pair of leggings. I pull on a pair of comfy boots to go with it before checking out my reflection. Cute but casual and still warm as fuck, especially with my big fuzzy socks on underneath my boots. I pull my hair up into a ponytail, because I don't have the energy to spend my time on it, and decide I'm done.

I head back downstairs to find the guys playing Xbox in the living room and laugh at how competitive they all get when they actually act like the boys they are rather than the men they're forced to be every single day.

Quietly, I sit on the stairs, watching them, knowing that nobody's realized I'm here, and it fills me with joy to see them being so carefree. Especially after everything that's happened lately. But it also pains me to know that a lot of the issues we've been facing have been because of me.

I have no doubt that they had stresses in their lives before I arrived, but I'm also very aware that a lot has changed for them since I showed up. More so for the twins than the others because I know that their parents were never really that forceful or that pushy, but it's hard to imagine because that's all I've seen of their parents. I don't want to think that I'm the catalyst for everything, because I'm very aware that the world does not revolve around me, but it's also hard for my brain not to trip out over the thought and instantly blame myself.

My phone buzzes in my pocket, pulling me from my spiral—yeah, my sweater dress has pockets, it's my favorite—and I see Penn's name on the screen.

Penn:

Leaving now, be there in about three minutes. You better be ready. *winky face*

I laugh quietly as I type out a response letting her know that I'm ready and waiting for her. She responds with a love heart emoji back and I pocket my phone again, standing so that by the time she gets here, I really am ready to go.

"I'll see you guys later. I'm going to dinner with Penn," I say, heading toward the door to pick up my purse that has my wallet in it. "I have my phone, and yes, location services are on so you can track me with ease like the little stalker boys you are." My last comment is aimed mostly at Travis, because he's the one that I had the argument with earlier today about having the location services turned on and not being some dog that he follows everywhere. But ultimately, I lost that argument.

To be fair, if it hadn't been for Sawyer playing dirty the way he did, I probably would have won, but that little ball of sunshine is a Sneaky McSneakster.

Travis glances over at me, rolling his eyes before turning his attention back to the screen.

"Have fun, Beautiful," Sawyer calls out. "Let us know if you need us." Not one of them turns to look over at me because they are wholly fixed on the shooting war that they have going on on the screen, and I can't help but laugh at them.

I've never really been a gamer girl, so I have no idea what it is they're playing, but it looks like chaos.

I shake my head at just how enraptured they are by the game. "Yeah, if I need you I'll let you know, but I'm sure I'll be fine."

I dash outside before they can make any other weird

demands just as Penn pulls up in front of the house.

"Let's do this, bitch!" she says with a wide grin as I climb into the car and pull on my seatbelt.

We end up going to an Asian fusion place out in the middle of Oakwood, which, obviously, I'm not sad about. When I see Tonkotsu on the menu, I do a little dance.

 I wish I'd known this restaurant was here because, despite the drive, I would have absolutely been here more. Hell, if this Tonkotsu is any good, I'm absolutely going to be dragging the guys back here on a semi-regular basis.

"So spill," Penn says once we've ordered our drinks, so I ramble on and tell her everything that happened with the dean, the brick being launched through our window, and basically fill her in on the shitshow that is my life.

Obviously, I have to leave out some details, because she doesn't know the truth about Crawford, and while I hate lying to her about it, I also don't want to drag her into my mess.

I can see the rage building on her face, the tightness of her shoulders growing more intense with every word that I spill, and by the time I'm done, she's practically shaking.

Unfortunately, the server arrives with our drinks just as she shouts, "What the actual fuck?"

I smile apologetically at the server. "She doesn't mean you."

The guy just smiles nervously at me before putting our drinks on the table and basically running away. Penn winces and calls out 'Sorry' to him, but I'm not sure he hears.

"Man, I hate when people are horrible to servers. I so didn't mean to be that guy."

I laugh softly and shake my head before I take a sip of my Coke. "You're not that guy. That was just really unfortunate timing."

She lets out a big sigh. "Yeah, maybe, but we're gonna have to tip him real well."

I nod my agreement. "We can do that. We'll pool it."

She spends the next couple of minutes ranting about the dean and all the bullshit that seems to have followed me around the last couple of weeks. By the time she's gotten it out of her system, I'm laughing so hard that I'm almost crying. "I don't get what about this you find so funny. This is actually your life. How dare they do this to you? The audacity of that man is overwhelming."

I try to take a breath so I can actually speak, but it takes me a minute.

"It's not what he did that's funny. It's the expression on your face while you talk about it. I've never had somebody get so angry on my behalf before, especially about something that, ultimately, isn't the end of the world."

She looks at me like I have two heads and makes this weird choked noise before taking a sip of her drink. "It's just... men are stupid."

I have a feeling there's more to that statement, so I ask, "Connor?"

She puts her drink down and nods once.

"Who else? He's been weird since Christmas, and even more so since his family turned up. I've only met his uncle once before when I was super young, but my mom didn't like him then because he gave her the creeps. She said as much when I went to visit for the weekend with him being back. Apparently, he just gives her the heebie jeebies. Which normally I would dismiss, but with Connor acting so weird since his uncle has been in town, I don't know what to think. It's like he's a completely different person. And outside of being in the dorm together, I've barely seen him. He hasn't been going to classes as much and he's barely keeping up with his course load. It's literally like he's been replaced with a pod person."

I frown deeply, because that doesn't sound like the Connor I know at all.

"Do you want me to speak to him?" I ask, knowing full well that she knows him better than I do.

She shrugs and lets out a deep sigh. "I honestly have no idea what to do anymore. I've tried to talk to him about it and he just says that he has a lot going on. That it will clear up soon enough. But that doesn't make any sense to me. When I ask him why he can't tell me what it is that's going on, he gets all weird on me. It's like the guy that I've known my entire life is gone and it's just someone who looks and talks like him. But it's… it's not the same human. If he had a twin, I'd be convinced that they'd swapped places."

"*Does* he have a twin?" I ask, mostly to try and lighten the mood, but she shrugs, her frown still firmly in place.

"Not unless they were separated at birth or something else equally as ridiculous."

I feel some of the positivity I was trying to muster fizzle away. I've been so wrapped up in my own bullshit that I hadn't even noticed all of this had been going on.

Like, I knew that Connor hadn't been in class that often and he'd borrowed a lot of my notes, but I didn't think much of it because I've borrowed enough of his. I figured he was just sleeping and dealing with stuff, but if it's *this* out of character for him and he's being weird with Penn, then I can't help but worry.

Especially since it does seem to line up with his uncle coming back into town. It definitely seems suspicious.

I make a note to ask Cole if his police friend has any information on Connor's uncle and tuck it away for later, once I'm home.

"Let's just forget about the stupid boys in our life and try and enjoy tonight," I suggest, trying to lift the mood again, and this time, it seems to hit.

"Hell fucking yes!" she says, lifting her glass to clink with mine. We giggle before toasting to us. "Here's to girls and their uncomplicated ways," she cheers.

I laugh and shake my head. "Oh yeah, because we're *so* uncomplicated."

I stumble out of the taxi, waving goodbye to Penn, a little tipsy from the after-dinner drinks we decided to go for. Who would've thought getting served with no ID would be so easy as a Kensington?

Not me, but it was, so we took advantage.

Kind of.

A few cocktails does not an advantage make.

I try my key a few times and miss each one, ending up with my forehead pressed against the door while I laugh.

Maybe I'm a little more tipsy than I thought.

I stumble back to try again, but the door opens *for* me and I find a stern-looking Travis standing in the doorway, arms folded over his chest, looking almost disapproving. "Where have you been?"

"Dinner, I told you that earlier," I reply, hiccupping once then giggling again. "Then drinks. I texted you all."

He rolls his eyes at me and moves backward, motioning for me to come in. I grin at him, probably wider than I should. "Damn you look hot when you're mad. That T-shirt doesn't exactly hurt things either."

I'm not even lying. The dark and brooding thing works for him, as does the black T-shirt that looks like it was painted on. I drag my gaze down his body to his denim-clad legs, which are also a thing of wonder, especially when they do nothing to hide that monster cock of his.

"Briar," he says, my name little more than a growl. "Get inside."

"Can I climb you like a tree if I do as you say like a good girl?" I tease. His eyes darken as he watches me.

"If you're a good girl, you'll get far more than that. It's been a long week and I could do with working out some frustration."

I swear all of my insides clench at his words.

"That shouldn't sound so hot," I say, practically panting as I move into the house. "You going to make good on that promise?"

I let out a squeak as the door slams shut and he scoops me into his arms. It's only when we're halfway up the stairs that I notice the other three on the couch, laughing. I wave as Travis stomps up the stairs, not even caring that they heard that little exchange.

Travis kicks open the door to his room before doing the same to shut it, then drops me onto his bed.

"You're wearing far too many clothes."

"Mhmm, maybe you should do something about that." Travis looms over me, his eyes dark as coal and his head cocked to the side.

"Good girls strip." I really want to be a good girl for Travis tonight. "Keep the ponytail; I have plans for that."

My boots are first to go flying across the room, followed by my leggings and panties. When I reach for my sweater dress to pull it over my head, Travis kneels at my feet and spreads my thighs as wide as they'll go, his face so close to my pussy that I have to clench my muscles to keep myself from pushing his head exactly where I need him.

I can't forget who's in control or else I won't hear those soul-soothing words that I love so much. Especially when Travis speaks them.

"You had fun without us?" It's not an accusation, but it's really fucking close.

"Am I not supposed to?" Fuck, I'm getting my arms stuck in the sweater as I try to pull it over my head, my hair tickling my nose.

"I'm not sure yet." Where the fuck is the hole? Ha! That's what *he* said! I start giggling at my ridiculous joke, but it dies in my throat when Travis buries his face in my pussy and his tongue is working me in the same way it does when he devours my mouth. Still struggling with the fucking dress, I'm grateful when one of his arms shoots up and pulls the damn thing off, his mouth never skipping a beat.

His talents are never-ending.

With his dark eyes on me, he palms my thighs, pushing me onto my back, and settles in for a long night of pussy eating. I'll never get enough of it. Never ever.

"God, yes. Oh, Travis, so good."

He moans into my pussy as his teeth graze my swollen clit

before he thrusts his tongue back inside me. He doesn't relent, just keeps feasting on me like I'm the royal buffet and he's been starved for centuries. All around us, the scent and wet sounds of sex are like a cocoon, making me inhale deep and driving me even further into my horny bubble.

One of his hands reaches up and roughly pulls the cups of my bra down, not bothering to take the damn thing off. He pinches my nipple just as he sucks on my clit and the double sensation is enough to make me scream his name out and fist the sheets like they're a lifeline to my sanity.

"Come, Briar. On my fucking tongue. Now." How does he do that? How do his commands have a direct link to my orgasms? My brain wants to analyze that whole situation but my body says fuck that and comes, exactly as he demanded of it. On his tongue. He laps up every ounce of what I give him as my hips fuck his mouth from below, riding my climax to the highest of highs.

"That's my good girl." Fuck me, I melt into a fucking puddle every time he uses that growly voice to tell me he's pleased with me. "Now, get on your knees and suck my cock." Yes, sir!

Travis stands at the foot of the bed, popping his button open and dragging the zipper down slowly as I get my bearings and crawl up to him. My tits are still out of my cups, swollen and needy, and when I look up to him, his gaze is fixed firmly on them, his tongue sweeping across his bottom lip like he wants to eat me alive.

Though I think he just did.

A whimper escapes me as Travis suddenly grabs on to my ponytail and his mouth crashes down on mine with nipping teeth and searching tongues. The taste of my juices on his lips is an aphrodisiac, the musk and the tanginess of my orgasm as it mixes with his own unique scent is priming me for another orgasm, and fast.

Suddenly, he pulls away, my bottom lip trapped between his teeth, his eyes fixated on me. The lust in the room is palpable, the need for more a living, breathing thing between us, and I can't wait for him to loosen the reins on his control and do whatever he wants with me.

As soon as that thought crosses my mind, he pushes me back down on all fours and feeds me his dick. There's nothing romantic or subtle about his demands: he wants me to suck him off and he wants me to do it rough. With my hair tightly wound around his fist, he pushes until we both hear me choking. I don't stop, though. No fucking way. Breathing through my nose, I close my eyes and envision his cock sliding down my throat, past any resistance, past my gag reflex, and soon enough, my muscles relax and I hear him sigh in satisfaction.

"You're doing so well, taking me like that." His voice is like honey, smooth and soothing. It warms every inch of my skin as my eyes water and my mouth fills with saliva. I'm sure I look a mess, but it doesn't matter because I'm his mess and he loves me like this. Powerless, submissive, at his fucking mercy.

Except I'm none of those things and deep inside he knows it. I'm in control of the pleasure I give him.

"Don't just stand there, look how beautiful she is when she's choking on my cock." At first I'm confused, but when I open my eyes, movement to my side gets my attention. Travis doesn't relent, doesn't even miss a millisecond of his punching rhythm. With controlled pumps, he fucks my face like he was born to do this.

Sawyer sits down on the chair to my right and, with spread legs, watches as I suck off his best friend. Fuck, that's hot. And now I want to please him too. I want him to get off on watching me. I want him to pull his dick out and come all over himself just from the sight of me.

The thought spurs me on and, with renewed motivation, I allow Travis to sink impossibly deeper inside my throat.

"Christ, that's good. That's it, Baby. Take it all like a good girl." The unmistakable sound of a zipper tells me I'm getting my wish. Sawyer doesn't even pretend he's not turned on. His cock is out and his hand is furiously stroking his hard dick.

"You look so hot with my cock buried inside your mouth that Sawyer's going to fuck himself raw just watching you." God, yes. The walls of my pussy are clenching, begging for something to hold on to. My clit is throbbing, aching for someone to put it out of its misery, so I rub my thighs together, hoping to alleviate some of the need.

"Did you see that, Sawyer? She needs to be filled." Pulling

my face off his cock, I whine at the emptiness it leaves me feeling without him inside me. Travis kisses me again, his tongue searching out his own taste as he licks and prods and bites. I'm so horny I'm afraid I'll spontaneously combust from the need that's been building inside me. All the while, Sawyer sits quietly, the only noise coming from his hand as he fucks into his palm with abandon.

When I turn to fully watch him, his eyes aren't on me. They're on Travis. More specifically, they're on his long, thick length as it stands there proud and aching. Travis sees it too and now I can't get the idea out of my head.

Looking up at Travis, I lick my sore lips and beg.

"I want to see him suck you off." Travis searches my eyes for any doubt, but he won't find it. No fucking way. The idea of watching them together is going to make me come without even touching myself.

Without taking his eyes off me, he speaks loud enough for Sawyer to hear him.

"You heard the lady. Get over here and suck me off." With a groan of lust, Sawyer stands, pulls his jeans up just enough to cover half his dick, then grabs onto my ponytail and gives me a bruising kiss. It's quick, but it says everything he doesn't with words. He wants this just as much as I do.

Sitting on the edge of the bed, he looks over at me and winks. Travis places a hand on the back of Sawyer's head and his other grabs my hair once again. Without hesitation, Sawyer licks the head of Travis's cock before he drags his tongue on the underside from root to tip. I whimper when he suckles on the slit, but groan when he opens up and takes his entire length down in one smooth move.

"Fuck, that's hot." The words are out before I can school myself, but it's not a lie. It's the hottest thing I've ever seen. My pussy is so needy that I wonder if I could get myself off as I watch them.

"Lick his mouth and my cock at the same time, Briar."

Oh fuck me. I'm going to come and there's no way I'll be able to stop, even if Travis orders it.

He doesn't have to ask me twice. No sooner are his words out, than I'm on all fours again, right next to Sawyer, who takes one of my hands and places it on his own dick while my tongue licks at his lips and the smooth skin of Travis's cock. I'm greedy, licking and sucking on whatever I can get my mouth on. We all moan at the same time as and there's no telling what's spit and what's cum anymore.

Travis pulls out and feeds me his cock without even trying to go slow. I swallow it wholeheartedly as Sawyer licks and nips at us. Then he switches it up again until Sawyer is the one choking on that massive dick. Next thing I know, Travis pushes my head down until I've got Sawyer's entire length in my mouth while Sawyer is working Travis's cock like a fucking pro.

"Make her come, Sawyer. Finger that beautiful cunt of hers and make her come while she sucks you to orgasm." His voice is steady, but I can tell he's affected by what we're doing just as much as I am.

Sawyer pushes two fingers inside me and it barely takes him a minute to get me off. I see colors and sparks going off behind my lids just as Sawyer comes inside my mouth. I'm trying not to bite him, trying really fucking hard not to choke on the sheer amount of cum he's pumping into my mouth.

When we're finished, Travis pulls me off of Sawyer and removes his dick from his mouth.

"Now, watch as I fuck the life right out of her."

In an instant, I get a fast, hard kiss from Sawyer before he returns to his place in the chair and Travis makes quick work of discarding his clothes.

Naked, he's fucking magnificent. All hard muscles and lean features. Licking my lips, I reach behind me and unhook my bra, throwing it to the side before I lie down on my stomach and present him with my eager ass. Grabbing onto the headboard, I spread my thighs wide and give Sawyer a perfect view of my wet, hungry, pussy.

"Look at you. So eager, so willing to take my dick deep inside. Such a good girl." Again, his words make me melt, but I don't have time to linger on his praise before his cock spears me like a fucking sword and hits that deep, aching spot that drives me crazy.

He fucks me hard, wetting his cock with my latest orgasm as his fingers dig into the flesh of my hips. The slapping of skin on skin is a heady sound that drives me closer and closer to another impending orgasm. How the fuck does he do this to me? One is great. Two is fucking fantastic, but three? I feel a little greedy at the thought that some women can barely get one.

Turning my head toward Sawyer, I watch him as he watches Travis fucking my pussy like a wild animal. He's back to fucking his own hand, his jaw set, his pupils dilated with lust-filled need. We must be a sight, the three of us getting our pleasure.

Travis reaches up and pulls me back by my hair until my back is pressed hard against his front. I'm riding his dick now, my tits bouncing to the rhythm of his thrusts, my moans fueling our need, his next words priming me for the next climax.

"What happens to good girls, Briar?" I know the answer to this without even having to think.

"They get to come."

"That's right, Baby. Do it. Take your reward." With a gasp, I let go as Travis places his mouth to my neck and sucks the skin into his mouth while his free hand snakes around and rubs tight circles around my clit.

Letting go of my hair, he cups my tit and pinches my nipple, which is the last drop before I go overboard.

It's like a detonation goes off in the center of my body. An explosion that starts deep inside me and takes over every extremity. I see colors, taste lust, feel the heat from every inch of my skin that touches every inch of his skin. The slapping sounds of Sawyer getting himself off again and the groan that follows all add to the spectacular orgasm that overpowers me.

Gasping and trying to breathe in oxygen, I scream Travis's name just as he gives me one more reward.

"You look so pretty when you come for me."

I come down from my high, my arms dropping forward to hold me up as Travis fucks me through my orgasm before he explodes inside of me. "That's it, take it. Take everything I give you." He continues to thrust into me, despite having come, as if he can't bear the thought of not being inside me. I drop onto my chest, my arms giving out, and he comes with me, lying over my back, still inside of me, holding his weight on his arms.

"Fuck," he groans against my skin before kissing my neck softly.

I let out a moan of agreement and nod a little, still unable to make words. I feel the bed dip as my eyes start to flutter closed, the murmuring of their voices the last thing I hear as I drift off, and I wonder if I'm already asleep when I hear Sawyer's voice. "Love you, Sunshine."

A TASTE OF FOREVER

EIGHT

TRAVIS

The front door closes as Briar skips out to meet with Penn, and I finally stop pretending that everything's okay. I put down the controller to the game that we've been playing as a way to distract us from the bullshit that's been raised today and grab my phone before heading into the kitchen.

I know that, just like her arrest, my dad is behind her conversation with the dean today. The problem is that I don't know what more I can do about it. He is the one with the contacts. He's the one with the money. I like to think that I have power, but really, I'm just a nineteen-year-old guy trying not to drown in this insanely choppy water that I've spent my whole life paddling in. It's just that these days I spend more time in the vast, open water that's trying to drag me under rather than playing in the kiddie pool like I have been for the years before now—oh, when I thought that was the hard time.

Before Briar arrived, I did everything my dad wanted because Katy was my main priority. She still is, but I can't let my dad bulldoze over Briar, either.

I think about calling Bentley to see if he has any ideas. He has navigated this insanity for a lot longer than I have and he also found a way to get out, but I already know the military is not an option for Briar or for me or Katy. So I'm not sure taking that particular escape route is exactly what I need to do. I think about calling Pops, but he never takes Dad's threats against Katy seriously and I'm not sure how much he'll care about threats against Briar considering how little he knows her currently. He already stepped in around the whole engagement thing. While he knows that I have feelings for Briar, I'm fairly certain that at this point, the fear my grandfather's power wields is becoming limited.

My father has too much power and that is the problem. If Carter was still here, then that might not be the case, but he isn't. He moved away years ago and since he left, my dad has just grown and grown with the contacts that he has and his connections to the seedy underground, as well as the authentic ones that come with business.

I grip my phone, telling myself not to throw it out because that isn't going to fix anything, as I grind my teeth in frustration.

The others finish on the Xbox and the TV turns off, the silence feeling louder than the sounds of shooting from the game, and it just makes me feel even more suffocated than I already am.

I shouldn't have to deal with this shit at nineteen, but I guess this is my life.

"I'm assuming that we're pretending we're all okay instead of crazy overwhelmed, yes?" Sawyer asks as he saunters into the kitchen. The death glare I give him just makes him laugh as he hops up on the counter, swinging his legs like the man child that he is. I keep my thoughts to myself, because I know that really, I'm just jealous of how carefree he is. I know he has weight on his shoulders, but none of them really know the extent of what my dad has had me do, or the threats that he's made. Because then it'd be everybody's problem rather than just my own. But even aside from all that, I've never been as carefree as he is right now sitting on that counter, at least not since my mom died.

"So what's the plan?" he asks as Asher and Cole join us.

"My plan," Asher says, "is to take these dogs out because they're driving me insane." He grabs the leashes and hooks everybody up then disappears.

The yips of the dogs that I'd managed to tune out finally disappear once he's gone, leaving me with Sawyer and Cole. I scrub a hand down my face and pour myself a cup of coffee. I think Briar is rubbing off on me a little too much, because my caffeine addiction has definitely increased since she moved in.

"I have no idea what the plan is," I tell them both. "The dean is working on behalf of my dad. There's no way that he would have asked Briar to sit out the remainder of the semester if my dad wasn't whispering in his ear, so I guess I need to speak to my dad to work out what his endgame is here."

"Do we think that me marrying her will exacerbate or resolve these problems?" Cole asks, running a hand over his buzzed hair.

"Honestly, at this point, it might be the only way for her to have some semblance of a normal life. But then we already know that marriage wasn't what she wanted."

"Actually," Sawyer says. "We don't know that. We know that she didn't want to be *forced* to marry someone, but at no point did she say that she didn't want marriage. She just didn't want to be dictated to by sweaty old men."

I look over at him as he grabs an apple from the fruit bowl and takes a bite, the juice running down his chin.

"I'm pretty sure that she didn't want it, period. You saw her response to it."

Sawyer just shrugs. "What I know is that our girl is romantic at heart, and there's no way that she doesn't want to get married at some point. What I also know is that it was dropped in her lap like a ton of bricks with zero warning. She also didn't like either of you, so being told that she had to marry anybody, especially one of you, added to the way she reacted. That's what sent her spiraling. I'm fairly certain that if someone just proposed to her, she probably wouldn't have the same sort of, you know, adverse reaction that she did to being confronted at dinner in front of a room full of people that she didn't feel comfortable with."

He shrugs and jumps off the counter. "I'm gonna go save Asher before those dogs break his arms. Work out between you what the plan is. We all know *I'm* not the guy with the plan, but if it's going to help her deal, I'm in for whatever. Ride or die, right?"

He grabs his jacket and slips on his shoes then runs out of the house. I look over at Cole, who looks as confused as I do. "Do you really think it would be that easy?"

I shake my head, letting out a small bark of laughter. "Since when has anything with this girl ever been that easy?"

I know it's a bad idea before I even get in the car, and the entire silent drive to my dad's, I tell myself just how much of a bad idea this really is. Because in reality, this is probably only going to make things astronomically worse.

But still, here I am, driving to my childhood house of horrors, trying to give the anger inside of me a chance to calm a little before I try to find out what the fuck my dad's problem is.

We can talk all the theory in the world about why he's doing any of this, but none of his motivations make any sense to me right now and my dad has never been anything but logical. Ruthless, yes, but still, every move had a logical decision behind it and I can't see this one.

I get that he wanted Briar to marry Cole for political gain, but if he's dropped that idea now and he's just trying to sell her off to the highest bidder—which is what he said at the gala that I've been trying to forget about because of everything else we've been dealing with—then why is he doing this to her? Why is he pushing so hard for Sophie to have another kid when he already has me as an heir? None of it makes any sense.

The drive passes in a blink of an eye and before I know it, I'm pulling into the garage under the house. I shut off the engine and sit in silence for a few minutes, trying to work out what it is I'm going to say to him to make him actually tell me what's going on. I try to play out all the different scenarios that could potentially happen as I attempt to prepare myself to face off with my dad.

It's not that I'm scared of him. I'm more scared of what he'll do to Katy. He could do anything to me and I wouldn't really care, but he knows that. Which is why it isn't me that he makes threats against. He could take away my entire life and obviously it would suck and I'd have to think of something quick, but I could survive. I know that much.

Katy however, couldn't. She doesn't know how the world works outside of her boarding school. She's too young to survive the loss of her cocoon, and I'm not sure I'd know where to start with protecting her beyond what I'm already doing.

I head inside and find Tobias vacuuming the basement level.

He shuts it off when he sees me and envelops me in a giant hug.

"You look far too burdened for someone so young," he says, concern etched into the lines of his face as he observes me. "Is there anything that I can do to help?" he asks as he releases me from the hug, his hands still gripping my biceps and squeezing.

"Not unless you have a magic genie to grant me three wishes," I joke, and his frown deepens.

"If I did, it would be yours," he says before releasing me fully, and I tilt up the corners of my mouth.

If Tobias had been my father, my life would have been very different. I'm just thankful that I've had him in my life since I was a young child. I'm fairly certain the few slivers of humanity that I have are because of him and Mom.

God knows my dad tried to beat them out of me once my mom was gone, and he would have succeeded too, if it wasn't for the man standing before me.

"Is my dad home?" I ask, already knowing the answer. He hasn't been in the Kensington offices for a while. I know because the PA has a sweet spot for me and has always kept me apprised of his movements throughout the day.

Not for any specific reason, but I can't help but wonder what it is that my dad is doing at home so much because, before Sophie, he rarely left the office. He slept there more than he slept at home some weeks.

"Yes," he says, a look of disdain crossing his face momentarily. "He is in the nursery with Sophie, picking out colors."

My eyebrows shoot up in shock. "They're picking out nursery colors? And he's actually helping?"

Tobias laughs dryly as he nods. "Yes, I was as shocked as you are. But the designer is up there with them now. Since Sophie started to show, your father decided that it was probably time to get the house ready for a small child."

Well, this is news. I didn't think Sophie was actually pregnant. At least, that's what she told Briar. But now she's showing? My skepticism runs high, but it wouldn't be the first time Sophie has lied to Briar to get her way, so I don't know why I'm so shocked.

"So really, what you're telling me," I start, running a hand down my face, "is that he has you running around like a crazy person trying to childproof the house?"

"Exactly that," he says, rolling his eyes. "Head on up. You know where I am if you need me. They're in the room by the master suite."

"Thanks, Tobias," I say, heading toward the stairs.

I really don't want to go upstairs and speak to my father, but I know that I need to make sense of some of this if I'm going to get out of it. Though, I'm still confused about the bump because, unless Sophie has a fake one, then she definitely lied to Briar.

I know that she was supposed to keep that to herself and she swore the four of us to secrecy. Her explanation being that, with everything we know about her, she figured we should probably know everything that's going on with her mom too. Just in case.

I head upstairs, following the murmurs coming from the small room next to the master suite, and find a woman I don't recognize with my dad and Sophie. There are color swatches painted on the walls, different pieces of wallpaper hanging around, and various pieces of wood painted different colors. And once again, I'm glad that kids aren't on my agenda because this looks like my idea of Hell. Picking out colors for a room just isn't the kind of guy that I am.

"Travis, you're home," my dad says cheerfully when he sees me. His tone puts me on high alert instantly. He's never cheerful. "Is everything okay?"

He looks light, almost carefree even, and if I didn't know everything he'd ever done, I'd think that I was wrong and that he wasn't behind everything with the dean. I'd think that I'd made up how much of a monster he can be. Because the man before me... he doesn't look like the guy that I know as my father. He looks happy and alive and full of life. Excited, almost.

It's suspicious as fuck.

I wish I knew what he was up to.

"Yeah, I'm fine. I just wondered if you had a few minutes for me so that we could talk."

He quietly murmurs something in Sophie's ear before kissing her cheek and turning back to me. "I've always got time for you. Let's go to my office."

He walks across the space, claps a hand on my shoulder and

strides past me, leaving the room and heading toward his office. I can only assume that the little show was for the designer, because it definitely wasn't for me.

I keep the mask of happy family on my face while I'm in the room with Sophie and their decorator before following him. Once we're in his office and the doors are closed, the façade that he was wearing drops and I see the man that I really know.

"What do you want, Travis?" he asks as he pours himself a glass of whiskey. He doesn't offer me one, he just throws the amber liquid down his throat before pouring another and sitting on the sofa next to the drink cart. I guess underneath that mask, he's a ball of pissed off, 'cause the waves of rage coming from him are palpable.

I take a deep breath and prepare myself for the potential backlash of what I'm about to say. I'm aware of the consequences of prying into his business—I have the scars to show for it. Both mental and physical. I haven't questioned him since the last time he made me bleed, but Briar is worth the risk.

"I wanted to talk to you about Briar and the dean's latest maneuver to have her not finish this semester."

He smiles at me and it sends a shiver down my spine. The sadistic evil that shines off of his face is almost terrifying.

"I couldn't possibly know what you mean, son. Why would I try to sabotage my stepdaughter's education?" he says before laughing so hard that he ends up choking and coughing, spluttering, "Oh, that was too good. The look on your face. That girl has been nothing but a problem since she arrived. She has derailed every plan of mine, so why would I continue the façade of letting her continue her education when she is doing nothing for me?"

I stare at him, jaw slack. He looks like he's lost his damn mind, and when he looks at me he just laughs again. "Why look so dumbfounded? You knew my plans for her to marry into the Becketts. That's why I was doing what I was doing for her. If she's not playing her part, then I have no need for her. Plus, any of the men that I tagged her with at the gala, especially those who have followed up, don't care if she's educated or not. They want a breeding mare. They're not wanting an educated woman who's going to sass them. Her education isn't worth the money. If she wants to be a pain in my ass, well, I'm definitely the bigger asshole here."

I pinch the bridge of my nose, trying to process his reasoning. I'm sure it makes sense to him, but mostly I'm trying to tamp down the anger at him talking about her like she's nothing more than a doll, an asset. It's the same way he's always spoken about Katy and the anger burns through me.

"What is the point in giving her to one of your friends?" I ask, dumbfounded. His reasoning still doesn't make sense to me.

"I told you, if she's not going to marry the Beckett boy and further my political gains, then at least she can be useful by buying me other connections. These men just want a young pretty girl on their arm who's going to give them an heir for their fortunes. She could be that for them and then they will put their substantial power and money behind my campaign run. I'm not sure what it is that you're not understanding about this. You're not ignorant and I didn't raise you to be this level of stupid."

I swallow the words of him not raising me at all, because that was definitely done by Tobias. All he ever did was reign with fear and try to lord it over my life. All I've ever done is try to live up to his expectations and stumble at every hurdle.

"Now, if you can convince the girl to marry the Beckett boy, I will allow her education to continue, but considering everything else that that girl has been up to since she came to Serenity Falls, I think marrying her off to someone is going to be substantially easier than covering up everything else, don't you think?" My stomach twists as he confirms what I already suspected to be true. He was behind the arrest. He knows what she did and he's willing to use it against her. I don't say a word, refusing to confirm what I know, and his slimy smile just grows. "That's what I thought. I suggest you pick which one of them it is that you want to save, because you can only pick one, Briar or Katy. The decision is yours but just remember, one of them can fight for themselves and one of them cannot."

Fuck my actual life.

I sit in the car, staring at the Mexican restaurant that I've pulled into the parking lot of, and lean my head back against the headrest. I knew that Chase was ruthless—it's the way he raised me. It just didn't quite stick—but for him to try and make me pick between Briar and Katy is a new level of low that he hasn't sunk to before.

The two sides of me are at war. The protective big brother who would happily die to save my little sister and the man who loves the girl, who would burn the world for her.

Normally, in any other world, I could be both, but now? No matter how much I want to pick Briar every single time, I know that she can survive if I don't pick her. I know that one of the others will pick her, will help her.

Katy only has me, there is nobody else. But that doesn't mean I don't feel sick, that my stomach doesn't churn at the thought of not picking Briar.

Having to pick between the girl you love and your little sister isn't something anyone should have to do, but this is the position my father has put me in.

My phone buzzes and I glance over at the phone holder, smiling as Briar's face appears on my screen along with her message.

Briar:

Dinner turned into drinks. We'll be back later than expected.

Will be safe.

Of course it did. I'm just glad that she's able to have some fun despite everything that we've got going on. Especially because I'm going to have to be the one who tells her that her mom actually *is* pregnant. Her mom either lied to her about not being pregnant as a way to try and manipulate her into marrying Cole, or she finally fell pregnant and she's gonna have to deal with that all over again. She didn't exactly take the news well the first time so I have no idea how that's going to go.

I facetime Cole and ask him what he wants for food, knowing that the other two will be with him and listening. Once I have their orders, I hang up and my phone starts ringing almost immediately. A smile stretches across my face when I see Katy's face staring back at me. I answer instantly and find her waving frantically at the screen.

She's getting so grown up, but when she talks to me, she's still just my kid sister.

"Hi, Travis! I'm still awake," she says like she's trying to whisper. I hear the giggles of other girls in the background and she joins them. "We're having a sleepover. Everybody's in my dorm tonight."

"Oh, really?" I ask, raising an eyebrow, pretending to be skeptical. "And which of the dorm mistresses approved this, huh?" My words draw another giggle from her and it's like a balm to my very shredded soul.

"Mrs. Winters said that we could all have a sleepover because it's my birthday soon. I get to see you for my birthday this year, right, Travis?" she asks, tugging at my heartstrings without even meaning to.

"I'm going to try and get you back home for it this year, Katy Bug. Don't you worry. Then we can do all of the things that you've always wanted us to do."

Her face somehow manages to light up even more at the prospect of it. "That would be the best birthday ever, Travis! I want to come home, to see you and Tobias. I want to see the puppies for real too."

My cheeks almost hurt with how much I'm smiling. Even as guilt floods through me at the fact that she's not here and that she's literally on the other side of the country. "I'm working on it, Katy Bug, don't you worry. I've even got Pops on board with trying to smuggle you home."

She claps her hands together and bounces on the spot. "I'm going to be a whole nine," she says excitedly.

Sometimes I wonder if being there is making her grow up too fast. I've seen her in class and walking the halls of her boarding school and it's like she's already a grown-up. I can't quite handle it. I can't help but mourn that she doesn't get to be a proper kid sometimes.

"Yes, you will. And nine means that we need to celebrate in all the special ways."

She nods her head excitedly. "Yes, please. Can we go

horseback riding too?"

"If that's what you want, then that's what we'll do." I know how much she loves the horses at school and I'm unable to deny her anything. I smile in the back of my mind because I know how much Briar loves horses too. Maybe that's something that the three of us can do together, and how I'll introduce Briar to her because I haven't mentioned her to Katy yet. God knows my father wouldn't have, that would require him actually speaking to her.

A knock sounds on the door on her end and squeals sound before I hear the dorm mistress's voice filter through. "You've got ten minutes to lights out. I suggest you get into bed." I hear the click as the door closes and the girls all giggle again.

Oh, to be that young and carefree.

I hope they will keep it for as long as they can, because all the girls there are similar to Katy. Which means they're destined for the life that I lead and that, unfortunately, means that their innocence isn't going to last all that much longer.

"I have to go now, Travis, but I'll see you soon for my birthday?"

"I pinky promise," I say to her, and she puts her little finger on the screen as I do the same. "Love you, Katy Bug."

"Love you too, Travis," she says before the screen goes dark.

I take a deep breath, knowing that I'll move Heaven and Earth to make sure she gets to come home for her birthday.

Seeing that joy on her face is enough to make me do almost anything. I put my phone back on the holder and head through the drive thru to grab food for everybody before heading home so I can eat while we wait for Briar to get home, because lord knows I'm not going to sleep until she gets back.

Who knows? Maybe she'll be in the mood to cheer me up when she gets there. Or maybe, even better, she'll do something to poke my anger and I'll get to play with her properly.

I smirk at the thought. Yeah, I'm definitely going to punish her later, and she'll enjoy every second of it.

LILY WILDHART

NINE

BRIAR

I wake up deliciously sore and more than a little bruised. Still trying to work out if what happened last night was real or a dream.

I'm alone in the bed, the sheets beside me cold, but the sun is bright as it filters through the windows. I check my phone and see that it's already lunchtime.

Holy shit, I guess I needed a lot of sleep after everything that's been going on lately.

I take my time stretching before I climb out of bed and go grab a hot shower, using the power of the water to knead out the kinks in my neck and ease some of the bruising from last night. It was hot shit, and I didn't think that I'd be as into everything that went down as I was, but I absolutely was. *So* here for it happening again. If the guys are up for it anyway. I should probably speak to Sawyer about that, and about what I thought about last night. Though how I'm going to bring *that* up is beyond me, and if it was just a dream, I'm gonna look like an absolute idiot.

God, I love being an overthinking type of girl. It's so much fun… said nobody ever.

Once I'm showered, I take extra care with myself, trying to pep talk my inner scaredy cat for a conversation that I probably should have had with the guys long before now, but it's not like we haven't had a lot going on to keep distracting me from this particular thing on my doom list.

Once I feel like I have my armor on, I pad downstairs. My fluffy socks muffle the sound of my footsteps on the hardwood. It's only when Shadow and the other puppies announce my arrival that the jig is up and I find the four of them huddled around the island in the kitchen, talking while Asher makes sandwiches for everybody.

"Morning, Sunshine," Sawyer calls out, smirking at me.

"Morning," I call back, smiling wide as I head over to them. I jump up onto the stool at the end of the counter and my stomach gurgles. Asher laughs at me, shaking his head. "I'll make you one too."

Sawyer bounces over to the coffee machine and starts making me a coffee. "Peppermint or black forest?" he asks, and my grin wilts the tiniest bit over them doing everything for me. It's still weird.

"Peppermint, please," I respond, trying not to feel like I'm taking advantage of his kindness. Once the coffee's in front of me, Sawyer goes to kiss my cheek, but I turn my head before his lips land and kiss him properly. When he pulls back, he wags his brows at me, making me smile. "I can definitely deal with starting the morning like that every day."

I can't help but giggle at his silliness before he hops back up onto his stool, and Asher lays out plates in front of everybody before he takes a seat himself.

I take a deep breath and say the words that nobody ever wants to hear. "So, we should probably talk."

The silence that emanates through the room is so intense that you could hear a pin drop. Even the puppies have gone deadly silent. The four of them just stare at me with looks on their faces varying from amusement to sheer horror.

"It's nothing bad," I say, trying to claw back some semblance of normal. "I just figured we should probably talk about this thing between the four of us and how it translates into real life. I don't know what we're doing or what this is. My brain needs clarity on something in my life right now and, unfortunately for you guys, that gets to be this."

Nope, didn't ramble on with that at all.

It's like the four of them let out a deep breath all at once, and Sawyer starts to chuckle.

"Dude! That's not a 'we need to talk' conversation. We save that line for the real stuff... for the heavy stuff," he says before taking a giant bite from his sandwich.

"Yeah, are you trying to give us all a heart attack?" Asher asks as he slides chips into his sandwich. Pressing down on them, the crunch... it makes my mouth water. I definitely need to try that.

"I wasn't trying to do anything other than have a conversation," I say, attempting to keep as light as they appear to be about the whole thing. "I just need some clarity, some understanding, because, obviously, I've never done this before. Your entire world is new to me, and I have no idea how to navigate any of this and all the things that we're dealing with. I feel like I have no control over anything in my life right now. I need some semblance of control. So I need to have this conversation."

"Well, what do *you* want this to be?" Travis asks, leaning back on his stool as the four of them look back at me, and I feel like someone just lit a fire under my ass.

"This isn't exactly how I saw this conversation going. I mean... I have no idea. I've never done this before. Is this something that even manages to translate into real life, considering the high-profile exposure you and Cole have with the world you live in? Is something like this even reasonably acceptable in your worlds? Where I come from anything goes, but the rules here are different."

Sawyer chuckles at me while Asher smiles. Cole doesn't say anything, but that's not surprising, considering who he is as a human.

"The way our world works is like this: with power comes doing whatever the fuck you like. So we tell the world what is acceptable; that's the joy of our circles. If we tell the world that we're doing this, but it's wrong, then that is how they will view it. But if we tell the world that this is who we are, and this is what we're doing, and that this is absolutely the way forward, then that is also how it will be accepted. Of course, there are going to be some people that turn their nose up at the idea of a poly sort of relationship. But again, that's how the world works in general," Asher says.

Sawyer nods in agreement. "Everything he just said."

"So I ask again," Travis says, drawing my attention to him. "What do *you* want this to be?"

I look to Cole, who watches me intently and takes a deep breath. "I want exactly what we have. The four of us don't want to have to choose, then you don't have to choose."

Travis nods. "We all agreed to share you and that hasn't changed for us. And if you're on the same page as we are, then fuck what anybody else thinks."

I smile, my heart fluttering in my chest, surprised that this was as easy as it was. Sawyer reaches over and squeezes my thigh and, as if reading my mind, says, "Easier than you thought, hmm?"

I roll my eyes at him, and he leans over and squeezes my thigh again. "One day you'll learn that you can tell us anything and it will be okay. I mean, you literally killed a man and we covered that up. Why wouldn't asking about our relationship status be okay?"

I try not to laugh at how casually he talks about what happened on Thanksgiving and shake my head. "Only *you* could take possibly the worst thing I've done in my life and make it sound like a day at the fair."

"We've all done things that the world would frown upon. We're not about to judge you for what you did to survive." He pauses, looking at me intently. "Eventually, you'll find out all of our deepest, darkest secrets, but just know there isn't anything you could tell us that would change how we feel about you."

I look down at my lap because there's still so much that they don't know. "And one day, you'll know all of *my* deepest, darkest secrets too," I say before grabbing my sandwich and standing. "I'm going to head back upstairs and study. You guys are way too distracting."

Travis laughs once, Cole nods, and the twins just smile at me.

"Yeah, we know we're hot. Way too hot, which is good for us, because it makes it way too easy to distract you," Sawyer calls out, and I shake my head as I make my way up the stairs, tapping my hand on my hip to call my monster, and Shadow runs up beside me.

"Could be that, or it could just be that this guy's the only company I want for the rest of the day," I say as I turn to look back at them over my shoulder and stick my tongue out.

"Never thought I'd be jealous of a goddamn puppy," I hear Sawyer grumble behind me. I can't help but laugh as I close the door to my room and Shadow jumps on the bed.

Maybe this day won't be so bad after all.

My conversation with the guys went so much better than I thought it would. And while things are still a little fuzzy about everything else in my life, at least I know where I stand with them. It's made me feel like I'm not just walking through my entire life with blinders on. I lie on my bed, reading through my textbooks, considering I now have to do all of my studying myself, with Shadow curled up beside me.

When a knock sounds at the door, I look up and find Travis hovering in the doorway, seemingly unsure about whether or not he actually wants to be here, which is unlike him.

"What's up?" I ask him, and it's as if my words cement whatever decision it was he was trying to make. He steps through the doorway, closing the door behind him.

"Not to use your own words against you, but we should probably talk."

My heart drops and my stomach twists. It's almost ironic,

because I know I used that line earlier this morning and they laughed that it wasn't meant to be a bad thing, but they were right. Just hearing that one particular line does make you want to vomit.

"Is everything okay?" I ask as I sit up and push my textbooks to the side. He comes and sits opposite me, cross-legged, keeping distance between us. I can't help but think that he's changed his mind, even though we only had the conversation a couple of hours ago.

"We need to talk about your mom," he says, and my stomach twists a little more. At least it's not about anything between us, but if it's about my mom, it can't be anything good. "I went to see my dad the other night, to see what he was up to with the dean, and I found him at home with your mom and a decorator for the nursery."

I let out a sharp laugh, shaking my head. "The nursery? She's not even pregnant. I have no idea how she's going to keep up with this."

"Well, that's just it," he says, a frown on his face and the lines on his forehead deepening. "She's showing."

I feel my forehead furrow as puzzlement zips through me. "What do you mean, she's showing? She told me she wasn't pregnant. She told me that's why I needed to marry Cole, so that your dad didn't kick us out, so we wouldn't be left with nothing."

He shrugs and runs a hand through his shaggy dark hair. "I

don't know why she said that, but she's definitely showing and that's why they're decorating the nursery. I don't know if she lied to you, or if she's become pregnant since, or if she's somehow managing to fake the bump, but she is definitely showing."

I sit and chew on the inside of my lip, trying to work out how I feel about the fact that she actually could be pregnant again. I'm not surprised about the fact that she might have lied to me. That's her entire M.O. Telling the truth has never been her strong suit, but for her to try and manipulate me like that and use protecting her as some sort of sword to wield just makes me hate her a little more.

"Briar," Travis says, drawing my eyes to his. He just watches me as if he's trying to figure out what's going on inside my head.

"I'm okay," I tell him. "I mean, I'm not okay. This is beyond wild. But in the grand scheme of things, I'm okay. I already knew it was a possibility and that she was trying. You finding out that she lied to me pisses me off a bit, but being pregnant, I just... I don't really have anything for her. My biggest thing is being worried about the kid if it survives, because she might just be the worst mom on Earth. She isn't fit for motherhood; she doesn't have a maternal bone in her body."

I let out a breath and shake my head. "That might not be fair, considering what she told me about my conception, but if she was a warm mother, at any point, it's not something I remember."

"What do you mean?" he asks, and it occurs to me that, while

I told them she confirmed Crawford was my father, I haven't told him, or any of them, about the rest of the conversation that I had with my mom.

So I tell him what she told me about the fact that Crawford raped her and that that was why she never told me that my dad wasn't my dad.

He doesn't say a word. He just sits and listens to me explain everything like a robot, because I still haven't worked out how to process what my mom told me, or even if I believe it. I would never lie about rape, and I'd never question a victim, but my mom's history of lying to me is rampant. Case in point: the pregnancy that she very obviously has.

"Briar, I'm sorry. I didn't know."

I shrug. Because what else can I do?

"It's fine. It is what it is. He's dead now, so yeah…" I run a hand through my hair and pull my textbook back in front of me, trying not to let any kind of emotion overwhelm me. "I should probably get back to this," I say to him, and he looks at me like I've lost my mind.

"Are you sure you're okay?" he asks. I nod, knowing full well that I am not okay, but there isn't any room for me to be anything but okay right now.

"I'm sure," I tell him. "Do we have any plans tonight?"

He shakes his head as he stands. "No, I don't think so."

"Okay, well, maybe I can cook for everybody," I say to him. "It's been ages since I got to cook a real meal and I kind of have the urge for it."

"Okay," he says, still looking at me like I've lost my mind. "Just let me or one of the others know what you want to make and we'll make sure we've got the stuff for it."

"I can go to the store," I respond, but he just looks at me like I'm stupid.

"Briar, tell me or one of the other guys what you need and we will make sure that we have it for you."

I still feel squirrely about the fact that they don't let me pay for anything. It's not like I have any money to pay for it anyway, but it's the principle of the thing. But I nod, which seems to appease him, and he leaves me on my own.

Once the door is closed, I throw the textbook to the end of the bed and flop backwards so I'm staring at the ceiling, and Shadow moves to curl beside me again.

Yeah, I'm not getting any studying done today because all I'm going to think about is the fact that I might have another little brother or sister, and the thought of leaving a small human with my mom and Chase absolutely terrifies me.

After spending most of yesterday evening going back and forth about what Travis told me, I decided that the only way to know for sure was to ask my mom. I mean, she could lie to me, God knows she's done that plenty, but maybe she won't.

It's a huge maybe, but if I don't try, I'll drive myself insane thinking about it.

Thinking about the very tiny human who is going to be at the mercy of her and Chase turns my blood to ice, but I also don't know if I can survive going through what happened with Iris again. It's not that I won't want to know them, but I don't know if I can get attached again.

Not knowing the sort of life they'll have, especially in *this* world…

I'm powerless to protect myself, let alone anyone else.

That is exactly how I find myself sitting in the booth in the kitchen, the place where I met the guys for the first time all those months ago—well, second time all those months ago—sipping on a chocolate milk as Tobias flits around the room while I wait to speak to my mom.

Apparently, she's out shopping this morning. My own fault for not checking in and seeing if she was home, but I didn't want to give her notice to plan her lies to me. I've found that, usually, with her, it's easier just to drop in on her because I'm more likely to get the truth of the matter.

I've already been here for about half an hour with no idea when she's coming home, but at least if I'm here, I can see her rather than going back home and continuing to spiral in my own mind.

I can say I'm okay with everything, that I'm totally fine, out loud as many times as I like, but just because I can wear a mask and show the world that I'm okay doesn't mean that I am underneath. Masking is exhausting and I just don't want to do it.

So I'm sitting here sipping on my chocolate milk, waiting like a child for my mom to get home. A few minutes later, the kitchen door swings open and I think for a minute that it might be her, but it's Chase who walks through the door.

He pauses when he sees me sitting at the table, but his stride only hesitates for a moment before he heads for Tobias. "Tobias, I have people coming for dinner this evening. I need us to prepare a meal for ten."

My eyes go wide at the very little notice that he's given, but Tobias just nods. "Of course, that's not a problem at all. Who's coming so I can ensure that the menu suits."

Chase reels off names, some that I recognize like the St. Vincents and the Becketts, then others that I don't, but it's none of my business so I keep my mouth shut and sip on my milk.

When he's finished with Tobias, Chase turns to me, his heels clicking on the hard floor as he comes over to where I'm sitting.

"Why are you here?" he asks, any pretense of friendliness very much absent.

"I'm waiting to speak to my mother," I tell him, trying not to look as intimidated as I very much feel right now.

"Come with me," he commands and, without missing a beat, turns on his heel and walks out of the room. I guess he expects me to follow like a dog called to heel, but really, what else can I do? So even though it chafes at me to be spoken to and treated like this, I get up and rush out of the room to follow Chase toward his office.

By the time I get there, I find him already sitting behind his desk. "Close the door," he says sharply and, instinctively, I do as he says. I guess a man who wields the power that he does on a regular basis just has that authoritative air about him. And I, being a typical worker, naturally cave to it. But that doesn't stop it pissing me off.

"What did you want to speak to your mother about?"

"I just wanted to speak to her about the baby," I say to him, trying to be as honest yet brief as I can. Because part of me still doesn't want to drop her in the shit if she isn't pregnant and he thinks that she is. I don't know why I'm still trying to protect her, but it's ingrained into the very fiber of my being.

"Well, obviously, she's not here. And you don't need to concern yourself with the child," he says to me. "If I were you, I'd be more worried about my own life and prospects."

I clench my fists, my shoulders tightening as I look at him from across the room, still standing by the door as he reminds me about the shit with the dean. "Your prospects are getting slimmer and slimmer, and I've only shown you a *taste* of the power that I hold, the things that I can do to you."

He quirks a brow and smirks at me, so I take a deep breath, trying not to rise to the bait, which just seems to infuriate him and he continues, "I've had you arrested once. I can have you arrested again. I'm sure Travis told you about the evidence that

I have against you. But just in case he didn't…" He pauses, reaching over and opening one of the drawers in his desk. He pulls out a file and throws it onto the desk, pictures scattering across the hard wood and onto the floor.

I move forward a few steps, but I don't need to get any closer to know what's on the images. I can see it clear as day.

Me running, Crawford behind me.

Me struggling with Crawford.

The boys carrying Crawford's body away.

A part of me would like to think that he wouldn't share the pictures of the boys, but I also don't know him well enough to trust that to be the complete truth.

"What do you want?" I ask him, and he smiles like a Cheshire cat who got the cream.

"What I want is for you to start doing as I've fucking told you to do. You either marry the Beckett boy or you marry one of the other men that I put you with and you stop causing problems. *And stop fucking my son.*"

I take a step back in shock, not even meaning to move. I didn't know that he was aware of my relationship with Travis. But I suppose if he has these pictures, God knows what else he has on me and the rest of us. I open my mouth to speak, but nothing comes out and Chase laughs harshly at me.

"Don't speak now, you don't want to say the wrong thing. This could be the end of everything for you, and for everybody you love, or just the beginning. I suggest you take some time to think on it. Come back to me by the end of next week. That's all the time I'm going to give you, but trust me, not doing what I'm telling you to do has far bigger consequences than those I have laid out before you right now."

TEN

BRIAR

I have spent the entire day stress cleaning. The guys are out attending classes and God knows what else. Cole has been having an absolute mess of a couple of days because he has a super important game next week, apparently.

I am, obviously, the worst human in the world because I keep forgetting that he even plays for the team, despite the fact that he disappears each morning and some weekends. We've barely focused on any of his wins or losses because of the shit I've had going on, and I feel terrible about that, but I'm told this is nearly the last game of the season and it's super important with scouts and stuff.

Not that I have any idea what any of that means. Sawyer

filled me in on that—and the fact that he and Asher have been summoned by their parents for dinner tonight, alone—before he left at ass o'clock this morning when everybody headed out to train with Cole.

So I've spent most of my time spiraling about being a terrible human and about having my head so far up my ass that I've barely noticed things going on with the people around me, including Penn, who sent a message to me this morning because, despite going out for dinner earlier in the week, I haven't talked to her since then. Because, hello, I am a terrible person and everything seems to be about me at the moment.

I hate that this is who I've become.

I haven't even told the guys about my conversation with Chase yesterday because that's just making it about me again.

At least I actually got to speak to my mom after Chase and his bullshit yesterday. It turns out she is actually pregnant and that she did lie to me before. Her standard reaction of rolling her eyes and telling me not to take things so personally—so seriously—is what had me leaving, wishing her well and regretting that I'd ever turned up there because, obviously, my conversation with Chase wasn't enough to tell me that yesterday was going to be a crappy day.

I spent the rest of last night curled up in my room pretending to study, which just made me feel worse when I realized how much stuff the guys have going on today.

My head is basically mush at this point. My brain almost

feels like Swiss cheese.

Holey as fuck.

I turn the volume up louder when *Fuck Your Labels* by Carlie Hanson comes on my playlist and blasts through the speakers in the house. I scream the song at the top of my lungs because every single word feels like it resonates with me.

I dance along as I vacuum, having put the dogs out in the backyard while I'm doing so because vacuuming is a pointless task when you have six giant dogs running around after you. Once I'm finished with the vacuum, I pause and look around the sparkling space. I've dusted and scrubbed every inch of the kitchen and lounge to within an inch of its life, and it still hasn't done anything for the prickly feeling underneath my skin.

That feeling like my blood is gonna bubble up like a volcano and rupture out of me with all of the crazy that's going on in my life.

I grab the mop and run around the floors once more before I head upstairs. My phone buzzes in my pocket, and I giggle-snort when I see the message on my screen.

Penn:

TOTM. Cramps are the worst. I need chocolate. SOS. Send help.

Me:

That's the worst. I can bring chocolate. You want anything else?

Penn:

Heat pads. Pain killers. ALL OF THE THINGS, BRIAR.

Me:

Let me get dressed and shit, then I'll swing by the store on my way to you.

Penn:

You rock. Going to crawl back under my rock now.

I laugh, shaking my head, never more thankful for my IUD and the fact that it stops my periods. I was never one of those girls that overly struggled with them—could be the major malnutrition I had in early puberty, who knows—but I definitely don't miss them.

Not even a little bit.

I jump in the shower because *man* am I ripe after a day of cleaning. I've left the boys' rooms alone, after threats of bodily damage, but my stress clean started in my bedroom and bathroom, so this place already smells like a dream and practically sparkles.

After my shower, I put on jeans and a T-shirt and a pair of fuzzy socks because I don't have anywhere to go today but to see Penn, so why not? I love it; I'm so rock and roll.

Padding back down the stairs, I decide to let the dogs in now that the floors are dry. I head back to the island where my study materials are from earlier, after I decided to jump back into trying to focus on something that isn't Chase and his not so idle threats, when there's a knock on the door. I grab my phone and drop a message into our group chat.

Me:

Were you guys expecting anyone today?

There's no response straight away, so I head to the door. I'm startled when I find Travis's pops staring back at me.

"Briar, there you are. Just the girl I was after," he says as he strides past me into the house, and I just kind of stare at him, blinking, dumbfounded.

"Is everything okay?" I ask once I manage to get my wits about me.

"Of course, everything's fine. I just thought that you and I should talk, all things considered."

"All things considered?" I ask, my brain not exactly functioning at full speed right now.

He smirks at me, and it strikes me how much he and Travis look alike. "Yes. You know, things like my son trying to have you thrown in jail and my grandson being half in love with you. Those things."

"Ah," I squeak, not knowing where to look or what to do

with myself. "Yeah, I-I guess we can talk about that stuff."

He fusses with the dogs, who haven't let him be since he walked in the door. "Don't worry, dear girl, I'm not here to wring you out. I understand my son's been doing plenty of that. I'm here to see if I can provide any solutions."

"Oh," is all that falls from my lips, because what sort of Twilight Zone is it that I've just stepped into?

"Well, get your shoes and your coat. No point in discussing everything here. I'm a hungry man, and I imagine that you probably haven't eaten yet today either, so let's go get some food and talk this out, shall we?"

"Erm… Yeah. Okay," I say before running upstairs and grabbing some socks and my Converse. My phone buzzes in my pocket with messages from the guys. After I scroll through them, I quickly type back.

Me:

It was just Pops. He wants to take me out to lunch. We'll fill you in later.

I hit send and pocket my phone again. Quickly checking my reflection before I go back down, I confirm that I do not look like I'm ready to go and eat with the suited and booted man that is down in the living room right now, but this is what I've got and he didn't say anything about changing, so I don't intend on doing so.

I head back downstairs and find him sitting on the floor with the dogs, laughing as they attack him.

"Are you ready?" he asks when he looks up and sees me. Still feeling super uneasy, I fight the urge to shuffle as he climbs to his feet.

"Come on then. We have a lot to discuss and food always makes everything better. Steak?" he asks, and I nod, not knowing what else to do.

"Oh, but first, can we swing by the store? I need to do an SOS run for a friend."

He smiles at me and brushes off the dog hair from his suit. "Of course, but uh, what is an SOS run?"

"Time of the month store run," I tell him, trying not to smile.

"Ah, yes. Definitely an SOS run. Grab your things and we'll do that, then lunch."

Grabbing my purse and keys as he walks out of the house, I follow behind and climb into the black sedan that he has parked out on the street. This could either be the answer to all my prayers or go horribly wrong. Who wants to take the bet that it's the latter?

That went… weirdly better than I expected and I have a total pep in my step. So when I enter the house and find Travis and Cole working out—they've turned what was the empty space behind the stairs into a gym—I am not exactly sad to find them half naked and sweaty.

"Looking good, boys. Keep it up," I tease as I move toward them.

"You want to join us?" Cole asks with a grin, because he knows exercise is not my thing.

"Not a chance. I can think of much better ways to get sweaty than a treadmill or lifting weights."

Travis drops the bar he's holding to the ground and stands up tall again before grabbing a towel and rubbing it down his face and chest. "Then why don't we do that instead?"

He takes two steps toward me and straight up lifts me over his shoulder in a fireman's carry, spanking my ass for good measure. I let out a yelp of shock, but there's a huge grin on my face.

Yeah, this is a good day.

"You coming?" Travis bellows, and I hear Cole's chuckle as we head up the stairs.

"You know I am."

Moments later, I see Cole a few steps behind us as we reach the landing, and I just hang like some damsel in distress, ready to be ravaged.

Oh no, two evil villains in their sweatpants are going to defile me. What on earth shall I do?

I let out a giggle-snort before clamping my hands over my face, and a slap stings my ass again while Cole chuckles from a few steps down.

A door opens and moments later I'm being flung downward, bouncing as I land on the bed. When I've got my equilibrium back, I look up to find them both watching me. They couldn't be more different, and yet... oh, I know I'm going to enjoy this.

Brat mode: Activate.

"You really think the two of you can handle me?" I ask, quirking a brow as I sit up and fold my arms over my chest.

Travis turns to Cole, one dark brow raised in question, and it's like they're having an entire conversation I'm not privy to.

"That's not fair. You're always harping on about 'use your words'," I make sure to imitate Travis's voice with a little snark thrown in for good measure. Well, that gets his attention back to me.

"Bro, I'm pretty sure that's the definition of 'asking for it'," Cole says, his head cocked to the side like he's calculating all the different ways he can devour me and still leave some leftovers for Travis.

"I'd go so far as to say 'she's begging for it'." Now, it's Travis's turn to roam his gaze over my body, lighting every inch of it on fire.

"I am not! All I'm saying is, you don't play fair." Two pairs of eyes snap up to mine with matching smirks planted firmly on their lips.

"Oh, Baby Girl, no one ever said anything about playing fair when it comes to fucking the sass right out of you." It's like

Travis knows exactly what words will make me instantly wet and he's not afraid to use them. Quite the opposite, really.

I'm eyeing them both as Cole's eyes spark just before he walks around to the side of the bed, grabs my ankles, and turns me over until I'm on my stomach and lying crossways. Meanwhile, Travis just crosses his arms over his chest and smirks like he's already scripted this entire fucking scenario right down to the tiniest detail.

"Like you ever need an excuse to fuck me within an inch of my life. Sass or no sass." Cole's hands are now on the waist of my jeans, two nimble fingers snapping the button open and the other hand pulling the zipper down until all he needs to do is slide the denim right off of me.

When I see the look in his eyes, it makes me glad I wore my favorite thong. That look sends a shiver down my spine in the most delicious of ways.

"Well, look at that. She was planning for this." Looking over my shoulder at Cole, I catch him raising a brow up at Travis.

"Briar, Briar, Briar. Did you think you could manipulate us into giving you free orgasms?" Travis reaches down into his low hanging sweats—thank fuck for sweatpants season—and runs his big, capable hand over his already monster of an erection.

I snort at his scolding comment.

"Like I need to do much to get either one of you hard and ready to fuck." I slap my hand over my mouth, realizing that I've actually said that out loud.

Fuck me.

"Well, well. They say the truth comes out of the mouths of babes." Cole's words are punctuated with a long, slow lick from my clit to just below my asshole before he snaps the thong right back into place. "Hmm, and Briar is nothing if not a hot as fuck little brat." Then he takes a handful of my ass cheek and bites down on my flesh. Hard.

Clenching my teeth, I try really freaking hard to show indifference, but Travis is too observant; he knows exactly what I like, and that little bite of pain from Cole is the perfect amount of foreplay.

"Make sure she doesn't come. She hasn't earned it yet." Travis's wolfish grin, especially as he cocks his head to the side, infuriates me. But not enough to keep my mouth shut, apparently.

"That's bullshit!" I think Travis was right earlier. I am the very definition of "begging for it". In a nanosecond, his hand is in my hair, fingers curled around my long strands as he pulls back until all I can see is the ceiling and his vibrant—almost violent—blue eyes.

"Was that addressed to me, my little slut?" I bite my lip, not quite knowing if I should answer or if that was a rhetorical question.

A slap to my ass has me grunting and closing my eyes with pleasure.

"He asked you a fucking question, Briar." Cole's deep tenor

travels through my core and warms my entire nervous system.

"No, sir." Sir? Am I that person now? Yep, apparently, I am.

When I finally open my eyes back up, Travis's smile is like a fucking gift from the gods and suddenly, it's the only thing I ever want for birthdays and Christmases. That genuine smile of pure, unadulterated satisfaction.

"There's hope for you yet, Baby Girl." His mouth is suddenly on mine, his tongue demanding entrance, lips bruising and possessive as he takes what he wants and gives zero apologies for it.

Behind me, Cole buries his face in my pussy, feasting on me like he's been starved for a lifetime as he eats me thoroughly without ever ignoring my throbbing clit.

My legs are suddenly boneless, my muscles unable to cooperate as Cole and Travis assault me from both ends. I moan into Travis's mouth, and he swallows down the sound like it's the icing on a very naughty cake.

Cole spreads my ass cheeks, the hot, humid air of his breath teasing my puckered hole right before he dives right back into my pussy with renewed fervor.

Neither one of them is kissing me right now. No, they're both fucking me with their tongues, pushing in and pulling out as they dominate me with the sheer power of their mouths.

A whimper escapes me as Travis pulls away, leaving my mouth cold and empty, which only makes him chuckle at my frustration.

"Now that you're nice and warmed up, it's time to suck my cock, my beautiful little slut. I want to see it buried in your throat. I want you to choke on it while I watch the tears stain your cheeks." I'm guessing any normal person would be screaming "red flags" from the top of her lungs, but all I do is get impossibly wetter with every dirty word that leaves Travis's perfect lips.

Cole has been using my thong as a tool of punishment, snapping it back in place every time he's done licking me to the brink of orgasm, but he's clearly bored of that since he's now pulling the lace over my hips and down my thighs. Raising one knee, then the other, he discards the material before bringing his cock up to my pussy lips.

Travis steps closer to my mouth, my hands gripping the edge of the mattress as Cole kneels right behind me. I'm about to get speared on both ends and I can't fucking wait. My eyes are on Travis, watching his every move, his every tic as his gaze darts up behind me—probably communicating something to Cole—before he gives me his full attention once more.

"Open up that pretty little mouth for me, Baby Girl, so I can destroy it with my dick." I moan at Travis's words and grunt when Cole speaks.

"Fuck yeah, she's so wet right now, I could fuck her ass using only her juices as lube."

Yes, please!

"We'll see. First, she needs to earn it." Without another

word, Travis brings his cock to my lips, spreading his precum across my top lip before smearing my bottom one and pushing his entire length into my mouth without stopping until his groin is pressing against my nose.

The musky scent of his sweat and everything deliciously male about him is like a fucking drug at this point. I'm barely coherent with the amount of pheromones swirling around me.

Just as Travis places both of his hands on the sides of my head to direct his thrusts, Cole's cock slowly slides into my pussy, nudging that perfect spot deep inside me.

I'm officially getting fucked on both ends and the fullness, the possession, the complete dominance is my favorite high. No drug equals the ecstasy of being wanted this much.

Just as Travis predicted, tears start falling from the corners of my eyes, trailing down my cheeks and dripping off of my chin as I concentrate on not choking on his cock. Except, that's what he wants, right? To hear me gagging? To know he's the reason I can't breathe, that he's got that power over me?

As Cole's thrusts alternate with Travis's, I take in a deep breath through my nose as one dick slams into my pussy and the other pulls out, almost completely, from my mouth. Staring into Travis's eyes, I can see the pure, unbidden lust that shines in them. He's daring me to disappoint him, to be predictable like all the others in his life, but the idea of being subpar for him makes me feel physically ill.

Without lowering my gaze or closing my eyes, I challenge

him right back. Just as he pushes himself completely down my throat, I gag all around him, choke on the thick shaft that invades my esophagus and let my saliva coat my lips to make it even easier for him to get his wish. And there it is. The pride, the satisfaction that he's causing all these reactions. That he could orchestrate my life or death, it shines bright in his unmoving gaze.

"You're such a good girl, taking us both like this. Opening up your pretty little pussy for Cole and gagging on my cock." As he speaks, Travis uses his thumb to wipe away my tears before bringing it to his mouth and licking off the saltiness. Just as Cole pulls out, Travis thrusts his cock back inside my mouth one last time, grinding his groin over my face and grunting like a possessed animal. "Take it!" And I do. I take everything he gives me, but when Cole enters me again as he reaches around and pinches my clit as he empties himself in me, I groan around Travis's dick because screaming is impossible. My entire body shakes with the orgasm Cole pulls from me—without Travis's permission I might add.

When Travis slides out from between my lips, he bends over and kisses me so tenderly it belies the roughness of moments ago. It's crazy how he's capable of such gentleness just seconds after showing such ferocity, but I fucking love every minute of it.

Cole pulls out of my pussy, and I suddenly feel empty, cold even.

"You said you wanted to play, right Briar?" Travis's words are whispered in my ear as his hand slides from my chest to my collarbone and straight to my neck where he curls his fingers around my pulse points and squeezes just enough to get my full attention.

"Yes, sir." Again with the sir thing but I don't regret it, not when I can see how delighted my little word makes this larger-than-life man who has the power to love me and kill me in the same breath.

"Cole got your pussy, now it's my turn." In a quick move, I go from all fours to lying on my back, Travis pushing me down into the mattress at the only place he's touching me for now: my throat. "Grab the lube." His words are aimed at Cole but his eyes never leave mine, as if he's weighing my reaction, judging if I'm up for it or not. Testing me.

Well, I'm an excellent fucking student, *sir*, so bring it the fuck on.

A cruel, majestic grin lights up his entire face as he adds pressure to my neck seconds before he spears me with his cock without a second's notice. I gasp, but the sound is snuffed out by a quick flex of his hand from his position above me. From the corner of my eye, I can see Cole discarding his sweat pants just as he reaches into the drawer of the nightstand and pulls out the lube. Travis continues to fuck me hard and fast, his cock pistoning in and out of my pussy with unrelenting grunts. The force of his movements makes every single one of his muscles contract, the dips between his abs and the veins in his neck all proof of the power he's keeping leashed in. What would happen if he just let it all go? If he unleashed his power over me? How far would he actually go? Fuck, I want to find out.

Pulling out of me, Travis leans in and kisses me, our teeth and tongues battling it out like the clashing of titans. We groan into each other's mouths and right before he pulls away, he whispers, "I'm addicted to your taste."

I don't have time to register his words before I find myself kneeling over Cole, my back to his chest with the head of his cock nudging my puckered hole as he pours generous amounts of lube over my crack. It slides between my ass cheeks, and the slick sounds of his hand over his cock make me wetter by the second.

"Lean back, little brat." There's no venom in Cole's words, only lust. Travis nods and I follow their instructions, leaning back and realizing that Cole is sitting up against the headboard. Just as my back touches his chest, the head of his cock clears the tight ring of muscles, earning them both a small whimper from me. It burns just enough to make the pleasure of it that much more intense.

Travis brings two of his fingers to my pussy and scoops up the proof of my arousal and what's left of Cole's.

"Dirty little slut, indeed." He brings his fingers to my mouth and coats my lips right before he devours me in a kiss so intense I forget I'm about to get a huge dick fully inside my ass. In fact, it's not until Cole's completely seated inside me that Travis relents and pulls away.

He was distracting me and it fucking worked.

"Fuck, she's so tight. Not sure how long I'll last in this delicious little ass of hers." My cheeks flare from the compliment, but it doesn't last long. Cole's hands slide from my hips to my stomach then up to my tits, where he curls his fingers around them and pulls me down harder onto his cock.

"Oh my God!" My words sound far off, every single nerve in my body concentrated on the feel of Cole's invasion.

"Fuck yeah, this feels so fucking good."

"Just wait, it's about to get even better." Travis's words are ominous as one of his hands comes back to my throat, the other latching onto my hip just as he positions his cock at my wide-open pussy and plunges inside without any hesitation.

We all groan together in unison. I'm so fucking full that it's almost painful. Two cocks, two huge dicks, planted firmly inside both of my holes, is equal parts pain and perfection.

Travis has all the control. He fucks me, fast and hard, while Cole grinds against my ass, his hands squeezing my tits harder and harder the faster Travis fucks me. Every thrust equals a grunt from Cole and me. I try to hold on for dear life, my arms reaching back, planted on either side of Cole's chest.

Travis pushes me back and turns my head so Cole can kiss me, tasting, no doubt, the juices from my pussy. The more we kiss, the harder Travis fucks me, the wetter I get. It's like he planned it like this. Like he's the master of my body's every reaction.

Fuck, maybe he is. Who the hell knows?

"Make her come," Travis commands Cole, who immediately releases a nipple and brings his hand down to my clit.

It takes exactly one second for me to completely detonate. My chest heaves as Travis keeps the pressure on my throat, fucking me with abandon, taking his own pleasure with every thrust inside my cunt.

"That's it, come all over my cock."

Cole pinches my nipple just as his entire body goes stock still, his breathing hot on the side of my neck as he brings his mouth down on my shoulder and bites me hard enough to make me whimper.

I clench down on them both, squeezing my muscles until I can feel Travis coming inside me as he freezes and stares directly into my soul.

When they both pull out, I'm just a ragdoll that falls to the side, barely aware of the warm cloth between my legs, the soft kisses across my skin, or the heated bodies cocooning me into a deep, deep sleep.

After crawling out of bed at ass o'clock because I couldn't sleep, I headed into the yard with Shadow, but even that wasn't enough. So I quietly grabbed his leash, hooked him up, and take him out for a walk after dropping a message to the guys to let them know that I was okay and I'd be back soon.

I'd have taken all of the puppies, but I don't have the strength that the guys have to walk with that many almost-fully-grown dogs at this point. Walking around Serenity Falls isn't something I've done much of. Hell, I've barely explored anything beyond campus, but I needed to clear my head and try to work through some of the things that have happened to me that I just keep pushing down, pushing away.

The walk is beautiful and it's perfectly crisp outside, but it doesn't clear my mind as much as I would have liked. Regardless, by the time I get home I'm ready to talk to the guys about everything that's happened over the last couple of days. I know I need to stop shutting them out and start telling them all of the little nuances... including Chase and his threats and lunch with Pops yesterday.

They all know I went to lunch with Pops, but with the twins being out last night and Travis and Cole getting more than a little distracted when I got home... well, I haven't filled anybody in on anything.

I take a deep breath before I open the front door. Letting go of Shadow's leash as the door flies open, I let him bound off into the house before me. Winter is finally starting to disappear and spring has begun showing its face, but it doesn't mean that I don't still need my beanie, coat, and gloves along with my boots and scarf. I discard all of it, smiling at my pink fuzzy socks, and once my boots are off, they are the only color pop in my entire ensemble.

I head straight for the coffee in the kitchen, because I swear I'm cold in my goddamn bones, and blow on my hands while rubbing them together as I wait for the coffee machine to warm up.

"You're back," Sawyer says as he walks into the kitchen before hopping up onto the counter beside me. "Everything okay?"

I look up at him and smile. "Yep. Everything's peachy. I just needed to work through some stuff in my head."

"Anything you need to talk about?" he asks, and I nod.

"Yeah, I should probably tell everybody all at once though. Is everyone home?"

He glances at his phone then looks back up at me. "Not quite, but Cole should be back from practice any minute and it's a Saturday so everybody else should be home. Nobody else has anywhere to be."

"Practice? But it's a Saturday."

"Yeah, it's the end of the season. Big game's coming up so everybody's putting in extra hours," he explains.

Once the coffee machine's finished heating up, I make my cup of mocha and decide to add black forest to it today, then top it off with a huge, heaped pile of whipped cream. Yes, technically this is breakfast, but dessert for breakfast is always a good idea.

I go and curl up in what I have unofficially claimed as my corner on the sofa while Sawyer putters around in the kitchen, doing God only knows what, and wait for the others to appear. I don't have to wait long before Cole comes running through the front door, calling out a good morning as he jogs straight up the stairs and into his room. I watch his ass as he jogs up the stairs, smirking to myself because that's definitely not a terrible sight to see early in the morning. You could literally bounce a quarter off that thing.

Goddamn.

Sawyer comes and joins me, plopping down on the sofa beside me. "The others will be down in a minute. I sent them a message," he says.

I shake my head, laughing softly. "You didn't have to do that. I could have waited."

"Well, maybe you could, but I couldn't. The suspense is killing me," he says, a teasing smile playing on his lips. "You sure you don't want to tell me before they get here?"

"I'm sure," I say to him, laughing again. "I'd really rather not have to go through it all twice."

He twists his lips in a weird frown thing but nods. "I can appreciate that. I don't like explaining myself more than once either."

A few minutes later, the three of them descend down the stairs in various states of sleep. Travis has sweatpants on and nothing else. He smirks at me as he makes his way down the stairs, glancing at my throat which is covered by my turtleneck, hiding any and all of his marks and he knows it. Asher looks like the message woke him up and is possibly the most unkempt that I've ever seen him, but it's kind of adorable how sleepy he looks. Cole is the last one down, freshly showered and dressed, looking more relaxed and alert than any of us.

"Coffee," Asher mumbles as he pads into the kitchen. Cole heads straight for me and sits on the chair to my left.

"So, why did we need to get our asses down here, Sawyer?" Travis asks, the snark in his voice thick.

"Ask our girl," he says, pointing a thumb at me.

Travis turns to face me, his brow quirked. "Well?"

Asher appears and sits on the sofa opposite, clutching his coffee, and I can't help but giggle. "You okay there, Asher?"

"Oh, I'm fan-freaking-tastic. Drank too much whiskey with Dad last night. I'll be fine," he mutters as he pushes his glasses up his nose.

Sawyer barks out a laugh beside me. "Too much whiskey? I had to basically carry you up the stairs, bro."

Asher flips him the bird and I press my lips together, trying not to laugh at them both.

"Briar?" Cole says my name more of a question than anything.

"Right, yeah. So, a few things…" I start, before trailing off and taking a deep breath. "Chase."

"What did he do now?" Travis grumbles as he sits next to Asher and pinches the bridge of his nose.

I give them the run-down of Chase and his threats, the fun conversation I had with him on Thursday, and then about how I spoke to my mom before tagging on at the end, "And then... well, my lunch with Pops yesterday."

"Well, isn't my family just stellar?" Travis grumbles. "Please tell me Pops wasn't awful."

"He wasn't," I reassure him, shaking my head. "And to be fair, Cole's dad isn't exactly a peach either," I tease, winking at Cole. "The twins' dad is the only parent who's been any semblance of nice to me since I got here. Apparently, I'm not a parents kind of person."

Sawyer rolls his eyes and pulls me under his arm so I'm tucked against his body. "You're the best kind of person. Now tell us about Pops."

I make them laugh by telling them about him running errands with me for Penn first, lightening the mood a little before I dive into our conversation over lunch.

"He basically said that I need to learn to fight my own battles. That he'll help as much as he can, but in this world, you really can't win everything. That making concessions is the best way to survive, at least until I have the things I need to live life on my own terms. He gave me some sage advice, but he also said that flaunting what we are out in the world probably isn't a good idea yet either. He had solid reasoning too, since technically none of us have our own power yet. Everything we are relies on the power and money of other people. I'm not saying I like it… but he did make sense."

I pause, not really wanting to keep going, but I do anyway. "He also said that I should probably try to bend to some of what Chase wants, just to make my life easier, because what am I really sacrificing? My response being, 'Other than my free will' made him laugh, but…" I trail off and shrug. "So yeah, that was my few days."

The four of them just sit, staring at me, and I start to squirm under the weight of their intense gazes.

Travis breaks the silence by standing and shouting, "Fuck," before he heads to the back of the house and goes into the yard, slamming the door behind him.

Well, yeah… that definitely could have gone better.

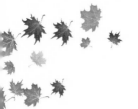

ELEVEN

COLE

This is so stupid. Why am I stressing this so hard?

Travis was already on board for this once, and I'm sure the twins will see reason… so why am I stressing about talking to them about this so much? It's all for her, not for me. If it could be them, I'd support it, but it makes the most sense for it to be me.

It was always meant to be me, even when I hated the idea and didn't know who she was. I'd accepted it then. This time, I just get to actually enjoy the idea. Be excited about the possibilities. But first… well, first I need to speak to the guys.

And then I need to speak to Briar.

I'm not thinking about that part yet though. I feel sick at just the passing thought.

"Beckett! Get your head out of your ass!" Coach screams at me as I miss yet another pass at this morning's practice. "Do you want to lose this fucking trophy? Because that's what you're going to do if you keep throwing crap shots like that!"

"Sorry, Coach," I call back and suck in a breath. Sunday practices are not for the weak and I am seriously off my game today. With everything we've had going on, I've somehow managed to not let it spill over into the game. I've kept my head on straight and used the laser focus my dad drilled into me to separate life from the field.

I try to focus, but after missing another dozen passes, Coach bitches me out and sends me to the bench. Now is not the time to lose focus. If I can just get through today, I'll be able to get my shit together.

I grab a shower after Coach calls the practice and get dressed in the locker room, dropping the guys a message to tell them we need a family meeting… code for, *do not tell our girl yet*.

"You okay, man? That practice was… well, it wasn't like you." I look up and find Dante in nothing but his towel, watching me as I sit on the bench with my head in my hands.

"Just a rough night's sleep. I'll be fine, Reed." The lie rolls right off my tongue and I know he believes it. Everyone always does. Another thing my dad taught me. If you believe the lie, so will they.

He watches me closely for a minute, then accepts it, nodding.

"Okay, man. Try and get some rest. We've got a few big games coming up and can't afford to have you off your game. Though, I mean, it'd mean the scouts aren't distracted from how awesome I am if I'm cleaning up your mess."

"Keep dreaming. Even off my game, they'll all be looking at me."

He smirks at me and winks. "You keep telling yourself that, QB." He laughs before getting changed. "How's Briar doing? Penn said she's been having a rough time of it, and the rumors round campus... well they haven't exactly been stellar."

"She's fine," I grumble, not wanting to talk to him about Briar. His hard on for her has been obvious since the first time I saw them together. I've never been the jealous type, but knowing he knew her before? Knowing they were together, albeit just for one night... yeah, apparently that's enough to make me a little Hulk-Smash-like.

Who would've thought?

He must hear it in my voice because he raises his hands in surrender. "I'm just asking, man. Briar's a cool chick and I haven't seen her around much unless she's with Penn, and I know all too well how girls like her hide their shit all the way down."

"Uh-huh," I grunt back as I pull on my T-shirt. "She's fine, but we appreciate you looking out for her."

The lies taste like ash on my tongue, but I'm used to that. Lying is something I've always been good at, thanks to my father.

"I've always got her back, so if anything ever happens, and you're not around, hit me up. I'll play the white knight." He laughs when I flip him the bird and finishes getting dressed as I shove my gear back in my locker. I need to get the fuck out of here and clear my head.

Which means just one thing...

I need to go and talk to the guys.

It's taken a whole week for Sawyer to stop going back and forth with his plans, for me to stop feeling like I'm going to puke every time I see Briar, and for the other two to finally stop bitching. I get that it isn't exactly what everyone wanted, but my point still stands.

Doing this gives her the power to make a choice, and she hasn't had many of those. I am so stupidly in love with this girl that even if she says no, I'm not going anywhere. But if she says yes? Well, it's going to make some things in her life get a lot easier.

Chase, for one, will get off our case, which should mean she stops getting hauled in by the police, and the evidence he showed Briar... well, that will disappear because my dad would never allow images like that to exist, let alone be in Chase's hands. Not when it could affect him and his political career.

God forbid anything get in the way of that.

But it also means the dean should take back his bullshit ruling about her classes. She's been going along like it isn't bothering her, but at this point, we all see behind the mask.

If I can make life easier for my girl, why wouldn't I?

I would've done it already but Sawyer has insisted we do this properly. The candles, the dinner, all of it. He even hired caterers.

She's out shopping with Asher right now until we give him the all-clear to bring her home.

Which is exactly why I'm here with Travis who is grumbling about moving furniture to meet Sawyer's grand plan while he's bringing the dogs over to his parents.

Having six Rottweilers running around a bunch of burning candles didn't seem like the greatest idea.

"You know this still changes nothing with the five of us, right? Even if she carries your name." Travis's statement is one I've heard a dozen times.

"I know," I tell him as we drop the table down near the back door. "And you know that if it could be anyone else, I'd happily let them step in. But it can't be you. You have Katy. The twins' surname doesn't carry the same clout with your dad as mine, which means it's me."

"Mhmmm. Just because I see the logic of it, doesn't mean I have to like it."

"I'm not asking you to like it," I tell him, scratching at my freshly buzzed hair. "I'm just asking you to get on board with it, *if* she wants to go ahead with it, because it's going to make life easier for her. If we're not all okay with it, she's never going to be okay with it either. You heard her the other day. She doesn't want to give any of us up, but being in our lives hasn't exactly been easy on her. She's got your dad breathing down her neck... and I can help with that."

"Hardly a reason to marry her," he grumbles in response.

"People in our world marry for far less, but you know that isn't the only reason I'm doing this for her. I don't need to tell you how I feel about her."

"I know you don't. We're all absolutely mindless when it comes to her."

"Exactly."

"But that doesn't mean I have to be happy about the fact that you get to be the one to tell the world that she's yours."

I let out a deep breath and nod. I can't say I'd be exactly overjoyed if it was any of the others either, but I'd also let it happen if it was what she actually wanted.

"I'm not going to stand in the way, but I'm not going to skip and dance about it either."

"Okay," I respond, nodding again.

"Are we done here?" he asks, and I tell him yes even though we're not even close to ready, because I can tell that he doesn't want to be here anymore. Emotions aren't exactly easy for any of us, but T... well, emotions have always been harder for him.

Considering his dad, I'm surprised he emotes at all.

I watch him leave, the door slamming behind him, and question again if this is the right thing to do. I know we all agreed it was, and on a logical level, it is… but if this is going to come between the four of us, it's not going to work. Because that'll just make Briar even more miserable, which is not the point.

But I'm not going to let any of that detract from this day. I grab the chairs and the fancy shit Sawyer got to decorate the table and get it set up as best as I can before shooting him a picture.

Sawyer:

Looking good, big guy! I'll be back to help in about 10. The three of us should bang it out real fast.

Me:

Two of us. T bailed.

Sawyer:

Course he did. It'll be fine. He's just all up in his jealousy and doesn't know how to deal. This isn't about him. Don't stress it.

Me:

Stressing it. This is supposed to help, not break things. I feel like such a fucking chick right now.

Sawyer:

Getting in touch with your feminine side isn't a bad thing, dude. As for the rest, it'll help. You'll see. Now start laying out those candles, see you in a few.

I go to pocket my phone but it buzzes in my hand again.

T:

Sorry, don't mean to be such a dick. Good luck, not that you need it.

Me:

Don't sweat it.

I pocket my phone and head to the kitchen to find the six million candles Sawyer got for tonight and groan as I scrub a hand down my face. I do not know how to do this shit. Romance, flowers, candles… not exactly my usual style.

Hell, I've never even had a long-term anything. I didn't want it until she walked into my life.

"Never fear, Big Daddy is here!" Sawyer announces as he enters the house with a hilarious flourish. I burst out laughing as the stress that was starting to build disappears at his antics and he grins wide at me. "Let's get this done, shall we?"

"Let's do it," I agree.

Thank God for Sawyer, because I have no idea how I'd be

doing this without him.

I finish buttoning my shirt, praying that my hands stop sweating at some point soon, because this is insane. It shouldn't be this terrifying. It's not the end of the world if she says no. All of this is purely a solution to help her out of a few different sticky situations we're in at the moment and get our fathers off all our backs since this was what they wanted in the first place.

So why the fuck am I so nervous?

Could it be her visceral reaction the first time an engagement to me was discussed? Most probably, but this isn't that. Far from it… well, kinda. At least this time it's a question rather than a demand… and I can totally handle her saying no and rejecting me…

Yep, totally.

My ego can take the hit because I know if she says no, it's not because she doesn't want me…

At least, that's what I'm going to keep telling myself if she *does* turn me down.

Goddamn, I am being such a chick right now.

My phone buzzes in my pocket and I swear I fumble my phone just trying to get to it.

Asher:

On our way.

Shit.

I guess it's go time.

"Come on, big guy!" Sawyer bellows from downstairs. "Candles are nearly lit, it's game time!"

I let out a deep breath and pocket my phone before shaking my hands out. This is ridiculous.

I shouldn't be this nervous.

And yet... I don't remember ever feeling this nervous in my life.

Go figure.

"Cole!" Sawyer yells again, annoyance bleeding into his tone and pushing me to jog down the stairs. I hit the landing and take in the extreme fire hazard that is our house.

"We all know that Briar can be clumsy, right? Is this many floor candles a good idea?"

Sawyer turns and deadpans me. "Do not fuck with the vision. Pick her ass up and carry her if you need to, but do not fuck with the vision."

"Sawyer, man, it's awesome, but how long is it going to take to blow these out?" I ask, chuckling.

He shrugs and flips me the bird before muttering, "Doesn't matter. The vision is what matters. Now, will you help with the last few? They're going to be here any minute."

I take the lighter he throws at me and light the few candles on the mantle that are unlit before I hear a car pull into the drive.

"It's time," Sawyer says excitedly. "I'm going to bolt out the back, house is yours for the night, big guy. Have fun! I'd wish you luck, but you don't need it!"

"Thanks, man," I call out as he runs down the walkway he created in the candles to the back door, disappearing, just as I hear a key turn in the lock.

I turn to face the door just in time to see Asher smile over her shoulder and nudge her inside. The door closes behind her and she just stands there, her focus torn between me and the room around me.

"Hi," I murmur, taking a few steps toward her so that she has to look up at me and I can steal her entire focus.

"Hey," she whispers, breathless. "What is…"

She trails off as I wrap my arms around her waist before leaning down to kiss her. She gasps as my lips touch hers, and I swear it turns something inside of me almost feral as I move one hand up into her hair, tilting her head back to give me better access to her mouth as my other arm locks around her waist to press her against me.

Her hands clutch at my shirt. The press of her nails into my chest does things to me and it's all I can do to resist picking her up and taking her right the fuck now.

Instead, I pull back from the kiss, leaving my hand in her hair to make sure she's looking up at me.

"Sawyer is going to kill me for ruining all his plans," I murmur, and she smirks at me.

"What plans?"

"Proposal plans," I answer, releasing her so she can take in the room. Instead, she sucks in a gasp of breath, making an 'oh' squeak.

I run a hand over my buzzed hair and take a step back, pulling the little black box from my pocket before I get down on one knee before her. This isn't how it was intended to play out, but fuck it.

"Briar, we've been through a lot in a short amount of time, but I don't need any more time to know that I love you and want to spend the rest of my life with you." I look up at her as she just blinks down at me and I swear the seconds stretch into eons.

"Briar...?"

She blinks at me like I just told her the sky is orange and the sun is blue. I clear my throat and try to find the words I've rehearsed a thousand times over.

Before I get chance to say anything, she blurts out a, "Yes!"

"Really?" I ask, stunned. She just laughs at me like I've lost my mind. Which, in all reality, I might have.

"Yes, really, you big dummy." She shakes her head and rolls her eyes like *I'm* the outrageous one here.

"You're sure?" I ask as I stand up. I'm aware that asking this is stupid, but I never claimed to be the smart one. I leave that to Asher and Travis. "Because honestly, I wasn't expecting it to be this easy…"

The twinkle of her laugh sounds again, and I scratch at my head.

"You want me to say no?" she asks, her brow quirked.

"No, ma'am, I absolutely do not."

"Then stop questioning me, you crazy man. You asked me to marry you, and I said yes. Take the win."

She's right, I am absolutely being an idiot. I didn't clear the guys out of here and spend hours doing all of this with Sawyer, just to question her. I slide the ring onto her finger, and she stares at it in awe. I already know she's going to have something to say about the ring, so before she gets the chance to object to the money spent on it, I open my big mouth.

"Technically, I didn't ask," I say with a smirk, and she sticks her tongue out at me. "You might just make a smart man out of me yet." Before she has a chance to say another word, I lean down and scoop her into my arms, throwing her over my shoulder. I'll deal with the candles and the food later.

"Oh my God!" she squeals, and I swat her ass just for fun. "Put me down!"

"Not a chance," I say with a grin so wide my face almost hurts as I jog up the stairs. "We're celebrating. You're mine, you officially just agreed, so I'm going to show you what being mine really looks like."

Opening the door to my room, I stride through the darkness, flicking on the lamp in the corner before I lower her to her feet so she's standing in front of me. I cup her cheeks in my hands and kiss her in a way I haven't let myself kiss her before. Like she's actually not going anywhere. Like there's nothing we can't do if we do it together.

I know that nothing at home is really going to change, but this... I'm the one who can protect her now and that's unleashing something deep inside of me, and I know I need to claim and mark her as my own.

"This dress has got to go. Too many clothes," I tell her between kisses down her throat, moving my hands down her sides and around her waist to pull down the zipper without actually having to let her go.

The zipper jams and she giggles as I groan. "Stuck?" she teases, and I nip at her with my teeth in response.

"If you like this dress, then help. Otherwise, I'm going to just tear it from your body."

She sucks in a breath, and that one movement alone makes my heart pound harder.

"Do it," she murmurs, breathlessly, and it's like she releases that beast inside of me that I keep locked down. "Take whatever you want from me."

"Don't say that if you don't mean it, Briar." The words are strained as I try to not break the zipper.

"I mean it," she responds, and it's the final lock being undone.

I grab at her dress and pull, the zipper crumbling under the pressure. I relish the sound of fabric tearing before the dress flutters to the floor, leaving her standing before me in almost nothing.

Hot fucking damn.

My gaze follows the flawless line of her body from her bare feet to the apex of her thighs, barely covered by a lace thong, before I take in the curve of her waist and the perfect swell of her breasts, nipples hard and pressing against her dainty bra. It's when I reach her face, our gazes crashing like two unmanned freight trains, that our lust becomes a living, breathing thing between us. Chests heaving and skin flushed, my heartbeat thunders against my eardrums and I know it's only a matter of seconds before this hunger will consume us.

"Cole?"

"Yeah, Baby?" My tongue darts out to dampen my lips as my hands reach back behind her, and with a flick of my fingers, her bra is sliding down her arms.

"Show me your beast." And that's it. Her words are the keys that let my darkness free and the honesty behind her gaze destroys every ounce of my control.

With a wolfish grin, I curl my fingers around her waist, picking her up and throwing her on the bed, watching as she bounces once, twice, then settles. Giggling, she watches me with desire spelled out across the curve of her smile, the dart of her tongue, and the bite of her lower lip. Every move she makes tells me she can't wait to feel me, the real me, inside her. On top of her. All around her.

Reaching back with one hand, I pull my T-shirt up and over my head before throwing it on the chair behind me. My pants are next, abandoned at the foot of the bed. We're naked within seconds, save for Briar's sexy as fuck thong that I plan to use wisely.

Crawling up the bed like a predator sizing up its prey, I nudge her sweet-smelling pussy with my nose before biting the inside of her thigh. Briar makes a yelping sound mixed in with a moan, like her body isn't sure if it felt pain or pleasure.

Without taking my eyes off her, I hook my index fingers around the strings at her hips and slowly—oh so fucking slowly—pull down her poor excuse for underwear.

"Spread." She doesn't even hesitate, her thighs open up as wide as they can go, giving me a breathtaking view of my own personal heaven. The sight makes my entire body hungry for her but my mouth is the first to relinquish control.

As I hover over her, I circle my arms around her thighs and lift her just enough to bring her level with my face before my lips descend on her and I'm devouring her like a starved animal. I bite her and lick her and I suck her swollen lips into my mouth until she cries out for more. I fuck her with my tongue and I pinch her clit between my teeth, but only when I see her fighting against the urge to come, her entire body strung tight, her muscles clamping down on my tongue, do I take a small measure of mercy on her.

"Come all over my mouth, Briar. Make it count." It's like I just opened the valve to her orgasm. Her body convulses as her pussy contracts and relaxes in a steady rhythm as she releases her delicious juices right into my mouth.

But before she's finished, I take her lace undies and stuff them in her cunt, making sure they're nice and soaked. Only when she's relaxed and breathing hard do I take them out and slide my body up hers until we're face-to-face. She's dazed, her lips tilted up in a drunken smile, her lids hooded as she watches me watching her.

"Such a good girl. Got a treat for you, Baby. Open up." She opens her mouth without question, giving me the chance to run my tongue around her lips before shoving her thong inside her mouth. At first, she's surprised, her eyes suddenly wide and alert, but then she relaxes again.

"This is my addiction. Your taste. The scent of your pussy on my lips makes me fucking crazy. So suck on my favorite drug while I fuck that gorgeous pussy of yours." She offers up her pelvis, her lower body arching into me as I slide inside her without pause until I hit the deepest, darkest inches of her body.

"Ahh…" She can't speak, but the noises that come through the fabric only make me harder, make my lust grow rampant.

"That's it, squeeze my cock, Baby." My lips fall onto her neck as I clamp a hand on her mouth, forcing her to suck on her own cum. I kiss her and lick her and leave teeth marks that brand her as mine all over her neck, her collarbones, her tits.

All the while, I'm pumping in and out and fucking her with the force of a titan, barely able to protect her head from slamming into the headboard.

The bed creaks with every push; it slams into the wall over and over again with the force of my thrusts. Still, she takes it. She begs for more without saying a single word. It's in the way she wraps her legs around my waist, the way she digs her heels into my ass, the way her pussy clamps down on my dick every time I bottom out.

It's in the way she looks at me like I'm the beginning and the end of her pleasure. I'm the king of her orgasms and she's kneeling at my feet hoping I'll give her more.

"Come, Baby." I rip the underwear out of her mouth and swallow her screams while I fuck her hard enough that I'm pretty fucking sure I'll leave bruises.

Good. She's mine and the whole fucking world needs to know it.

We kiss like horny teenagers who can't get enough of each other while I give her everything I've got until she begins to go limp from the effort.

"Come, Cole. Brand me from the inside." If I hadn't already been ready to spill my seed, those words would have been my undoing. Slamming into her one last time, we stare at each other as I fill her completely with my cock and my cum. I coat her with the very essence of me and watch as she takes it all and grins like a satisfied little kitten.

"We're doing that again. Soon."

Because, yeah. I wasn't lying or exaggerating when I said she was my drug.

I'm just the addict that never wants to quit.

LILY WILDHART

TWELVE

BRIAR

I am engaged.

Have been for a whole week… and what a whirlwind of a week it has been. After that night—and oh what a night it was—Cole and I spoke about the realities of what being engaged to him meant. How it would get Chase off my back, how his dad would protect me from any further allegations, how I'd be able to go back to school… and I started to feel a little like he didn't actually want to marry me, he was just trying to help me.

But after much, much persuasion, he convinced me otherwise.

The next issue was Travis, which is still a work in progress. While he *has* been supportive and hasn't exactly taken a step back, he also hasn't been as present as normal. I've tried to talk to him about it, and I've talked to the others about it, but they just told me to give him time. So that's what I'm trying to do.

The twins have been fully on board with everything—not that I'm even remotely surprised that they're uber supportive—and once Sawyer got over the fact that his proposal didn't go to plan, he jumped in with both feet, helping me deal with what's to come.

I'm trying to be respectful of everybody and their feelings, but it's really hard. I never expected to be in this place or this situation. I have exactly zero idea of how to navigate everything and keep everybody happy. People pleasing has always been a skill of mine—hi, hello, thanks, trauma—but on this occasion, I am failing very, very badly.

It turns out getting engaged to a Beckett is a whole thing, and I've been more than a little distracted with everything going on. There have been photoshoots and interviews and a whole host of shit I never thought I'd have to deal with. I've been dressed by designers, plucked and primped to the point where I nearly punched some woman out because leave my fucking eyebrows alone. Circa 1990 pencil-line brows is not a thing I want, thank you very fucking much.

Today is my first day back on campus after Cole cleared everything up with the dean, and I am meeting Penn before my class. I'm trying to find all of the joy in finally getting back to some semblance of what I've been pretending is my real life for the last couple of months.

I park the Batmobile and find Penn waiting for me by the entrance to campus. She squeals when she sees me and wraps me up in a hug. "Girl, I am so glad to see you again. It just hasn't been the same wandering these weird and lowly halls without you."

"It's good to be back," I tell her, squeezing her hand. "We need to catch up, though, because I feel like everything's been an absolute whirlwind this last week or so and we've barely talked."

"Bitch, you got engaged! We're allowed to have barely spoken. Now show me that fucking ring." I laugh at her, lifting my hand so she can see my new bling. She lets out a squeal again at the ridiculously sized sparkler that currently sits upon my ring finger. "Oh, the boy did good."

I smile at her and nod. It *is* beautiful. It's nothing like what I would have expected him to buy for me—if I would have expected anything at all—but it is exactly me. The moss agate pear-drop stone is set in platinum so delicate that it looks like an elvish ring. He totally nailed my nerdiness when he picked this ring, and it's absolutely everything I could have even attempted to dream up for what I would want from an engagement ring.

"No diamonds, but diamonds aren't always a girl's best friend," Penn says with a wink before linking arms with me as we head onto campus.

I feel so much lighter already just being back here and being with her. Like life might actually start to work out.

Cole told me that his dad's already dealt with Chase, the police, and everything to do with Crawford. That my name being linked to everything going on is no longer a problem so I can finally breathe easy about that, even if the guilt does still eat away at me about the fact that I killed my biological father.

He also reassured me that Chase will no longer be all over me about anything because we don't answer to Chase Kensington anymore. Our new adversary—for lack of a better word—is going to be Senator Beckett and everything that he requires from us now that we're engaged.

Which I'm sure is going to be a whole new fuck bucket of fun.

But that's for future me to figure out. Right now, I get to breathe easy for a minute. At least that's my hope.

I'm jolted to a halt when Penn stops suddenly, staring off into the distance. Concern rushes through me as I try to scan the crowd for what could possibly have made her stop like that.

"What's wrong?" I ask her, but she doesn't answer me, which is strange for my very talkative friend. She just continues to stare into the distance.

I look around again to try and find what she's so focused on and find a woman staring at us from across the quad. I blink in shock, looking at the woman who could easily be Penn's twin if she wasn't obviously at least twenty years older than we are.

"Penn? Are you okay? Is that…" I trail off as she nods,

confirming my suspicion. This is her bio mom.

She's never really spoken to me much about her bio family. Hell, she only mentioned in passing that she was even adopted. I've never pushed her on it because I know how hard it can be to talk about some shit, but I get the feeling in this very moment of regret that I probably should have at least asked the question.

"Yeah, that's my bio mom." The words fall from her lips as the woman in question takes a step toward us. Her step falters for a moment before she squares her shoulders and lifts her head as if giving herself a pep talk before making her way over toward us again.

She stops mere steps from where we stand, quickly glancing at me before turning her attention back to Penn. I feel like I should put Penn over my shoulder and run the fuck away right now, but since we've never talked about her family, I don't know if running or standing our ground is the right decision here.

"Penelope," the woman says, and I feel awkward as fuck right now, but I'm not going anywhere because my friend is squeezing my hand so tight that I'm fairly certain I'm going to lose all circulation in my fingers. There's no way I'm leaving her right now, even if I could. She needs me and I am not that person.

"Why are you here, Erica?" Penn asks, her dismay and snark fully audible.

The woman lets out a deep sigh and almost folds in on herself before looking back up at Penn and speaking. "It's Joey.

He's dying and I need your help."

I swear the world pauses, and I hear Penn suck in a breath then just stop breathing all together. The sounds stop as my heart races in my chest, but then everything speeds back up as Penn releases my hand before gripping it again as I stand here questioning who the hell Joey is.

"What do you mean, he's dying?" Penn asks, sounding confused even as that fiery personality of hers that I've grown to love shines through.

"He needs a bone marrow transplant and, thus far, we've been unable to find him a match." Penn opens her mouth as if to say something when my guys appear out of nowhere, rocking up behind us.

"Is everything okay?" Cole asks as he moves to my side, staring down at the woman who takes a step back under the glare of the four guys that just surrounded us.

"This is Penn's birth mother," I tell them, and the twins both glance at me before Sawyer reaches up and squeezes Penn's shoulder.

"I'm assuming you want me to test to donate," Penn says to her mother.

Cole frowns. "Donate?'

Erica clears her throat as if finding her voice again. "Penelope's little brother is dying and needs a bone marrow transplant. We haven't found a match yet that can donate, so I came to ask Penelope to donate. To her *little brother*." The emphasis she puts on those last two words sets my teeth on edge.

Penn glares at the woman, hissing, "He is not my little brother in anything but science. You made that much *very* clear. But of course, now that *you* need something you're here."

"Penelope, don't be such a brat about this. I'm trying to save his life." Penn lets out a dry bark of a laugh, her spine straightening, and the girl I've come to know shows herself.

"Yes, of course. I'm being the brat after you turned me away and told me never to look for you again. *I'm* the one that's the problem here. Lucky for you, Joey isn't the monster that you are and he's too young for me to make him pay for the mistakes of his mother. So I'll get tested, but you don't get to speak to me again."

Erica clasps her hands in front of her and nods before reaching into her handbag and pulling out a piece of paper and a pen. "This is the hospital that he's in. Just let them know that you're coming to be tested. You don't have to speak to me. You don't have to see me. But I had to ask."

"Of course you did," Penn snaps, rolling her eyes. "Now leave." She takes the piece of paper, still grasping my hand with her other, and we watch as the redheaded woman walks away from us.

"So... that was intense," Sawyer says, trying to break some of the tension in the way that he always does, and I glance over my shoulder at him, smiling.

"You could say that." I turn back to Penn, squeezing her

hand while I try to get some feeling back in my fingers. "Are you really going to get tested?" She shrugs, releasing my hand and pinching the bridge of her nose before letting out a deep breath.

"I guess I kind of have to. Joey isn't old enough to understand the politics of it all and I'm not about to let a kid die just because I'm pissed at the parent we share."

"Do you want me to come with you?" I ask, and she nods.

"Yes, please. I'm not sure I'll make it through the doors on my own." I take her hand again and squeeze it.

"I got you, always."

"We will be there too!" Asher adds on, and Cole nods as he squeezes my shoulders from behind. "Yeah, we got you. We'll all get tested if it helps."

A tear slips down her cheek and she swipes it away almost as quickly as it appeared. "Thank you, guys. You don't have to do that."

"Of course we don't," Sawyer says. "We're still going to. When do we need to go?"

Penn looks at the piece of paper, taking a second to glance her eyes over it. "It doesn't say, but I'm guessing sooner is better than later."

"Then we'll go tonight," Travis backs up. "We'll finish class and meet back here and head straight to wherever the hospital is." He reaches out for the piece of paper in Penn's hand and she passes it to him. "This hospital is only about an hour away," he confirms. "We'll easily be able to get there after class. Cole, you might just want to mention something to Coach if you're going to be getting tested."

"I can do that," he says with a nod, leaning down and kissing the top of my head. "I've gotta go, but I'll catch you guys later."

"We should probably all head in, otherwise we're going to be late," Asher says, and the other guys nod at him. "We'll see you guys later. Let us know if you need anything."

"I will, thank you," I respond as the three of them walk away.

"What would I do without you?" Penn asks with a sad smile.

"Oh, you'd be just fine. You've survived plenty without me. Now you just happen to have extra backup."

"In the form of you and your hot men," she says with a giggle snort. Who would have thought having the four of them on her side would ever make her smile?

"Come on, let's go and pretend to focus in class so we can get this done. Is Connor going to come?" I ask her, and the small smile falls from her face.

"I haven't heard from Connor in days, again," she tells me, and I frown. I really do need to speak to that boy, but for now, I need to focus on my friend.

After what was probably one of the most painful experiences

of my life last night, we all decided to take the day off from class. Except for Cole, who ended up not getting tested at Penn's insistence, because it would have meant that he would have to sit out the last few games of the season and nobody wanted that for him.

He might have his life set out for him by his dad with politics, but I also know that football is a huge thing for him. Penn being the follower of the game that she is also knows that, so she refused to let him get tested.

We're going to have to wait until at least the end of the week to find out if anybody's a donor for Penn's little brother, but chances are Penn will be the best match anyway because she's the sibling. The chances of any of the rest of us being a match are slim, but I'd rather get tested and be there for my friend than not.

Though that's exactly why the four of us are lounging around in the living room while the puppies lose their mind in the yard. None of us can quite find a way to get entirely situated, because who would have thought that having bone marrow extracted from your pelvis was quite as uncomfortable as it is? I mean, anyone with two brain cells probably would have, but hi, hello, I obviously wasn't thinking everything through quite fully.

A knock on the door steals my attention from the pain currently emanating through my ass, and Sawyer jumps up, groaning at the fast movement before heading over to the door.

He opens it and his entire posture changes as he folds his

arms. "What do you want?" he asks, sounding the most un-Sawyer like I've ever heard him.

"I need to see your girlfriend."

I hang my head, trying not to groan as I stand up and head over to the door. "What do you want, Emerson?" I ask once I reach her, the other guys' attention perking up at the sound of her name.

"We need to talk," she says, smirking at me in that cold, manipulative way she has, and I already know that this isn't going to end well for me.

Just when I thought my problems were finally getting under control. Of course, she blows back into my life. Note to self: Don't make frenemies, it always bites you in the ass. "Okay, let's talk," I say to her, stepping out onto the front porch and trying to shut the door, but Sawyer keeps his foot in the way, looking at me like he thinks I'm insane for trying to close them out of this conversation.

"Oh, I'm fairly certain she doesn't want you to hear what I have to say, Pretty Boy," Emerson says to him with a smirk.

"Anything that you say to her can be said to any of us. She knows that," Sawyer says, glancing at me with a raised brow. While I know they've seen me at my worst, there's still so much that they don't know about me that Emerson does. And while they literally covered up murder for me, that doesn't mean that I'm proud of some of the things from my past and don't expect that they won't judge me for it no matter how much they say they won't. It's just like Emerson to blow in and set off another chaos bomb in my life right as things were starting to get back to normal.

"What do you want, Emerson?" I ask again. She folds her arms over her chest, leaning back against the porch railing.

"I need more money," she says. I let out a deep breath, laughing under it.

"I don't have any money," I tell her, and she cackles.

"I read the papers, you know. Your face has been splashed all over them. I know that you're engaged to the senator's son. Don't try and tell me you don't have money. Just look at the rock on your finger."

"I don't have money, Emerson. They have money, but I still have nothing. Nothing has changed in that respect. Any money that is surrounding me doesn't belong to me."

"You're trying to tell me that you don't get an allowance from your darling boyfriends? Or fiancé, should I say? How does that even work? Does he enjoy being a cuckold?"

"Emerson…" I say, growling. "Don't fucking start with me. I don't have any money. Last time you came here asking, I told you it was the only time that that was going to happen."

"Yeah, well, I'm renegotiating our terms. Or maybe you want me to start spilling secrets to the tabloids? God knows that you've got enough skeletons hiding in your closet."

I feel Travis arrive behind me, knowing that it's him without needing to turn around purely from the static rage that comes from him. "You're not going to say shit to anyone about anything. People have ended up dead and buried for much less." The cold rage in his tone is enough to turn my blood to ice but she just laughs at him.

"Oh, please, Pretty Boy, I've faced much scarier men than you and won. You think death threats are new to me? You try living my life and be afraid of death. Death would be welcome at this point."

"Emerson, I keep telling you I don't have money and any secrets that you want to sell to the tabloids…? I mean, really? Who's going to believe them? If it comes down to it, *I'm* the fiancée of the senator's son and you're just the drugged-out whore selling herself for her next fix." I hate myself as the words fall from my lips, especially because I've never judged anyone for anything they've ever chosen to do to survive, but I can't keep doing this with her and I can't have her threatening me like this.

I don't even know what it is that she's talking about this time but like she says, God knows there's enough hiding in my closet.

"Oh, I'm sure that the tabloids would love to know about our darling friend, Allison, that was OD'ing and you just let her die there on the cold pavement in the snow rather than calling an ambulance because you didn't want to get into trouble." I suck in a sharp breath, glaring at her.

"I'm not the one that gave her the drugs," I fire back. "I

didn't even know that she was OD'ing until you came and got me. That one's on you as much as it's on me."

"Yeah, but I have nothing to lose," she says, her eyes lighting up, and I can't help but wonder how we got here. We were friends once, but after Iris... I know things changed, but to end up here, it's like I don't even recognize her anymore.

"Maybe not, and maybe I do have something to lose these days, but again, who's going to believe you?"

"I'm sure I can find someone," she says. "The internet is a wonderful place. Haven't you heard?"

"How much do you want?" Travis asks her, and she turns that cold, calculating smile over to him.

"I want enough to survive. I want at least three grand a month, every month, and then I'll disappear from your lives and you'll never hear from me again. I don't want this life. I never did. I just need a way out."

"Emerson, there is no way that you're getting that sort of money from us. I keep telling you I don't have money."

"Consider it done," Travis says from behind me. "I'll have a contract drawn up, but know that if you utter one breath about anything to do with her or her past, that you will disappear down a very dark hole and you will regret having ever mentioned her name or looked in her direction."

"Oh, Pretty Boy, your threats are so sweet. She has my number. She knows how to get in touch with me."

She blows me a kiss, wagging her fingers at me before

skipping down the porch steps and walking off into the distance. Once she's out of eyesight, my shoulders sag. I look up at Travis. "You don't have to do that. I can't afford to pay you back."

"You don't have to pay me back," he says. "And you don't need to worry about it, it's done. Three grand a month is nothing to my father. And nothing to my trust fund. I can't do much for you right now, but this I can do. Consider it an apology for me being an ass for the last week." He pulls his phone from his pocket and taps away at the screen. "I've got a call to make to my lawyer," he says before disappearing back into the house and heading upstairs.

I follow him inside and Sawyer closes the door behind us. I find Asher standing just on the inside of the door.

"I knew she was going to be a problem," Asher says, shaking his hand.

"I know. I knew it too, but we all have a past, the difference is that I have people willing to spill mine."

"Not anymore," Asher says. "Travis really will bury her if she utters another word. But maybe we should all have a big talk and come clean so that we don't have any more surprises."

I chew on the inside of my lip, not really wanting to get into my past. Sawyer squeezes my shoulders from behind before wrapping me up in a hug. "She doesn't have to tell us anything she doesn't want to, brother. When she's ready, she'll tell us and even if that's never, that's fine by me. I'm sure we don't want to dig into all of the regrets of our pasts either."

Asher frowns but nods. "Fine." Sawyer squeezes me tighter. "Plus, it's easier this way. We've got plausible deniability. If we don't know, then we can't be held liable for any of it."

"What he said," I say, leaning my head back on Sawyer's shoulder, slightly relieved that I don't have to get into everything about my past. "You guys know pretty much everything about me now anyway, even if not the nitty gritty details. I've told you about the traumas of my childhood. You know about Iris, you know about Crawford, and now you know about Allison; they're probably the worst things that have happened to me in my life."

Asher nods. "You know we're here if you ever need to talk about any of it, right?"

I nod, reaching out a hand and taking his before squeezing it. "I know, but talking about it doesn't change it. It just means that I have to talk about it and drag it all up, and I'd rather leave it locked away where it belongs: in the past." He nods and moves to hug me so that I'm in a twin sandwich and I giggle as they squeeze against me from either side.

"Now this is a party," Sawyer says, and I can practically feel him wagging his brows even though I can't see him and I laugh again. I love these guys for always being able to make our situation seem not so world-ending. "Now, let's head upstairs, shall we? I say we take this sandwich to a whole new level."

After what has to have been one of the most tumultuous days that I've had in a hot minute, I find myself in the kitchen comfort cooking. Travis appeared back downstairs after his conversation with his lawyer and looking about as happy as a bear who got stung by a wasp, though I'm fairly certain that could be because I was off upstairs with the twins too, but we're not going to think about that too deeply right now.

The four of them are laid out in the living room relaxing now that Cole is finally back from practice while I make chicken Alfredo, because I've been craving pasta since this afternoon's fun. Plus, I haven't cooked this in ages and there is just something about chicken and cream and pasta that is ticking all of my boxes right now. I could legit just eat this entire pan with a fork and not even care.

A knock on the door sounds and my heart sinks because every time someone knocks on that door, something bad happens. But I let one of the guys answer it and stay focused on my pasta because I'm not letting whoever that is ruin my joy for this food. I already made my own roasted garlic butter so that I could do cheesy garlic bread with the pasta and I put some of the roasted garlic in my Alfredo too. Nothing is ruining this pasta dish for me.

That's what I'm thinking when I hear Asher's voice. "Emily?" he says, shock very apparent in his tone. "What are you doing here?" I glance over my shoulder, shocked to hear the twins' little sister's name fall from his lips just in time to see her sashay into the living room. She looks exactly like them and not at all, all at the same time. She is everything a beautiful ballerina is shown to be in all the movies.

Her hair is even pulled back in a slick bun and she has a gym bag over her shoulder. She looks like she's just come from a rehearsal.

"I decided to drop out of Juilliard," she says casually, quickly followed by an 'oh fuck' from Sawyer's direction.

"What do you mean you decided to drop out of Juilliard?" Asher asks, closing the door. "Have you talked to Mom and Dad?"

"No, of course not," she answers. "I thought I'd come to you guys first so that I could have, you know, backup when I talk to them. You'll back me up, right?"

"That depends. Why, exactly, did you drop out of Juilliard?" Sawyer asks, his voice going up a couple of octaves, his fear obvious.

"I'm just bored of it. The girls are all bitchy because I'm younger and 'technically' shouldn't be there and the teachers are assholes for the same reason. I'm sick of the life of a dancer. They've stolen my joy for it. All I ever wanted to do was dance and now I dread waking up and going to class every morning. That isn't what I want my life to be."

"And what is it that you want your life to be?" Asher asks, blinking at her like he doesn't recognize her at all.

"I want my life to be fun and to have meaning. I want to help people. You guys are training to become doctors and lawyers and businessmen and I'm just out here dancing. Don't get me wrong, I know that arts are important and life wouldn't be the same without it, but also, the entire environment is so toxic and I'm over it."

I blink over at the sixteen-year-old girl, shocked at how grown up she sounds. It's at that point she looks over in my direction and realizes that I'm in the room. All warmth drops from her as she glares over at me. "I guess you're Briar."

I press my lips together and nod, not exactly sure why she's had such a reaction to me.

"So you're the one ruining my brothers' lives?" My jaw drops as she stands there glaring at me, and Asher scolds her.

"Emily, you don't get to talk to her like that. You don't know her. You don't know anything about our lives. All you know is whatever bullshit Mom has fed you, so dial back the cold bitch act and play nice."

I chew on the inside of my cheek and turn back to the pot of pasta because I've dealt with enough hatred from these guys' families for a lifetime. Here I was hoping that there wouldn't be any more of it. I guess I was wrong.

"Good to see you're in top form as always, Emily," Travis bites coldly, before moving into the kitchen. "Do you need any help?" he asks me, and I shake my head, keeping my eyes focused solely on the pan in front of me.

"No, I've got it. Don't worry." Cole follows him in and

stands on my other side, like they're both protecting me from the girl who just walked in the house.

"This is your home, Briar. You don't get made to feel uncomfortable here," Cole says, the words little more than a rumble from his chest as he glares in the direction of the twins' sister.

"It's fine. She doesn't know me," I say with a shrug. "She can think whatever she likes." I can hear the twins arguing with their sister as they move upstairs, their voices fading slowly, and my name is impossible to miss the dozen or so times that it's thrown out in the conversation. *Well, that could have gone better,* I think to myself before turning down the heat and moving my focus to making the garlic bread.

"Hope you guys are hungry," I say to them, because I'm fairly certain I just lost my appetite.

"Don't stress about her," Travis soothes. "She's always been a cold, vapid little bitch. I'm not certain that she isn't adopted because she's nothing like the twins at all. I chalk it up to the ballerina lifestyle," he says with a shrug. "It's exactly why I never wanted Katy to be anything like that."

I nod, knowing that the pressures of dancing and Juilliard must take their toll on a person, especially one so young, but also, who is she to judge me when she doesn't know who I am?

I can make excuses for her all day long but that doesn't make it right. I finish up dinner and Travis heads upstairs to get the others once I start serving and Emily comes down with them.

"I'm sorry, Briar," she says as she walks into the kitchen and takes a seat at the counter with the twins. "I don't mean to be such a bitch; it just kind of happens sometimes."

I shrug. "We all have the capability to be a bitch. Most of us are just better at keeping the lid on it, I guess."

She smirks at me and nods. "Maybe I like you more than I thought I would."

I shrug and hand her a bowl of pasta while dishing out the rest to the others, grabbing the bowl of garlic bread last and putting it on the counter for everyone.

I try to tune out the conversation and just focus on my pasta that was supposed to be my comfort for the day after everything with Emerson earlier. Two crazy bitches in one day are two too many for me and I'm exhausted. I kind of hoped to get along with the twins' little sister after they spoke so highly of her, but fuck it. I don't need more friends.

My appetite has all but disappeared, so I eat as much as I know I can get away with without making myself sick but without the guys complaining at me before making my excuses and heading upstairs to my room. It feels like I haven't been in here in forever because I've been bed hopping between all of the boys' rooms, so when I drop onto my bed alone, without even the puppies for a change, I close my eyes and let out a deep breath. Today did not go to plan at all, and I still need to talk to Travis about the deal that he made with Emerson because I'm still not happy about it. And I should probably let Cole know what happened too. But all I want to do right now is curl up in a ball and go to sleep, so I grab a quick shower and change into the fluffiest pajamas I've got before doing exactly that. Just when I thought today was going to be a good day.

Maybe tomorrow will be better.

THIRTEEN

BRIAR

After what I'd hoped would be a peaceful week, more chaos bombs continued to drop all over my life. Which is exactly how I find myself at the mall with Penn on this gray and rainy Saturday morning, pretending to shop as we sip smoothies and act like we're just regular humans. It's better than dealing with the nerves of waiting for results on the bone marrow test and Penn dealing with her birth mom popping back up in her life again.

I pretend that none of my problems exist and solely focus on hers, because that is how I'm going to get through my own.

"What do you think of this?" she asks, holding up an emerald-green body wrap dress in front of her.

"I think you'll look fucking amazing in that, that's what I think," I tell her, and she smiles at me, though it doesn't quite reach her eyes.

"I don't know that this is working," she says as she puts the dress back on the rack.

"No, I don't think it is either, but what else are we supposed to do?" She shrugs and moves over to the next rack, thumbing through the different coats on it.

"I have no idea. But I *do* know that if Connor ignores one more text message and if I hear one more person at home utter my birth mom's name, I'm going to lose it and probably end up institutionalized because I'm going to flip the fuck out."

I can't help but giggle-snort at her and she glances at me, smiling. "At least one of us can get some amusement out of this."

I shake my head at her, smiling. "Like you didn't giggle-snort the entire way through the drama of Emily St. Vincent turning up to my house after dealing with Emerson. What a fucking clusterfuck of a week it's been for us both."

"Oh, yeah. Neither of us have exactly had a week of sunshine, rainbows, and puppies, but I'm still gonna say that this week, just this one, I get to wear the *my life is shit* hat."

"Oh, feel free to take it. I've been wearing that crown for far too long," I tell her, and she laughs at me softly.

"Do you want to just go get ice cream and, like, maybe massages or something? Shopping is not quite the fulfilling distraction I'd hoped it would be," she says to me, and I nod.

"When have I ever said no to ice cream? You think I got an ass like this saying no to ice cream?" She laughs softly again. I feel better about being such a crappy friend because I'm able to actually put a smile on her face, even if the one on mine is nothing more than a mask.

We head back to the car, swinging by the 7-Eleven to grab a couple of pints of ice cream before heading back to the house. Once we're home and situated on the sofas, she laughs as she scrolls through her phone. "Do you reckon dial-a-masseuse is a thing?"

"I have no idea," I say to her, trying not to laugh again. "But with the amount of money these guys have, probably." I grab my phone and send a text to Sawyer, because he is the frivolous one of the bunch and is going to be able to tell me the answer to this one.

Me:

Is dial-a-masseuse a thing?

Sawyer:

I have no idea where this is coming from.

Me:

Penn and I are trying to relax. We have ice cream, figured we'd have a massage too.

Sawyer:

I can send you a gift certificate for the spa in the city?

Me:

No, we have ice cream, just wanted a massage.

Sawyer:

Fine, it's totally a thing, but I'm sending you female masseuses.

I laugh and Penn glances up at me, so I show her the message from Sawyer and she shakes her head.

"Of course he wants to send a female masseuse."

Me:

I can order it. Just give me the details.

Sawyer:

It's already done. They'll be there in half an hour. No naked hanky-panky without me being there. So I can watch, please and thank you.

Me:

You're an idiot.

I sit laughing as I type it out, showing Penn the messages

again, enjoying the smile that actually seems real on her face.

"So have you set a date yet?" she asks, and I groan, shaking my head.

"No, we absolutely have not. I'm so not ready to. The engagement was intended to be a helping hand, but with all of the chaos that keeps going off in my life, I'm not sure that I'm ready for an actual wedding yet. The media circus that happened just the week of the engagement was bad enough. And that doesn't include the paparazzi that I've noticed around the campus taking pictures this last week. Do you know how hard it is to make sure that I don't look like an absolute fucking mess each day in case one of them captures me? Because the last thing I want to deal with is Cole's dad bitching me out for looking like shit while I'm being spread across tabloids, even though I didn't give permission for that to happen."

"Oh, the problems of the rich and the famous," she teases, and I roll my eyes.

"Oh yeah, 'cause I'm totally the rich and famous."

"I hate to break it to you," she says, raising her brows at me. "But you kind of are now. You're a Kensington *and* you're about to be a Beckett. Like, it doesn't get much more rich and famous than that in this part of town."

I groan at her because the reality of it is, what she's saying is true. I just don't feel like that person and I don't know if I ever will. She shrugs when I say as much.

"I mean, it's probably not like life will change that

drastically," she says. "But you do have to face some new realities. You're going to be the wife of a politician, because we all know that's where Cole is going to end up, and even if he doesn't by some form of miracle, he's still going to be in the spotlight because there's no way a football scout isn't coming for him over these next couple of weeks. Dante hasn't shut up about it since Coach told them that scouts were coming to these next few games."

I kind of blink at her, shaking my head. "I didn't realize it was such a big deal."

"Oh, girl. You have no idea."

My phone pings and Sawyer's name pops up on the screen again.

Sawyer:

*Masseuses will be there in five minutes, strip down to robes.
And I repeat, no hanky-panky unless I get to watch.*

Me:

*Yes sir, *winky face**

I respond, laughing as I show Penn the message again. I might have a new reality out there, but this is my reality in here.

"Let's go strip, I guess," she barks out loud.

"If Sawyer could hear you talk now, he'd race home faster than a bolt of lightning."

"Oh, I have no doubt he would. I'm not convinced that he isn't already in the car on his way here just to watch any hanky-panky, as he calls it."

Our dial-a-masseuse appointment is interrupted by Sawyer and Asher bursting through the door a few hours later. At this point, I'm not sure how much more relaxed I could get, so it's probably a good thing that they came home.

Sawyer apparently booked these two women for the entire day, so we have just been enjoying all of the things since they arrived. The twins are laughing and joking around, the puppies rushing to meet them all to say hello, and I tell the two masseuses that we're good for the day and thank them for everything.

Asher tips them as they leave, having packed up their beds, and they leave Penn and me with the twins. I pull my robe tight around me, while Penn runs upstairs to get dressed properly, and collapse onto the sofa with the guys. Sawyer turns on the TV and I snuggle into his side while Asher fusses with the dogs.

"This was a good day, thank you," I murmur to Sawyer, who kisses the top of my head, squeezing me tighter into the side of his body.

"You're welcome, Sunshine. Anything I can do to make you feel better is a good thing. How's Penn doing?"

"She's pretending she's okay," I tell him. "But she doesn't

have her results yet and I think the whole her mom prioritizing her little brother's life over hers when her mom didn't even want anything to do with her is really starting to get to her. She's told me a little about it, but nothing major. Though I want to bash Connor's skull in because he's been completely MIA the entire time this has been happening and nobody seems to know where he's been."

He frowns down at me and pulls his phone from his pocket. "Do you want me to have people looking for him? Are we concerned?" I let out a deep breath and sit up, folding my legs underneath me.

"Honestly, I don't know. Penn seems more angry than concerned and Connor's apparently been acting real weird since his uncle showed up in town. But I don't know if it's my place to go so far as to look into it, or if I should just be a friend to her and let her vent about it and bitch him out when he finally does show up."

He puts his phone back in his pocket and nods. "Okay. Well, if you want us to do anything, just ask. What's the point in having all these people to help us and all this money if we can't help the people we care for?"

"I kinda love you, you know," I say to him, and he grins down at me.

"I kinda love you too."

Penn reappears and drops into the chair beside the sofa just as a news alert flashes up on the TV. Another body found in the strangler case. Still no suspects with the killer at large.

It feels like time stops as I read the headline and the woman on screen starts talking. Sawyer turns up the TV and Asher stops playing with the dogs to pay attention.

"This is horrific," Penn says. "I don't understand why they've been focusing on you. You're *obviously* not involved. Too many people have died now, they really need to sort themselves out."

It occurs to me that she has no idea about the truth of anything. At this point, I don't know the truth of much beyond the fact that I killed Crawford either.

"The police department really needs a kick in the ass over this one," she adds before grabbing her bag. "I'm going to head back home and try to get on with some studying. Thank you for today, B."

I stand up and give her a hug. "Anything for you, Penn. If you need me, you know where I am, okay?"

"Thank you," she says quietly before I walk her out, open the door, and find Travis and Cole on the other side of it. They move aside to let Penn out and down the steps. Once she's in her car, I close the door. The guys have already gone inside and everyone's still watching the news. When I turn back and see the picture of the girl on the screen, I gasp.

"Holy shit." The words fall from my mouth and I take another step toward the TV. "I know her," I tell them, shock flooding my system.

"You know her?" Asher asks as Cole pinches the bridge of

his nose.

"Of course she knows her. Something about this has to do with her, we just haven't worked out what yet."

"How do you know her?" Travis asks, muting the TV.

"I went to high school with her. She was someone who tormented me on a daily basis for absolutely no reason. I hated her and that wasn't any secret, but I would never have wished her dead, not like this."

"So everybody knew that you hated her and that she hated you?" Asher asks, and I nod.

"Yeah, it was no secret. She was the queen bee; I was the lowly poor outcast. Even in a school full of poor kids, there's still a queen bee who runs everything and there is still always an outcast. She lashed out daily like it was her favorite sport and I was her favorite prey. I can't believe she's dead."

"This isn't good," Cole tags on and instantly pulls out his phone. He taps on the screen before putting it to his ear and striding out of the room toward the backyard.

"Chances are the police are going to want to talk to you again if another body is linked to you, Briar," Travis adds, before typing away on his phone. "I might call Denton in, just for some extra help. He did well enough last time and you guys got along, right?"

"Yeah, Denton was good. He was nice enough, but do you really think I'm going to need a lawyer? I have an alibi for today."

"Better to be safe than sorry," Travis responds, bringing the phone to his ear and disappearing upstairs, leaving me with the twins and the dogs. I drop into his old chair and hang my head. One of these days I'll get an actual entire good day. Just one, maybe.

After the news last night and Travis speaking to Denton, who had already spoken to the police and any contact that they require of me will have to go through him, I feel a little better that I'm not going to get dragged out of class again. But at the same time, he is a little terrifying.

Travis also spoke to Bentley last night, who has been doubling down on everything that he can look at and, apparently, he has a trail on the emails that have been coming to me from whoever this crazy psychopath is. So I'm hopeful that maybe we might have some answers soon and if Bentley can work with the police, then all the better for it.

While I haven't been living my life in fear, now that everything else is starting to settle down, it occurs to me that I should probably be a little afraid of everything that's going on since it keeps leading back to me. From Serena, to Becca, to the girl who died yesterday, to the notes and the emails, it's very obvious, like Cole said, that this has something to do with me. We just have no idea what and there isn't anything that I can think of that would link me to all of this beyond the whole Crawford thing. But at this point, I don't even know how that links into any of this. None of it makes any sense and I'm not exactly a criminal mastermind. I don't have the brain capacity to sit and work it out.

Hell, I barely have the brain power to make it through my classes, let alone try and work out a serial killer mastermind who seems to be evading the law at every turn. Needless to say, the guys have made sure that one of them is with me at all times now. Which means Sawyer is back to taking my classes for psychology and the others are tapping in when they can.

Somehow, Sawyer's class loads seem to be lighter than everybody else's, which makes zero sense to me because he and Travis are going for the same degree. I tried to ask questions and object, but I was overruled—shock, horror. Four against one on that voting system and I got overruled.

I spoke to Denton briefly this morning too, who told me that if anybody contacts me, I should let him know immediately and he'll jump on a plane. He also happened to vote for the protection, so I was majorly outvoted and I'm still not happy about it.

Thankfully, I don't have classes today, it being a Friday, so I haven't had to leave the house. The dogs don't count as enough protection, apparently, so Asher has been studying from home. I feel really bad that he is having to stay here and babysit me when we have the alarm system that's been installed and I quite literally have six Rottweilers here to defend me should I need it.

I glance at the clock again, making myself another coffee before heading back to my own books to try to catch up on everything that I keep missing with all of the chaos bombs that keep going off in my life. The others should be home soon, since Cole doesn't have practice tonight because he has an away game tomorrow. It was meant to be held on campus but something to do with a washed-out field and needing a change of venue… they did explain, but I still don't understand it entirely. I don't think sports will ever be my thing.

However, it means that he's going to be gone and since I'm his fiancée now, apparently I have to go with him. Upside, at least we get a road trip this weekend. Maybe a change of scenery is exactly what we need.

Just as I sit down and start reading through the same paragraph I'm pretty sure I've read four times at this point, Travis gets home with Bentley close behind him.

Travis's face is thunderous, and I can only imagine what news it is he got from Bentley.

"Everything okay?" Asher asks, and Travis glares at him as he storms over to where we're sitting. Bentley closes the door behind them and waves hello at me before coming to sit next to me.

"Depends on your definition of okay," Bentley responds to Asher, while Travis just sits and broods in silence. Surprise, surprise, the angry guy went into quiet mode.

"What did you find?" I ask, tentatively, almost not wanting to know the answer if it has Travis this worked up.

"I found the IP address that the emails are coming from and when I gave Travis the name, well, you can see how that went." I glance over at Travis, his arms are folded across his chest.

"Oh, yeah, I can see exactly how that went. Who was it?"

Bentley glances at Travis before looking back at me. "Apparently it's somebody that you know, so I'm not sure what to do with the name, whether to hand it off to the police or just tell you who it is."

"Well of course we hand it off to the police," Asher says. "Even if we know the person, the police deserve to know where the emails are coming from. I'm assuming that Denton's working with someone higher up than the detective that had an agenda against Briar, so the threats against her can be safely forwarded as evidence?"

Bentley nods his head. "Yeah, we can do that, but it does put a little bit more scrutiny on your girl. I'm pretty sure Denton can handle the heat."

"Is someone going to tell me who the IP address belongs to?" I say, trying not to sound as frustrated as I feel, especially when I know that it's partially just fear of the idea of finding out who it is that's been doing this to me. Especially when they've told me it's somebody that I might know.

Bentley lets out a sigh and looks over at me with a sad smile on his face. "The name is Reed. Dante Reed."

A TASTE OF FOREVER

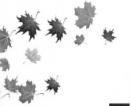

FOURTEEN

ASHER

Well, wasn't this just the clusterfuck of the century to walk into when I got home today?

"Are we sure, like, without any reasonable doubt, that it was him?" I ask, while Travis and Cole yell at each other in the other room. Briar's been sitting in silence on the stool in the kitchen since I got in, her knees pressed against her chest, her arms wrapped around them. Like she's trying to process that Dante could be the one that's been doing all of this to her.

I don't know the guy very well beyond him being on the team with Cole and the fact that Briar knew him from her old life. I'd like to say he doesn't seem like that guy, but when does that guy *ever* seem like that guy?

227

People are good at wearing disguises and hiding their true nature; it's literally how we were raised in this world.

"I'm as sure as I can be. What I know is that the IP address definitely belongs to him. Could he have been hacked? Possibly. Could it be somebody else making it look like him? Also, possibly. But I think it would be remiss of us to just assume these things when you don't know him that well and this is where the trail is leading us. It would take someone fairly genius level to layer the encryption that I had to get through to mask the IP, and why do that if you're not hiding who you really are?"

"This doesn't make any sense," Briar says quietly. "None of it makes any sense at all. There's no way. I get that it *could* be him, but I don't understand *why* he would do any of this. None of it makes any sense to me."

"The why is always the most fucked up," Bentley says to her softly. "I've seen many people do many things, and their reason for why has never made much sense to me, but it hasn't been any less true."

I push my glasses up my nose, itching the bridge of it before taking them off and putting them on the counter, trying not to lose my shit about all of this.

"So, how do we take this to the police?" I ask Bentley, trying to ignore Travis and Cole's voices getting even louder. Thank God Sawyer took the dogs out, because I'm not sure that we could deal with their noise on top of everything else right now.

"I can't do this right now," Briar says, standing. "I'm just gonna go upstairs and try to sleep, because that's the only way that I can get through this today, I just need to sleep it away. I know I'm resilient, and I know I'm strong, but if Dante is the one who's done all of this, I don't know how to process that yet."

I open my mouth to speak, but she just walks away and heads up the stairs, leaving us watching after her.

"She'll be okay. It's just been a bit of a shock," Bentley says, trying to reassure me, and I nod as I turn back to him.

"Everything in her life since she got off that plane has been shock. I'm surprised she's even still standing."

"Like she said, the girl is resilient. It's one of the worst traits that a person can have because it means that they've been through so much that they've learned how to cope, but she'll be okay and she *will* get through this. As for how we go to the police, Travis has already called Carter and Denton and I believe that they're on their way. Denton is going to deal with the police and how we give them the information about the notes without getting Briar more mixed up in everything."

"This is such a fucking clusterfuck." I let out a sigh and drop onto the stool that Briar just vacated. As the front door opens and Sawyer returns, he lets the dogs off their leashes and they all bound toward the garden and he heads toward me.

"I see we've made no progress."

"No, not really. Everything's still a mess."

"Where's our girl?" he asks, and I motion toward the stairs.

"She needed a timeout, so she's just gone to bed for a bit."

"I don't blame her," he says, dropping onto the seat beside me. "I think if I had the option between being awake or sleeping through the bad shit, I'd want to sleep through it too. How do we fix this for her?" he asks Bentley, who smiles sadly.

"There is no fixing this for her; there's just being there for her while we get through it. If it turns out that it is this guy, then at least she might finally get some answers, and if it's not, we are one step closer to finding out who it is that's been messing with her for so long."

"Are you okay?" I ask Briar for maybe the twelfth time today. Dante being taken in for questioning isn't sitting well with her... especially since they tackled him on campus and dragged him away. The fact that her and Penn were with him at the time despite us telling Briar to stay the fuck away... yeah, it's been a bad few days.

"They released him, said there wasn't enough evidence. I just don't understand why these detectives go in so hard. You know for a fact that if it was you or Travis being arrested it wouldn't happen that way." She lets out a sigh of frustration and I nod, because she's not wrong.

"I know. One day things will change, but right now, I'm more worried about you."

"I just need to burn off this anxious energy… but I do not run, and I can't think of anything else to do."

I smirk at her as Sawyer walks down the stairs. His gaze bounces from hers to mine before he grins and rubs his hands together. "Well, I appear to have arrived just in time to save the day."

A laugh rips through my chest, because of course he's going to save her day.

"Save the day?" Briar asks, looking up at him through her lashes from where she's sulking on the stool at the counter.

"Well, you look pissed off, and my dearest brother looks a little lost… which means, obviously, I'm going to save the day. What's on your mind, Sunshine?"

"She wants to burn off some energy," I say out loud, while telling him the rest with a look, and his grin widens.

"Oh, I can definitely help you with that, Sunshine," he says to her, wagging his brows. "We don't even have to let my twinny twin twin in on it."

"And what do you have in mind?" she asks, a smile playing on her lips, because she knows him as well as I do. And if he thinks he's leaving me out of this fun, well, he has another thing coming.

"Well, the construction in the backyard is finally finished… which means the hot tub is available. And I might have an idea about how to really get you relaxed."

I quirk a brow at him. I didn't realize the construction was finished. But then, I haven't really been paying attention. It's been his thing and I don't even really know what he had built out there, just that he made it happen really fucking quickly.

"Do I need a suit?" she asks playfully, and I laugh.

"Oh I doubt that very much," I answer her, knowingly.

"Last one out there doesn't get an orgasm," Sawyer shouts and hauls ass toward the back door while Briar blinks at me in shock.

"Snooze, you lose, Pretty Girl," I say with a wink before running out after Sawyer, hearing her laugh behind me as her footsteps thud beside mine.

I wait at the door and scoop her up over my shoulder before running across the yard, her laughter like food for my soul.

Sawyer waits for us by the door to the new building, shaking his head at me. "That feels like cheating."

I shrug and Briar laughs harder. "Orgasms for everyone!" she shouts as I put her down and runs inside.

Just as I reach the entrance, Sawyer grabs the top of her lounge shorts and pulls the silky material down, exposing her delicious, tight ass. The next thing I hear is her high-pitched squeal as his teeth sink into her flesh, his eyes dancing with delight.

"You're an ass." I realize my mistake as soon as the words escape my mouth.

"I'm an ass lover. Nuance." Shouldering my way inside, I take a second to look around. The place is bigger than I expected, with the in-ground hot tub front and center and gym equipment just beyond it. All around the tub is an elevated wooden surface, like a sun deck, and my mind immediately sees Briar laid out, naked, and sucking on my cock like her life depends on it.

Suddenly, I'm impossibly harder and of-fucking-course Sawyer notices right away.

"You just imagined her naked and riding your dick, didn't you?" Briar slaps my shoulder as I scowl at my twin. "I mean, her lying naked and riding my cock was my entire motivation for making this place so, no judgment here." I grin at him when Briar slaps his shoulder too.

That's when our twinning minds switch on, sharing matching smirks and a fire in our eyes that only Briar can tame. Slowly, we both turn our gaze to our little prey just as she's huffing and puffing and pulling up her irrelevant shorts. Once she sees our faces, she freezes, her brows pulled down in confusion at first, but she quickly understands that playful twin time is over and the fuckery twins are omnipresent.

"I guess I won't be needing any of this after all, will I?" I bite my bottom lip as she pushes her shorts and panties down in one smooth move before crossing her arms over her midsection and pulling her barely-there silk top over her head, flinging it across the room.

"Fucking hell, brother. I don't know which hole I want to fuck first, but what I *do* know is that my dick is so hard right now, I'm in pain." Ah, Sawyer…

Ever the romantic.

"What he means is, get in that hot tub, right now. We need you nice and wet." I palm my hard cock so she can see just how much we do need her.

Her grin and saucy little wink only gets our blood flowing faster as she turns on her heel and skips—actually fucking skips—to the tub before immersing one foot, then the other, in the water. From the corner of my eye, I see Sawyer reaching for the control panel and seconds later, bubbles erupt all around her waist.

Briar's face lights up as she turns toward us, her tits on full display with nipples hard enough to cut glass, throwing us a sultry *come hither* look.

Sawyer and I are both naked in record time and sliding into the water beside her. My mouth is on hers as my fingers curl around her hair just as Sawyer's mouth latches onto one of her nipples. Our little minx moans into my mouth and I swallow the sound like a gift. Falling to his knees, Sawyer lavishes her tits with attention as my free hand wraps around her throat, my lips and tongue dominating her mouth. We kiss like this for minutes while my brother pushes her legs further apart and buries his hand between her thighs. I can't see him, but I know him, and his next words only confirm my theory.

"She's so fucking wet and it has nothing to do with the water."

Pulling away from her addictive mouth, I smirk down at

her, "Are you wet for us, Briar? Do you need your pretty little holes to be filled?" With lust glazing over her eyes, she flashes me a drunken smile and nods.

"Someone better start fucking me or else I'll have to go find the others to do the job." Christ, no wonder Travis likes to spank her tight ass. She loves the punishment, doesn't she?

"Well, well, brother. It seems our little vixen here is trying to make us jealous. Or maybe…" I pull her hair harder, her head falling back even more until she's nearly bent over enough for her head to touch the water. The position gives Sawyer the perfect angle to do as he pleases with her breasts. "Maybe, she just needs a big cock in her mouth to keep her quiet?"

Sawyer releases her nipple just long enough to answer, "I vote for the cock. She does love a nice throat fucking, don't you, Sunshine?" Briar doesn't answer him but she keeps her gaze steady on me as the corners of her lips lift into a victorious smile.

I mean, she can't lose at this game. She's either getting punished or fucked, both of which she loves. We may as well get off on it, too.

Pulling her along with me, I sit on the edge of the deck, legs spread enough that Briar can nestle between them, before taking her mouth in a scorching kiss once again. She tastes like strawberries and freedom, making it almost impossible to pull her away from me. Sawyer turns her face toward him and winks at her right before his mouth descends on her. I watch, enthralled, as their lips glide and suck as their teeth nip and their tongues dart out into each other's mouths. It's fucking hot. The way my brother makes her moan, how quickly he gets her heart rate up and how he commands her body to his will. I know he sees the same thing whenever I touch her, but this mirror effect makes my dick twitch and precum ooze from my slit.

"I think my twin needs his cock in your mouth." Sawyer trails his lips down the column of her throat until he reaches her collarbone, then makes his way back up to her ear, whispering. "While he fucks your pretty little face, I'm going to pound your pretty little cunt."

With a quick kiss to her swollen lips, I guide her mouth to my dick and slowly slide my head between her lips until my entire length is swallowed up and I can see the bulge of my cock thrusting in and out at the top of her throat. Fuck, that's even hotter.

Tearing my gaze from the erotic sight of Briar's lips wrapped tightly around my hard length, I meet my brother's eyes over her head. He's drunk on the sight too and I know that, below the surface of the water, he's gliding his dick between her pussy lips, teasing her, teasing himself, before he slams inside her at the perfect moment.

I lean back, holding myself up by my arms just as Briar's back is covered by Sawyer's chest and abs. I'm captivated by the sight of him wrapping her hair around his palm as he closes his fist and pulls her head back half an inch, giving me the perfect angle to fuck her throat. My hips are thrusting up, my feet planted on the seat of the tub, giving me the leverage I need to keep a tight rein on my movements. Hurting her isn't the name of the game, orgasms are.

Just as Sawyer pulls her back, the cool air hitting the overheated skin of my cock, I know he's just slammed inside her pussy. It's in the way he closes his eyes and moans into the space around us, in the way his entire body tenses and his fist tightens around the strands of her hair. Mostly, it's the way Briar whimpers around my cock, the vibrations bringing me dangerously close to spilling my seed right down her esophagus. But I need more. I can't just sit back and watch her lips slide up and down my cock. I need to own her.

My hand flies to her throat, my thumb pressing against her pulse point, and I squeeze hard enough to feel my dick every time she opens up for me. How the fuck am I supposed to last?

We fuck her like this until neither one of us can take it anymore. Everything about Briar is erotic. The curve of her spine as Sawyer spears her pussy, in and out, without mercy, the bounce of her tits as they splash in and out of the water with every thrust I give her mouth, the swell of her lips as she slides up and down my shaft and buries her nose at my root.

Sawyer looks up at me and I just know. He wants to change it up and I'm one hundred percent on board. We both slide out of her and suddenly, I'm fucking starving.

Grabbing her at the waist, I switch up our positions so that

I'm in the water and Briar is lying on the deck, legs spread out like a royal offering of her pussy. The sight makes my mouth water, my tongue sliding along my lips knowing exactly how fucking good she tastes.

"Appetizer before the main course?" Fucking Sawyer. Although, he's not wrong.

"Yeah, I need to whet my appetite." My brother laughs, which piques Briar's curiosity as she leans up, giving us pointed looks. I suppose laughing while we're admiring her gorgeous pussy—all swollen and dark pink with her juices shimmering on her parted lips—is not recommended.

I'm the first in, my mouth latching onto her flesh while I kiss and devour her, sucking on her cum and burying my entire face between her legs. Her scent is like a drug, her taste like a fine wine that can't be priced. I could spend my life between her thighs and still come back for more.

Except my fucking brother shoulders me off and grunts, "My turn, you greedy bastard."

I know he's enjoying her as much as I did, so I let my gaze wander to her face as I sidle up to her and take her nipple in my mouth, my eyes focused entirely on her. On her closed lids as her chest rises and falls at uneven breaths, her mouth open, her top teeth raking along her bottom lip. She's a fucking vision, all hot and filled with unbridled lust.

Closing my teeth around her nipple, I bite down just hard enough to get her attention right as Sawyer slides two fingers inside her ass. I know this because he's giving us a play by play, which is his way of distracting himself so he doesn't come in the tub like a twelve-year-old virgin discovering how good orgasms feel.

The first sign that Briar is about to blow is her body tensing, going completely still and rigid. Then it's her gasp as she inhales enough air to make her chest rise, giving me the perfect opportunity to suck on her tit. And I know she's lost the battle when Sawyer announces that he's about to suck on her clit while he fucks her ass with his fingers. Her cry is loud and long, a continuous stream of vocalized lust filling the air around us. Her body shakes, her toes literally curling along the edge of the deck as her legs fall to the side and her torso arches off the surface below. I keep sucking on her tit and Sawyer keeps eating her pussy while he fingers her forbidden hole. She's beautiful on any day, but like this? She's a fucking goddess.

"Dude, I'm gonna fucking blow. She turns me on like nothing else." I know what he wants so we don't waste time. Like a well-oiled machine, I sit on the bench of the tub while Sawyer steals a kiss on Briar's mouth. Picking her up, he places her on my lap, straddling my waist and wrapping her arms around my neck. Without any further foreplay, Briar sits on my cock and rubs her pussy on my groin just as she slams her mouth on mine. I kiss her like she's my oxygen and she lets me. She gives me her reins, her trust, and her pleasure. And like the greedy bastard I am, I take it all.

"Fuck, you're hot." I feel the pressure of Sawyer's fingers in her ass as he scissors his way inside her hole, pushing and pulling and widening her enough for his cock.

Soon, I feel her pussy getting tighter and tighter as he pushes more and more of his length inside her until we're both seated perfectly inside her body. Sawyer's head falls back, his hands resting on Briar's hips, his entire body shaking with the need to fuck. To fuck hard and fast.

"Baby Girl, I think we may have taken too long." My words are whispered, my eyes locked on Sawyer, hoping he won't hurt her with his need.

"Then fuck me like you mean it." It's precisely because I'm watching Sawyer that I see his eyes pop open and the lust invade his entire body.

All fucking bets are now off.

"You sure?" I'm asking Briar but also… I'm warning my brother.

"Fuck me like you mean it." She repeats her words and they're strong, sure. They're the words of a woman who knows exactly who her men are.

In tandem, I pull out of the warm cave of her pussy just as Sawyer slams inside her ass, his fingers probably leaving bruises on her hips with how hard he's holding her down.

We fuck for an eternity, the grunts and moans like a soundtrack to our scene. The water splashes more and more, wetting us higher and higher. Briar cries out that she's about to come but we don't slow down, we don't relent, we just continue the onslaught of our fucking over and over again, pushing and pulling and kissing and biting. We're a tangled, wet mess of limbs and flesh flying higher and higher until Sawyer pulls Briar's head back and I wrap my lips around her nipple and suck it hard enough to make her gasp.

We all freeze at once, our bodies convulsing like we've been jolted by an electric shock. I come deep inside her pussy as she coats my cock with her own orgasm and I know, without a fucking doubt in my mind, that Sawyer is emptying his sack inside her thoroughly-fucked ass.

We're quiet for a while, breathing hard and trying to clear our heads from the mind-blowing orgasms.

Once Sawyer pulls out, I lift Briar from my sensitive cock and sit her next to me, her head resting on my shoulder and her legs leaning on Sawyer's chest.

"So, did I save the day or what?"

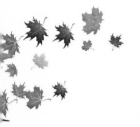

FIFTEEN

BRIAR

After everything last week with Dante being hauled in by police in the fashion that he was and Bentley finally singing to the police about how all of this seems to link back to me, Travis has Denton coming back to try and help navigate what it is that the police want from me because they, obviously, want to speak to me again.

I'm not sure what else I can tell them because I don't know anything. I know we haven't told them about Crawford and we never will, but I have no idea who's doing this. The police said earlier that the murders were happening before I even came to Serenity Falls, so I have no idea how any of this could possibly link to me. If there are two different people that just happen to be killing in the same way, then maybe somebody's a copycat and that's how they've all been linked and the copycat is somehow the one that's coming after me.

I pause my racing thoughts and take a deep breath. None of this is getting me anywhere. I've been spiraling down this rabbit hole for days, especially once the police cleared Dante, saying that there was no evidence on his laptop that any of the emails came from him, even though his IP was used, and that it wouldn't take a tech genius to be able to spoof an IP address. I didn't think it was him, he's been too nice, and he's related to Penn. Sure I had a sliver of doubt, but I mean who wouldn't. As soon as he was cleared, I believed it instantly.

So now we're back at square one, which I think is the other reason that Travis has called in Denton. That plus the fact that Cole's dad has had the two of us at a fancy dinner every night this week with different politicians and different networking people of his to show off the new toy that his son has.

I've been primped and preened more times this week than I care to think about but, apparently, I can't even dream of dressing myself or doing my own hair anymore for a function for the senator, because God forbid I should be anything close to myself.

This man has me dressed up like a freaking Barbie doll. Cole tried to speak to him about it, but threats were made and voices were raised and I ended up walking away. If I get to stay in school and Chase is off my back, I can deal with being paraded around like some sort of trophy wife. Even if it makes my skin crawl and my soul die a little on the inside. The only upside of it all is that I know that Cole hates it as much as I do, and that he would never make me do this if it were up to him.

I jump off the treadmill in the outbuilding that Sawyer had set up. We've got our own little gym and leisure suite back here now and, surprisingly, the treadmill has been my solace. I never really thought that I was one for running. It turns out that I'm not one for running when it comes to outside running but, in here, with my headphones in and nobody else around, running is a way to burn off all of the thoughts and all of the insanity going on inside of me and to focus on the burn of my lungs and the ache in my legs. It's like the rest of the world falls away.

I'm starting to understand why people take solace in things like this, whereas before I had no idea. I'm not saying I'm going to become an Olympian, but with the amount of stress in my life, maybe my ass might just shrink a little bit. Not that I want to lose my bubble butt. I'm pretty sure Sawyer would have something not very nice to say about that.

I take my headphones out, pausing Sofia Camara's *Never Be Yours* as I stop the treadmill and take in a few lungfuls of air. Today's run hasn't really helped clear my thoughts the way it has been the last week and I'm trying to let that not piss me off, but it's a war that I'm losing.

I step off the machine and grab my towel, rubbing myself down before turning off the lights and heading back into the main house. I open the back door and the sounds of voices hit me, that southern drawl coming through, and I can't help but grin.

"I see I missed the welcome party," I say as I walk through to the lounge area.

Denton looks up at me and grins. "Hey, Sweetheart! I thought we agreed that you'd keep yourself out of trouble."

My grin widens and I shrug. "Can't say I didn't try, but trouble seems to follow me everywhere I go."

A dry laugh pulls my attention to the man sitting on the end of the sofa next to Denton. Something about him makes me pause. It's like he radiates a magnetism that both terrifies me and intrigues me. If Denton is fire, this man is definitely ice.

"Briar, this is Carter. Carter, Briar." Travis introduces us, and I manage to unstick my feet and make my lungs start working again.

Carter's dark brown eyes bore into me like he can see into my soul and finds me wanting. Yeah, this guy is straight up terrifying. There is a cold, calculating way about him that screams serial killer, but Denton seems at ease next to him. I've heard Travis talk about him, but what I've heard about him I can't match up with the man sitting in front of me.

"Nice to meet you," I say with a small wave, trying not to wrap my arms around myself to protect against this man's stare.

"So you're the girl all the fuss is about?" Carter asks, leaning forward, his unblinking eyes never leaving me. "And what is it about you that makes you so special?"

"Don't be an ass," Denton says, nudging Carter. "She's a good girl. She just landed herself in some hot water."

"Hmm…" Carter says before leaning back and crossing his legs so his ankle rests on his knee. "I still would like to know what all the fuss is about for one girl to cause so much drama."

I shrug and slip back into the old defensive me, the one that survived on the cold, hard streets of New York. "I wish I could tell you, but I'll be damned if I know, trouble just seems to like me I guess."

The corners of Carter's lips tip upwards at my words before he lets out a small laugh. "I think I see it now. Girl's got balls of steel."

I quirk a brow at Carter and he laughs again, shaking his head. "Oh, yeah. You're definitely a magnet for trouble. You'd do well back home with us."

"Carter…" Travis growls. "Don't even think about it."

The two of them face off in a staring contest that I have absolutely no interest in, but it gives me a chance to study them next to each other and I realize just how alike they look. I'm fairly certain Travis doesn't have a big brother, but I don't know enough about Carter to understand any of this. I probably should have asked some questions before now. But I guess that's just the way this story goes.

"So, Sweetheart, you and I have an appointment at the police station this afternoon to go and talk it out with Detective

Douchebag One and Two. Do we need to cover anything before we go?"

I shake my head, chewing on the inside of my cheek. "No, I don't think so. Cole has kept me pretty up to date with everything and has coached me on what I should say and what I shouldn't be saying, but most of it's just common sense."

Denton nods. "Well, we'll go through it on the drive there anyway, but you go get yourself ready to face off with those assholes. Once you're good to go, we'll head out." I nod, glancing at Travis, who tilts his head once to let me know that he's good with everything, so I wave at them and head up the stairs to my room to shower and get ready for whatever this afternoon holds. I have a feeling if I'm facing off with Detective Douchebags One and Two, as Denton so lovingly called them, I'm going to need armor on, and right now I have nothing.

After an exhausting afternoon at the police station with Denton, I'm leaning against the wall trying to catch my breath outside while Denton's on a call. I didn't think this would be more exhausting than the last times that I've been in this station, but oh boy, was I wrong.

Denton lost his shit a couple of times because the detectives were being giant assholes and we ended up with the captain sitting in with us, rather than the detectives, because it really just seemed like one of them has a hard-on for making my life hell and I have no idea why.

I never met this guy before all of this happened, but he looks at me like I'm the guiltiest person on earth and all of this has to be my fault. Like there's no way in hell anybody else could possibly be responsible for what's been going on.

The sound of voices makes me stand up straight and I spot Connor and Jamie talking in the distance. Huh, there's two people I never expected to be friends. I have no idea how they even know each other. Jamie's from back home and Connor is very much from Serenity Falls, even if he is one of the supposed poor kids.

I also haven't seen him in weeks, so seeing him now is a bit weird.

Jamie sees me and smiles, waving at me. "Hey, Briar!" he calls out, and Connor's gaze whips toward me, shock filtering over his features before he manages to school them back into an indifferent-yet-somehow-friendly mask.

As they reach me, Connor says hello before asking, "You guys know each other?"

I nod. "Jamie and I go way back, though, I suppose I could ask the same question about you two."

Jamie lets out a weird laugh and rubs the back of his neck. "Yeah, I've known Connor for a good while, the joys of small-town life I guess."

I nod, trying to pretend that it isn't weird that they know

each other. I mean, it wouldn't be weird if Connor hadn't been so absent lately.

Speaking of… "Does this mean that you're going to be back around?" I ask Connor, and he shifts uncomfortably.

"Yeah, speaking of, I need to go and meet Penn. I'll see you in class this week?"

"Yeah, okay. If you need anything note-wise to catch up, just let me know. I guess." He gives me a tight smile before jamming his hands in his pockets and walking back off in the direction that they appeared from.

"So you and Connor are friends, huh?"

"Yeah, we've got a couple of classes together and he's dating my friend, Penn," I tell Jamie.

He leans against the wall that I was just on. "What brings you back down here?"

"I was just talking to the detectives again about the murders and stuff." His eyebrows rise just as Denton appears again.

"You ready, Briar?" Denton asks, and I nod, taking a step toward him, feeling uneasy about this whole interaction but not being able to put my finger on why. Maybe it's just because I'm tired from this entire day.

"We should meet up soon," Jamie says as I open my mouth to say goodbye. "Give me your new number and we'll arrange something." He hands his phone to me and I take it on instinct. My gaze quickly shifts to Denton before tapping my number onto the screen.

"Sure, drop me a message and we'll work something out," I agree as I hand it back to him. He gives me a brief hug before heading into the station. I turn to find Denton looking at me, eyebrow raised.

"You sure do keep some strange company, Sweetheart."

"My whole life has been one strange interaction after the next, so yeah, I guess I kind of do."

He watches me for a second before laughing and shaking his head. "Come on, let's get you home to those boys of yours before one of them thinks I've kidnapped you. Can't have the senator's men on my case now, can we?" He chuckles as he says it and I get the feeling that I'm very much missing something about this whole dynamic, but I just smile and shrug, mentally and emotionally exhausted.

He opens the car door for me and I slide into the back with him following quickly. Without even a word, the moment the car door is closed, the driver pulls away from the curb and I lean my head back against the headrest.

"Do you think I'm going to have to go back in there again?" I ask Denton, turning to face him.

"No, I don't think so. Especially now that the captain has gotten involved. He was able to see just how bad Douchebag One and Two were being to you so I think having answered his questions, you should be in the clear. The only reason you might need to speak to them again is if you get another little love note or email. But hopefully with the tech guys working with Bentley, that shouldn't be an issue anymore. Even if it is, Bentley can liaise with them for you. But I think Carter and I are hanging around for a bit anyway, just in case."

"So, what's the deal with you guys and Travis?" I ask, aware that I should probably be asking Travis that, but he's been tight-lipped on the whole Carter-Denton thing and I get the feeling that even if I asked him, he probably wouldn't tell me.

Denton's eyebrows rise in shock. "You don't know? Carter is Travis's cousin. Chase and Bentley had another brother but he died a few years ago, which is why Carter doesn't live in the city anymore. He changed his name to his mom's name and moved his entire operation further south."

"What do you mean, his entire operation?"

"That, Sweetheart, is not a question that you get to ask me," Denton says with a wink, "Now, do you want coffee or are we going home and getting food?"

I let out a small, disappointed sigh but really, I knew that Denton wasn't going to be the one to give me the answers that I want anyway.

"I need food and coffee, so we might as well just head home because we already know that the guys are going to have questions anyway."

"I bet they will. Those boys have got their dicks in a knot about you, don't they?"

I burst out laughing at his turn of phrase. "You definitely have a way with words, don't you, Denton?"

He winks at me with a mischievous smile on his face, "Yeah, but all the ladies love my way with words."

"Oh, I bet they do," I say to him, still chuckling, and lean my head back as I close my eyes. "I bet they do."

The entire journey home, all I've done is laugh at Denton. It turns out he's actually kind of hilarious when he wants to be, even if he is being tight-lipped about who Carter is as a human and what it is that he does. But I guess I can respect that. Him and Carter seem to have this bond that is of the unbreakable kind, a little like I see between my guys.

I'm still giggling as I open the front door, and I hear Carter speaking. "We still need to sort out this thing with Marco."

"I know we do, but I have no idea what it is that he wants. He had his guy destroy the evidence, but it wasn't all destroyed, so technically he didn't hold up his side of the deal and I don't know if we need him to now, but the deal has been made," Travis responds.

Normally, I'd pause and try to find out what's going on, but Denton pushes the door open from behind me, interrupting their conversation before looking down at me and shaking his head a little.

I stick my tongue out at him before walking into the house, and the conversation that was happening dies out. I know who

Marco is, but I have no idea what it is he wants from Travis or what deal it is that Travis has made with him, but I have this horrible sinking feeling that it has something to do with me.

So I decide to suck it up and just ask, "What deal with Marco?"

Carter looks at me and rolls his eyes, moving to drop into the chair that he was standing by while Travis just looks at me, uncomfortably shifting from foot to foot.

"It doesn't matter," he says to me. "It's nothing for you to worry about."

"It not mattering and it being nothing for me to worry about are two vastly different things," I say to him as Cole descends the stairs. I turn my attention to him and he pauses under my gaze. "Do you know about this deal with Marco?" He rubs the back of his neck and glances over at Travis, then lets out a sigh before I hear him drop onto the sofa too. "Oh, good. Apparently, we're being toddlers today."

"I-erm... no? Maybe?" Cole responds, and I let out a frustrated non-scream and turn back to face Travis. "This is because of me, isn't it?"

Still, nobody says anything, but I hear Denton moving around in the kitchen, fucking around with my coffee machine. "If you break it, I will break you," I call out to him, and hear him chuckling in response.

"Now, is somebody going to tell me what the hell is going on? I thought we were past the keeping secrets stage."

Carter snorts a laugh and slaps his hands against his thigh as he stands up. "Darlin', if you think that, you have no idea the sort of people that you're playing with." He pauses a beat, just watching me and I hold his gaze, refusing to back down. I don't know who he is, but I don't care. He doesn't get to tell me what is my business and what isn't, especially when it's so very obviously my business.

"Denton, let's head back to the hotel. We're done here for the day."

"Sure thing," Denton calls back then reappears from the kitchen with one of my tumblers, steam coming from the top.

"You mind?" he asks, looking directly at me, because, obviously, it doesn't belong to any of the guys in this house.

"Same rules apply. You break it, I break you." He grins widely at me, and Carter just rolls his eyes again. I get the feeling that Carter really has zero patience for me and I don't understand why. He barely even knows me, but then, I can't say that I know him either.

Hell, I only just found out that he's Travis's cousin.

"I'll catch you guys later," Carter says to Travis and Cole, completely skipping over me as he leaves. Denton shakes his head behind his friend and stares back at me.

"See ya later, Sweetheart. Try not to get into too much trouble for the rest of the day. Later, boys," he says before following Carter out of the house and closing the door behind them.

"So…" I say, my gaze bouncing between the two of them. "Who's going to talk first?"

SIXTEEN

BRIAR

"I feel like I've barely seen you," I whine at Penn over the phone, and I swear I can hear her eyes roll.

"Yeah, well, life has been a little crazy for you of late," she says sarcastically. "For a change, mine has been one chaos bomb after the other too."

I wince at the thought of everything that happened with Dante, knowing that she already had so much going on with Connor and with her birth mom.

"How is everything going?" I ask her. She lets out a sigh, and I hear a thud as she drops onto what I'm assuming is her bed.

"Everything is just kind of bad," she says sadly. "My

auntie flipped with Dante being hauled in, even with him being released. There is a lot of tension in their house at the moment, which means there's just a lot of tension in the entire family. Even though it's been proven now that his computer was hacked or whatever it was that happened. My auntie wants to know why he's the one that was targeted for that and everyone is also still angry at me for being your friend, because obviously it all links back to you. Plus, Connor is still basically MIA."

"Oh, I saw him the other day," I say, finally remembering to mention it to her. "He was at the police station, talking to an old friend of mine."

"Old friend?" she asks, and I tell her about Jamie and the run in that I had with them.

"Hmm, I don't think I know Jamie," she says. "Weird, but that means that you've seen more of him than I have."

"He said he was coming to see you," I tell her when it pops into my brain that that was how he left the conversation.

"I haven't seen him in like, a week," she tells me, and I chew on the inside of my lip. It was only two days ago that I saw him at the police station.

"What is going on with that boy?" I say rather than ask, because nobody has any answers.

"I don't know," she responds, "but I'm fairly certain that his uncle is leaving this week, so maybe we'll get the Connor that I know and love back."

"At this point, do you really want him back if he's not going to tell you the truth of what's been going on with him?"

"Honestly? I have no idea. Everything of late has shown me this boy has more red flags than I ever thought he did. But if he won't tell me what's been going on with him, then no, I probably don't want him back, because the world doesn't go round unless you can be honest with the person that you're meant to be in a relationship with. Speaking of honesty, are you ready for next semester now that it's exam season?"

"Absolutely not," I tell her, knowing that most of my exams were done in assignment form this year rather than actually requiring an exam. "I think I've only got two exams for the entire semester to get wrapped up, but I'm not ready to restart this process all over again. I know that summer isn't far away, but I was going to work through it," I explain to her.

"Girl, you're crazy. The best part about college is that we get summers off. Why on earth would you try and work through it?" I smile, laughing softly at Penn just being Penn.

"Because, originally, I wanted to get in and out of here as fast as possible and complete about five years' work in three years. I was not going to take any breaks at all. But maybe I should rethink that plan now that everything has changed."

"Bitch, hell yeah you should," Penn says, laughing out loud. "And then we can do a summer break together. You, me, Mexico, tacos and margaritas. Tell me something that sounds better than that?"

I grin widely. "Now I can't wait to do that, because that

sounds like heaven."

She pauses and calls out "Hello?" before her attention comes back to our conversation. "I've gotta go, somebody's here," she says, and a pang of worry flits through me.

"Okay, you know where I am if you need me, but I'm seeing you soon, right?"

"Bitch, of course you are. I love you. Bye." The phone goes dead and I drop mine, letting out another deep sigh. With everything that's been going on lately, my friendship with Penn has been somewhat neglected and I hate myself for being that girl that spends all her time with her boyfriends and fiancé rather than with her friends. But Penn's had just as much chaos going on as I have, and I realize that I didn't get any answers about her birth mom or her brother or her results from the marrow test that we did. I really do need to work on being a better friend.

"Where's Travis?" I ask when I get back and notice he's absent. The three of them look at each other like they're talking in that super-secret stupid boy code of theirs before Cole turns to me and shrugs.

"He went with Carter to speak to Marco. Something about Marco wanting to make a deal with Travis rather than Chase. I'd tell you more but that's all I know." He looks at me earnestly, and despite wanting to shout at Travis for having kept yet another thing from me, I nod and thank Cole for being honest with me.

At least someone was.

"Okay, well, let's hope it's nothing serious. I told you guys when he gave me his card that I wanted nothing to do with Marco Mancini. It's never going to end well." I let out a deep sigh. Today has already been exhausting and it's barely mid-afternoon.

"Speaking of things not going to end well… we're having an engagement party," Cole tells me, looking about as happy at the prospect as I feel.

"And on that note," Sawyer says, jumping to his feet and clapping his hands. "Asher and I should walk the hounds." He darts away, calling for the furry monsters. I look at Asher, who at least has the decency to look sheepish before he heads off to grab his coat and the leashes.

Once the twins have shepherded the dogs onto their leads and headed out with them, I turn my focus back to my fiancé, who is practically squirming where he sits.

"Engagement party? Why?"

"My dad, why else?" he says with a sigh, rubbing a hand over his buzzed hair. "Something about letting people know the dynasty is growing or some shit. Really, he just wants an excuse to throw a party and woo people, I'm sure. It'll be boring, exhausting, and absolutely not about us, even if we are the guests of honor."

I bark out a laugh and drop onto the sofa beside him. "Good

to know. What do you need from me?"

"To be there? Dad will send someone over to get measurements to have you fitted for a dress… they'll make sure we all coordinate with each other, the guys too. I made sure my dad was aware they would also be attending with us."

"It's going to be a disaster, isn't it?" I groan, putting my head in my hands. "I can already see it. I'll trip and spill a drink over someone important. Someone will get drunk and start a fight. Or, better yet, Emerson will rock up and start blackmailing us all again."

Cole chuckles softly beside me before wrapping his arm around my shoulders and tucking me into his side. "It'll all be fine, beautiful. Just you wait and see. As for tripping, we can tell the stylist no heels. That should help, right?"

"It might," I say, bringing my face into his chest, breathing in the calming scent of him to try and stop the panic before it begins.

"You took this all much better than I thought you would," he murmurs as he kisses the top of my head.

"When I agreed to marry you, I had a faint idea of what that would mean. I also know that complaining isn't going to do anything other than make you feel bad, because we have to bow to your father's whims… which, so far, are much easier than the hoops Chase wanted me to jump through, so I'll take it." I press my lips together, holding in the thought that it could be much worse, because I know that if I say it out loud, I'll jinx myself.

Hell, I might have already done it just by thinking it.

"When is it?" I ask, realizing I probably should have lead with that.

"Saturday," he mumbles into my hair, and I start laughing. "I know, I know."

"That's two days away," I say with a sigh. "When is this person coming to measure me up?"

"In about an hour?" he says, and I swear I feel him flinch.

I just laugh at him before pulling back.

"Be glad I have a game tomorrow, otherwise it would've been then."

"Big game?" I ask, and his shoulders tense as he nods his head. It takes me a second but I realize this is the game with all the scouts, that got rescheduled, that was meant to be an away game, and well, floods happened. Got to love winter on the east coast. "Well, then we will all be there cheering you on."

"Thank you," he says softly. "Now how about we fill the next hour with something fun."

He winks at me before standing and holding out a hand to me.

"Now there is something I'm definitely not going to complain about."

"I feel like someone's freaking doll," I complain to Penn as I take a sip of the champagne that the waiters at this party are handing out like water. "And the boning in this dress is enough to make a girl want to scream."

"I mean, you look good though?" she responds, trying her best not to laugh, but she doesn't quite manage it.

This entire night has been one fake smile after another. The very expensive heels that I was bribed into are pinching my toes and I haven't seen Cole or the others for what feels like hours.

I am so at the point of being done that I'm ready to walk out of my supposed engagement party, sans my fiancé, and run away with my bestie.

Damn that sounds so freaking appealing, but… "There you are, Briar!" I wince at the sound of my mother's voice. I thought I'd managed to evade her for a minute, but apparently not. She's been the show and tell committee all night, introducing me to the who's who of the political world.

So. Over. It.

"Briar, I'd love to introduce you to Ella Saunders. She is the president of one of the charity boards I sit on. It's for homeless girls in the city. I thought that might be something you'd be interested in." She smiles at me and it's so condescending that, even though I'd absolutely love to be involved in something like that, it still makes me clench my jaw and grind my teeth.

"Sounds good," I say to her before throwing what's left in my glass down my throat and turning to Penn. "I'll catch you soon."

"Have fun," she says with a giggle and a finger wave. I flip her the finger, turning her giggle into full laughter, before I turn back to my mom and motion for her to lead the way.

It takes every ounce of strength that I have to not wince as I take each step. My toes are definitely bleeding in these very expensive shoes. I've mostly tried not to think about the amount of money spent on tonight, but I am also fully aware that since Cole's dad is throwing this party, that absolutely nothing I said or did was going to make any difference to the cost.

"Ella, there you are! It's so lovely to see you," my mom coos when we reach the beautiful blonde, whose eyes are warm and smile seems genuine when she turns to us. They do that weird air kiss thing before my mom pulls me forward. "This is my daughter, Briar. I was explaining to her about the girls we work on behalf of, and she agrees it's something she'd like to be involved with."

Ella's blue eyes brighten as she turns to face me before pulling me into an embrace. I stiffen, startled, but recover as quickly as I can and hug her back. "That would be lovely, Briar. We can use every helping hand we can get. Homelessness in the city is an uphill battle, but the amount of young girls on the streets, and the extra issues they face... well, let's just say it's something near and dear to my heart."

Her smile falters at the end of her sentence, but her picture-perfect smile is back in the blink of an eye. "Your mom has my details, so get them from her when you're ready and we'll talk more about your involvement."

"That sounds great," I say, trying to sound as genuine as I feel. It's just this setting and these *goddamn shoes* are killing the vibe for me.

I turn to grab another glass of champagne as a server passes when I spot Cole across the room. He's moving toward me, practically pushing people out of the way, and the hairs on the back of my neck go up.

I catch his gaze and the panic reflected back at me makes my heart race.

What the hell?

I take a step back and bump into someone, so I turn to apologize and come face-to-face with a stunning woman with warm hazel eyes and waist-length black hair. "I'm so sorry," I say once I get over seeing her, and she smiles back at me.

Except the smile isn't warm.

It's cold and calculating. Her eyes narrow at me before her gaze sweeps over me from head to toe. The look on her face tells me she finds me lacking and I feel like a helpless deer caught in her trap.

"Oh, don't be. I've been looking for you."

"You have?" I ask, trying not to stutter, wondering why I'm so freaking panicked. "Who are you?"

As the words fall from my lips, Cole appears at my side and takes my hand, squeezing it.

"Briar, this is my mother, Catherine Barclay. Mother, I

didn't realize you were coming." The panic on his face recedes when he's at my side, replaced by a look of anger. I squeeze his hand back to let him know I'm okay when his words register.

Wait, what?

"Of course you didn't, I wasn't invited," she says, her words about as smooth as poison.

"Catherine," Theo says as he joins our merry little circle. Just what I wanted. To be caught up in more family drama. "I'd say it's lovely to see you, but it's absolutely not. What are you doing here?"

"Well, Theodore, as Cole's mother, I figured it was my right to meet the girl you were marrying him off to. I must say, I am disappointed."

I flinch at the comment, though I'm not sure why her opinion matters to me—I thought she was dead, for fuck's sake, sure the senator was a widower—and I feel Cole stiffen beside me.

"Mom, you don't get to speak about Briar like that," Cole says through a clenched jaw, but she just laughs at him in response.

"I should go," I say quietly to Cole. "I get the feeling that this isn't actually about me."

"I'm sorry," he murmurs to me before wrapping me up in a hug. "Don't worry about any of this. I'll handle it. Wait up for me?"

"I will," I respond, chastely kissing his cheek before turning to his parents with a tight smile. "Thank you for this evening, but I'm feeling rather unwell."

"Of course, Briar," Theo says, not looking away from Cole's mother.

I release Cole's hand and walk away from the toxic situation I just found myself dropped into and take a deep breath. I already wanted to leave this freaking party, but now I *really* want to go. It doesn't take long to find Penn at the bar where I left her, and after a quick catch up, we're practically running from the party.

If this is what the rest of my life looks like, I'm not sure that I'm ready for it.

I wake up warmer than should be possible for March, but when my eyes flutter open, I realize that Cole and Travis climbed into bed with me when they got back last night. The biggest problem I have is that I don't want to move, and I definitely don't want to wake them, but I think I might have heat stroke. I blow my hair back out of my face, trying to move the comforter down my body a little without disturbing them, but it's no use.

I am in a man-cocoon and it is *hot.*

In more ways than one, but it's the actual heat I have a problem with. They must have gotten home pretty late last night because, despite my attempt to stay up as per Cole's request, I have exactly zero recollection of them wandering in here.

"Stop wriggling," Travis grumbles as he pulls me tighter

against his chest.

Cole mumbles in front of me as he turns over to face me. "What he said."

"You guys are really warm," I whisper, since it's still dark out and I have no idea if it's even morning yet.

"No, you're just wearing too many clothes," Travis growls in my ear as his thumb strokes my ribs and his hand splays across my stomach underneath my tank top.

"That's easily remedied," Cole adds, his dark eyes like warm honey as he stares at me. I bite down on my lip, knowing that we should probably talk about what happened last night, but just being this close to the two of them has me all kinds of wet and needy.

"I guess you should do something about that then, shouldn't you?" I tease as Travis presses his hard dick into my ass. A breathy moan spills from my lips as Cole cups my breast, tweaking the nipple through my top.

"I suppose we could," Cole responds, and I swear a whimper falls from my lips without my permission.

With both of them already naked, I'm the odd woman out in this scene, but Travis makes quick work of my top while Cole practically rips my bottoms off like they offend him.

Then there were three. It's crazy how quickly they get me from sleepy to horny—a matter of seconds, really—without breaking a sweat. Yet here we are, all naked and ready for orgasms galore.

I spread my legs, my arms above my head so I can hold on to my headboard, and wait patiently for them to jump on me and fuck me into next week. Maybe we could break some kind of orgasm record. Three? Four? Five would probably put me in a coma, but hey, they don't call it the little death for nothing.

"Such an eager little slut, aren't you, Baby?" Travis is lying on his side, his head propped up on his palm like he's lounging on a Sunday morning waiting for his coffee.

"I mean, we're naked and ready, so… yeah." I'm confused. Did I misread them? Hell no. Since when do they not want to fuck?

Travis trails his index finger down my body, starting at my forehead, down my nose, and across my lips. I try to bite him but he *tsks* me away like a naughty child. Maybe if I call him Daddy, he'll hurry up and make me come.

My breathing picks up as his finger runs down the front of my throat.

"Have I ever told you my dick looks really good when it's fucking you right here?" I swallow as he says this and realize he's pressing down just enough to make my throat work harder. "It's erotic as fuck."

"What about when her tits bounce with every thrust inside her cunt? Makes me want to fuck her pussy and her cleavage at the same time," Cole muses, his eyes fixed on the apex of my thighs, his finger caressing my skin everywhere except where I actually want him.

"Good thing we are two, then, huh?" I glare at Travis because his playful tone never bodes well for my orgasms. Especially as his finger slides between my tits without even pretending to touch my aching nipples. When he reaches the top of my clit, he stops. Then, the fucker retraces his path all the way back to my lips.

So, this is it, isn't it? Death by anticipation?

I'm jolted back from my thoughts by a quick slap to my pussy.

"Thinking about more important things than us?" Travis smirks at Cole's words like he's waiting for something. Like he's waiting for me to sass back. Joke's on them. I'm too horny to be crazy enough to give them lip right now.

Travis blows on my hard nipple, his smiling eyes on me, the sparkle in them saying everything.

I'm not talking back. I'll be patient, a good girl, so they can both put their dicks in me and make me come. That's the plan. That is always the plan.

Oh, who the fuck am I kidding?

"Is this going to take all day? Maybe I should clear my schedule." Fuck, why did I just say that? Bad girl. Bad, bad, bad.

"There it is," Travis drawls out like he's been waiting for it since we woke up.

"Dammit! I really thought she'd have more restraint than that." At Cole's complaint, Travis quickly rises and straddles my chest, one hand on my throat and his face so close I can see the heat swimming in his mesmerizing eyes.

"When it comes to us, she has no restraint. Do you know why?" His tongue darts out to lick his lips before he takes a leisurely stroll across my open—I'm in shock at this whole fucking conversation—mouth. "Because her pussy is greedy and patience is missing from her list of qualities."

"And orgasms. I like them and you're always keeping them from me."

"That's because you're always being a brat." He squeezes my throat tighter, his mouth on mine, kissing and licking and biting on my flesh. "Don't tell anyone, but it's my favorite thing about you."

Travis slaps his free hand over my mouth and nose just as Cole grabs my legs and buries his face in my pussy, french kissing my cunt like he's searching for lost treasure.

I can barely breathe between my covered face and Travis's fingers pressing against my throat. Watching me, he comes closer, eyes darting from one eye the other, and I think he's weighing his options.

"I could fuck your mouth or maybe lube up your tits and fuck them while Cole is busy devouring your sweet little pussy. What do you think?" I can't answer and that's a good thing because I'd probably tell him to fuck off. Then tell him he can fuck me anywhere he wants and for however long he desires. Because he's right... I am their little whore and I love every second of it. I choose every second of it.

"Tits it is, then. Hey, Cole?" Cool air replaces Cole's hot mouth just long enough for him to respond with a grunt. "Know where any of her toys are?" Fucker knows exactly where they are but he doesn't want to move.

Mumbling a curse under his breath, Cole gives my pussy one last kiss before he rises and goes directly to my stash, taking out a variety of toys and placing them on the bed next to Travis. Then he makes himself comfortable and goes right back to eating me out. My back arches as he sucks on my clit just long enough to make me whimper but not enough to get me off. Dammit.

"Let's see…" Travis goes through the pile quickly, landing on a pair of nipple clamps and grinning like he's just found the holy grail. "These look convenient."

Bending at the waist, Travis circles one nipple with his tongue then sucks—hard enough to cause a little pain—until it's long and erect. Keeping one hand on my mouth and nose, he releases my throat to take the clamp and slowly presses the teeth on my tit. "Gorgeous. It'll soon be so full of blood you'll cry for me to take it off." He repeats the action on the other nipple before flicking the protruding flesh with his tongue, causing me to whimper. Between the two is a long chain, and I can only imagine the game he's going to play with that shit.

Just at that moment, Cole's teeth nip at my clit, and I shoot off the bed from the unexpected sensation. Screaming a, "Fuck," from behind his hand, I realize it barely makes any noise and is definitely not understandable.

Next, he grabs the lube and, with one hand, generously coats his dick and my cleavage with the thick, cold liquid before he throws it back to Cole.

"Play with her ass, it always gets her hot fast." Glowering at Travis, I curse at him in my mind, telling him he's cruel and mean and everything I love about sex. But the fucker already knows that.

Cole gives my pussy one last, long lick across my slit before he kneels and bends my thighs up to my waist as far as they'll go.

"Fuck, you're an image." Cole's voice is reverent, like he's looking at something glorious.

"Is she wet?"

"Fucking soaked." When I look up at Cole's face, I know he's speaking the truth, the evidence is all over his mouth.

"Good."

Once Travis has spread the lube all over his cock and my cleavage, he pushes against one of my swollen globes and slides his cock between my tits, beneath the silver chain.

"If you move too much, my shaft will catch on the chain, and since I'm planning to fuck you hard enough to bruise you, it may be a little painful for your nipples." His grin tells me he wants me to fight it and I'm proven right with his next words. "And I won't even be sorry for it."

Just as Travis thrusts his hips for the first time, I feel Cole's slick finger breach my hole. It's quick and practically painless, but it takes me by surprise, making my chest heave with the double sensation.

It also makes Travis's groin bump against the chain, flaring up white-hot pain from both of my clamped nipples. I scream behind Travis's hand, but all he does is grin and continue fucking my tits like it's his fucking job.

Cole adds another finger on the next thrust, then another, until the pressure is impossible to ignore. In fact, it feels so fucking good that every one of my muscles searches out for more as I squeeze and pulse my empty pussy.

"Greedy little girl, you want my cock in your pussy?" Cole drawls out his question, but I fucking know that if I say yes, he'll just keep it from me. So, like the good little slut I am, I say absolutely nothing.

It's getting harder and harder to breathe the more my body begs for their touch. Sucking in the air behind Travis's hand is now making me light-headed to the point that I might just pass out.

Travis rises a little on his knees, applying more pressure on my mouth and nose and fucking my tits rough and hard, the chain constantly rubbing against every one of his thrusts. The head of his cock hits the base of my throat at a regular rhythm, but Travis never falters, his gaze never leaving mine. His attention is only on me. On my eyes, my mouth, my bouncing nipples and his cock as it slides effortlessly between my globes.

"Lift your head and open that greedy little mouth of yours." As soon as he speaks, Cole pulls his fingers out and impales me with a rubber dildo, making me scream in surprise. Travis removes his hand and just as I position myself exactly as he wants me, I realize he's about to come all over me.

Grabbing his shaft and wrapping his finger around the chain, Travis gifts me his first spurt of cum and it lands perfectly on my tongue. My nipples are burning so fucking good, and I feel the tell-tale tingle of an orgasm beginning to spark just below the surface as his cum paints my skin and tattoos my soul.

"Don't you dare fucking come, Briar." Travis's tone immediately cools my body down and slows my heart rate. Cole continues to fuck my ass with my dildo, slow and agonizing, in and out as he coos praise every time my muscles contract for more, seeking out something to hold on to.

"That's my good girl." Travis knows exactly what I need to hear. In those four words, he tells me he's proud of me, he loves this, I turn him on… and it's exactly what's going to spur me on, what's going to keep me from disobeying him.

As Cole fucks me with the dildo, Travis scoops up his cum from my throat and coats my lips like he's putting lipstick on me then tells me, "Lick it all up."

And I do. My tongue greedily licks up every drop he gives me and just as I clean it all off, he bends down and kisses me, hard. He demands entrance and devours my mouth like he owns me.

Because he does.

They all do.

"I think Cole needs some attention; don't you think?" No sooner than his words are spoken, I feel Cole pulling out the dildo and licking up my slit while Travis unclamps one nipple then covers it with his mouth, taking away the pain and replacing it with the pleasure of his mouth. It takes everything in me not to cry from the sudden pleasure as he repeats the action with my other nipple.

"You must really love Travis's cum, Baby Doll, because you are practically a rushing river down here." God, I wish I were coming, but these two have decided to make my life a living hell.

Next thing I know, I'm manhandled and turned around until I'm on all fours, my thighs are straddling Travis's face and my pussy is grinding over his mouth as he digs his fingers into my ass cheeks, squeezing.

Cole grabs my hair and pulls until we are eye to eye.

"Suck my cock, beautiful. Choke on it like a good girl." My tongue immediately drops down, my eyes zeroing in on Cole's perfect cock, right before he pushes my head down and buries himself deep inside my mouth with a guttural grunt that makes my entire body tingle with awareness.

Beneath me, with his hands clamped on my thighs, Travis lets me fuck his face, grinding with each move of my mouth as

I suck and lick and whimper with delight. It's when Cole places both of his hands on either side of my face that he loses a tiny bit of control. His hips snap in rhythm with his thrusts, quick, hard fucks that have me gagging and barely able to catch my breath. He's praising, whispering words of love and gratitude mixed in with the occasional slur that only gets me hotter.

"That's it, my beautiful little slut. I love fucking your face, hearing you gag like a whore." Jesus, if he continues, I'm going to lose what little control is left in me.

"Fuck, man, I'm gonna come." At Cole's words, Travis bites down on my clit, making me fight the urge to explode. It's painful, this need for release, this physical push to come, and they're doing everything in their power to light up my body and then fuck with my mind so I don't explode.

It's cruel and it's delicious because I know when it does happen, it'll be fucking glorious.

Cole pushes my body back until I'm sitting up on my knees and Travis moves his hand so it's like a vise around my throat, choking me while Cole's cock is buried in it.

I can't breathe, I can barely see through the tears that are gathering in my eyes. My mouth is full of cock and my throat is completely closed off as Cole grunts his pleasure, the root of his dick grinding against my nose.

Just when I think I'm going to pass out, Travis releases me and Cole slides out of my mouth, saliva and cum dripping from his shaft onto Travis' chest.

"Lick it up." Blinking, I follow Travis's order, my tongue automatically seeking out Cole's gift and swallowing every drop of his cum.

"Fuck, I'm still hard." Cole's eyes are dazed, like he's been drinking all day, but he's right, his cock is just as hard as before he came down my throat.

"Well, I think it's time to give our little brat her reward for being such a good girl." Travis's words bring a huge grin to my face and, for the first time this morning, I can see the light at the end of my lust-filled tunnel.

Still on my knees, Cole lies down beneath me and it's Travis's turn to be behind me as he caresses my ass and pushes one, then two fingers into my ass.

"We have a surprise for you, Briar." For anyone else, Travis's words and his tone would be an omen, but for me, it means only one thing.

I'm going to love whatever it is.

Cole pulls me over him, making me straddle his hips, his still-hard cock gliding through the soaking wet lips of my pussy. Without fanfare, he sinks inside me with a long, drawn-out groan and stays buried there for seconds, or minutes, or maybe an entire lifetime. It's so good being filled by his cock and the only thing missing is…

Oh fuck.

I was expecting Travis to push into my ass, fucking me back there while Cole fucked my pussy, but that's not what's happening.

"Are you okay?" Cole's voice sounds worried. My gaze darts to his worried eyes and I'm quick to reassure him.

"I'm fucking great." Travis chuckles behind me just as he pushes his cock inside my pussy, right next to Cole's waiting one.

It hurts a little. A distinct burn of stretching tissue as they open my flesh as far as it can possibly go. And more.

I'm panting, my skin on fire with the need to move but also the need to stay stock still.

"Holy fuck, she's so tight." Cole closes his eyes, no doubt enjoying the moment as much as I am.

"Hell yeah, I knew it would be perfect." Just then, Travis pulls out as Cole remains buried inside me then, as he pushes back in, Cole retreats.

This is how they fuck me. Double the pleasure in my greedy pussy. I grab hold of the headboard to make sure I don't fall over or move too much, seeking out a faster rhythm. I have to follow their lead so that neither one of them pops out of me.

As their rhythm settles, I feel the return of my orgasm, hoping this time is the right one.

It's there, boiling under the surface, begging to be free.

"Travis, please, please, please." I can't disappoint them now. I need their permission first.

They keep thrusting in and out in tandem, fucking me with immutable concentration. I'm crying out, forcibly keeping my orgasm at bay when Travis pushes something—a butt plug?—in my ass and I fight with everything inside me to not come. Every cell in my body is honed in on only one thing… do not fucking come.

Finally, fucking *finally*, Travis's words liberate me.

"Come for us. Now."

My head falls back as I cry out into the room. My vision blurs, stars and comets and fucking meteorites explode behind my lids as my entire body shakes with violent abandon. Travis and Cole are both still fucking me, grunting and growling as I squeeze their cocks so tightly, I'm afraid they'll be scarred for life.

The last thing I hear before I completely black out is the roar of my men as they empty themselves inside my thoroughly-fucked pussy.

SEVENTEEN

BRIAR

After starting my day with a bang, pun fully intended, it seems chaos has reigned since then. Travis got a phone call not long after we came downstairs that had him hightailing out of here without a word to anyone—dude really needs to work on his communication game—and the twins took all the puppies out because the play fighting was getting to be a bit much, leaving me here with Cole.

He's been working out outside for the last half hour, and I've been hiding in my room like a coward after taking what I'm sure is the longest shower in recorded history.

I don't really want to talk about his mom showing up and what that might mean… he's literally never mentioned her, no one has. I genuinely thought she was dead. I'm convinced I read somewhere that Theo was a widower…

Not that it matters what I thought, because I was obviously very wrong, but I don't know if his mom is going to cause more problems for us, and lord knows we already have enough to worry about. Getting engaged was supposed to fix problems, not create them.

I pull on a pair of leggings, a tank, and a hoodie, pulling my hair into a ponytail while telling myself that I can put on my big girl pants and have this conversation.

I slide my phone into the pouch at the front of my hoodie and pad downstairs in my big, thick fluffy socks. It might be nearly April, but the air is still crisp and cold. We are not out of fluffy sock season yet and you won't find me complaining about it.

Procrastinating a little harder, I make myself a peppermint mocha, and once I take the first sip, I acknowledge that I have nothing else to procrastinate with, so it's time to face the music.

When I reach the new outbuilding that Sawyer had built, I find Cole at the weight bench, pressing more weight than I care to count, but goddamn it shouldn't be this hot watching him lift. The way his muscles ripple and his veins put themselves on display from the strain… yeah, way too hot.

Get your shit in check, Briar. Do not dry hump the guy, we're supposed to be talking.

Letting him finish his set, I slide down the wall and sit on the floor, sipping at my coffee, staring at my fiancé and the sheer beauty there is in watching him work out.

When he racks the bar and sits up, wiping down his face with a towel, he notices I'm here and removes an AirPod from his ear. He observes me, emotions dancing over his face before he starts to speak. "Morning, sleepy. You okay?"

I smile at him, blowing on my coffee. "I'm good."

"So why are you looking at me like you're sitting on nuclear codes?"

I laugh softly as he stands and walks over to where I'm sitting. He crouches in front of me and tilts my chin up so I'm looking directly at him. "What's wrong, Beautiful?"

I chew on my lip and he pulls it from between my teeth "Last night... your mom... are you okay? Should I be worried?"

He smiles at me, but it doesn't quite reach his eyes. "That woman is as much a mom to me as yours is to you. She birthed me, stuck around for a year, then left. She is not my mom. So no, you have nothing to be worried about, she's just being nosy. She probably already blew through her allowance from the trust for the quarter and is sniffing around my dad for money."

I chew on my lip again, but he holds my gaze like he's trying to will me to believe him.

"Briar, I swear, she isn't going to be a problem. Not between us. She might cause some issues with my dad, but I won't let her bullshit reach you, okay?" He swipes a thumb across my cheek before cradling my face. "I promise."

"Okay," I say softly, the knot of tension in my chest unraveling a little.

"Okay," he repeats back to me before standing and offering me a hand. He pulls me to my feet and steps into my space before wrapping his arms around me and pressing me against his chest. "Is there anything else you want to ask me? You know I'll tell you anything."

"I don't think so," I mumble against his chest. He laughs, his chest bouncing as he releases me a little so I'm not smushed against him.

"Good. Want to work out with me?" he asks, wagging his brows, and it's my turn to laugh. "Oh, come on, you could totally spot me."

"Only if you want to die." I shake my head and lean my forehead against his chest. "Strong is not something I am."

"Physically, maybe, but mentally, you're one of the strongest people I know." He kisses the top of my head before squeezing my shoulders and stepping back. "Did you hear from Travis yet?"

"Not yet, any idea what's going on?"

"Not a clue, but he'll check in soon, he always does."

"With you maybe," I mutter. "You think it could be something to do with Carter?"

He frowns, but shakes his head. "No, with Carter he'd usually tell us. Which means it's either his pops or Katy."

My heart does a weird skip a beat thing at the thought of

A TASTE OF FOREVER

something being wrong with either of them.

"I'm sure it's fine, Beautiful. As soon as I hear something, I will let you know if you don't hear from him too."

"Yeah, okay," I say with a sigh. "I guess I should work off some of this anxious energy. I can't spot you, but I can run while watching you work?"

He laughs once but nods. "Sure thing, but if I get distracted, I can think of much better ways for us to burn through that energy of yours."

After an intense, energy-charged workout with Cole, we head back inside just as Travis walks through the front door. He pauses when he sees us and then I hear her voice.

"Why did you stop, Travis? It's cold, let's go in and have cocoa!"

"Is that my Katy girl?" Cole calls out behind me before darting forward as a squealing, tiny version of Travis rushes into the house, arms wide. Cole catches her and spins her around, making her laugh and squeal more. Watching them makes my heart ache in the most beautiful of ways. She looks nothing like Iris, but she reminds me of her so much.

It's the light and joy that radiates from her. The innocence of youth. The lack of shadows.

Travis comes in, suitcase wheeled in behind him, and closes

289

the door before heading over to me. "I would have told you, but I didn't know she was coming. She called me when she landed. Apparently, my pops paid for her flight home for her birthday and everyone just forgot to tell me."

"It's okay. Is she staying here?" I ask as he takes my hand and squeezes.

"I have no idea," he responds, running his other hand through his hair. "I don't know if my dad knows she's here, how long she's here for. I've missed her like crazy, but with Carter here, and everything else going on..."

"It's not the best time," I finish for him, and he nods.

"Which makes me feel guilty as hell, because it's her birthday tomorrow."

I squeeze his forearm and lean my head against his shoulder while we watch Cole tickling Katy. "It's okay. You just want her to be safe, and with everything we've had going on lately, here isn't the safest."

"Exactly that. You want to meet her?"

I look up at him and roll my eyes. "What kind of question is that?"

He chuckles lowly and pulls me forward toward Katy. Cole sees us and puts her down on her feet. Katy looks up at me curiously, even more so when she sees Travis holding my hand. I crouch down to her height and offer her my hand. "Hi, Katy, I'm Briar. It's lovely to finally meet you."

She hesitates, looking up at Travis before offering me her

hand and shaking. "Hi, Briar. Are you Travis's girlfriend?"

I smile at her and look up at her brother for assistance.

"No, sweet girl," Cole interjects. "Briar is my fiancée, but your brother likes her a lot too. So do the twins."

She looks back at me and tilts her head. "So, they're like, all your boyfriends? Gross."

I laugh at her and nod. "Totally gross."

"Travis, can we go horseback riding? You said we could for my birthday and it's almost my birthday."

He nods at her and she jumps on the spot, clapping her hands. "We'll go tomorrow, on your birthday. How about tonight I call the twins and we all take you out for dinner?"

Her eyes light up and she nods vigorously. "Do I get to pick where?"

I press my lips together, stifling the laugh that threatens as I watch these two twenty-something men cave to the wishes of a nearly-nine-year-old. I can't wait to see her with the twins. Especially Sawyer. I bet he melts entirely for her.

"Of course you do," Cole says before Travis gets to answer. "You're the birthday girl."

"Yay!" She bounces again before turning to me. "Would you like to come to dinner, Briar? So it's not so many boys?"

"I'd love to, thank you." My heart warms at the look of concentration on her face as she nods.

"So, where are we going?" Travis asks, his whole demeanor softening when he speaks to her, and it's like seeing the man he'd have been without the pressures he has on his shoulders. It almost makes me sad for who he could be, but I remind myself that if he wasn't who he is, then I probably wouldn't love him the way I do. I kinda love his obstinate assholeish ways.

"I vote we go to Chenzos!"

I look at Cole, who laughs silently. "What is Chenzos?"

"It's all-you-can-eat food, of like every cuisine, a buffet," Cole answers while Travis tries to barter with Katy for somewhere else. Cole moves over to me and tucks me into his side. "Travis got super sick last time we were there, so he's going to try to persuade her with everything he's got."

"She doesn't look like she's going to budge," I respond, and he laughs, pressing his face into my hair.

"She's as stubborn as he is."

"So what you're saying is, we should get popcorn?"

He smiles widely at me and nods. "Oh, absolutely."

"Thank you for today," Travis says as he closes the door to his room. He hangs his head and I run my hands up his chest to loop them around his neck, making him look at me. We just dropped Katy off with his pops, since Chase refused to allow her to stay at his house. He went off about him not having approved the trip, so she wasn't his responsibility. Pops stepped up instantly, because the man is a godsend, and took the weight from Travis.

I can still tell he feels bad about her not staying here though.

"You don't have to thank me. It was fun. Thank you for taking me with you." I lift up on tiptoes and press a chaste kiss against his cheek. "But now I really need to shower because I am gross."

"You are never gross," he murmurs against my lips as he wraps his arms around my waist, holding me close before kissing me softly. "But I'm definitely not opposed to a shower."

I grin as I pull back from the kiss. "Oh, I'm sure you're not."

"Plus, I can definitely get you filthy in there." His eyes bore down into mine and my breath hitches.

"You know I'm yours. What do you have in mind?" I ask, curious and excited. I'm never going to tell him no unless it crosses a line for me, and well... I've always said I'll try most things once.

"That would be telling," he says as he moves to grip my chin, his thumb stroking against my lip. "But if you don't want to do anything I suggest, you tell me."

I nod, despite his grip, and his eyes light up. "Good girl."

A shiver runs down my spine at the praise. I don't think it'll ever get old for me, hearing him call me that.

"Now kneel at the end of the bed. I'll call you in when I'm ready for you." He kisses me after giving his instructions before he strides to his bathroom, leaving me needy and wanting.

But I do as he asks once the door to the bathroom shuts, anticipation running through me. I'm not usually a follow orders kind of girl, but I'm not sure there's much that man could tell me to do that I'd say no to at this point. Especially if there's the possibility of an orgasm on the table.

A thousand scenarios run through my mind, from sucking his cock to getting fucked in the ass, but for some reason, none of them sound ominous enough to ring true. With every image that flits through my mind, my body temperature rises, sweat begins to trickle down my spine, and heat builds between my thighs.

The guy hasn't even threatened or teased me, yet here I am, panting for him and his filthy mind.

Without giving it a single thought, I cross my arms at my waist and pull off the hoodie in hopes of lowering my temperature but nothing helps. The heat is within me and has nothing to do with exterior forces.

Biting down on my bottom lip, I look to the ceiling and think of puppies and grandmothers making hot chocolate with marshmallows floating on top.

There, much better. I can breathe again without the fear of self-combustion.

"I don't recall giving you permission to undress." And… there it is again, the fire licking at my skin from just the sound of his voice. His stern, commanding voice.

I clench my thighs together, hoping it'll alleviate the sudden rush of desire that stirs at the base of my tummy.

"I was hot." *Lame, Briar. Seriously, is that the best you've got?*

"Since when has that been an excuse?" My eyes find his and the electric current that crosses the empty space between us zips me to my feet.

I watch, mouth agape, as he reaches behind and pulls his t-shirt over his head before throwing it to the side. Every one of his abs is on full display, every ridge and dip begging for my touch. The smooth surface of his skin calls for me to run my tongue up and down and across until I've tasted every inch and he's as affected by me as I am by him.

"We've had this conversation, Briar. Good girls come. Bad girls are treated like the whores they are." He's now only a couple of inches away and if wanted to, I could reach out and run my fingers over his tight body.

I still haven't decided if I'm going to play the good girl or the whore. Both parts end with a mind-blowing orgasm, but there is something to be said about being worshiped by his touch all the while being degraded by his words; the contrast gets my body primed for orgasms every single time.

Reaching out with his thumb and forefinger, Travis pinches my chin hard enough to pull a wince from me before he leans in and whispers into my mouth. "I can see it in your eyes, little slut. You want to see how far I can go, don't you?" I hold his gaze, not answering right away. Mostly, I have no fucking clue what I should be doing because a horny Travis with a degradation kink who is left with carte blanche is a dangerous, dangerous man.

He's also hot as fuck and that's what I want.

"I see." Pulling me closer just from his hold on my chin, he slides his thumb against my bottom lip before he invades my mouth and pushes down against my teeth. "Open, I want to inspect your mouth. Make sure it's clean enough to suck on my cock."

My entire body tightens with need, my muscles pulsating with want as he angles my head just enough for his penetrating gaze to look around my mouth.

"I guess it'll do." Closing my mouth, he winks then places one hand on top of my head and pushes me to the floor. "Now, crawl to the bathroom and keep your head down. You haven't earned the right to look at me naked yet."

Why the fuck is my pussy so wet from his words?

Maybe because I know it's a game. Because I know for a fact every word he says is about my pleasure and, outside of this scenario, I'm his fucking goddess–well despite him being a grumpy shit lately. At any other time, I'm the one in charge. But for right now, I welcome his game and if the wetness seeping from my pussy is any indication, my body is craving for us to continue.

Still dressed in jeans and a tank top, I do as he orders and get on all fours. With my head down, my eyes fixed on the floor beneath me, I follow the path to the bathroom door. I'm just about to cross the threshold when Travis *tsk*s and stops me with his bare foot on my shoulder, pushing me back.

"Strip. And don't you dare look at me." Okay, I'm about two seconds away from sassing him but then I remember that I asked for this, so I rein it all in and close my eyes to avoid the temptation of ogling his perfect body.

"Nah uh, eyes open, gaze down. I won't repeat myself." Grinding my molars into near powder, it takes everything in me not to roll my eyes at him. I mean, he should be so lucky that I admire his body. If anything, it's a testament to his beauty.

"Careful, Briar. I can almost hear your sass. Don't force me to add orgasm deprivation to the list of things I want to do to you right now." My nipples perk up at the threat, like any type of suffering at the hands of Travis Kensington is a reward instead of a punishment.

I decide it's in my best interest to follow his instructions, for now. Looking down at my lap, I pull off my tank and bra then make quick work of my jeans and panties, breaking my position as little as possible. Without a stitch on me, the temperature is, indeed, much cooler, my skin pebbling as the air caresses my naked skin.

"You were right. You are positively filthy from head to toe, but only I'm allowed to degrade you. You don't get that luxury. Do you understand?" I'm a little confused. What the fuck is he talking about?

I gasp as the sudden sting at my scalp gets my full attention.

"I'm talking to you, you little slut. Are you ignoring me?" His minty breath dances over my lips and instead of feeling shame from his words, I get butterflies in my stomach and warm juices coating my folds and inner thighs.

"I'm sorry."

"You will be."

The urge to look up at him is strong but I keep my eyes averted as he grabs me by the hair and pulls me inside until we're both closed off in the shower, the hot water raining down on us.

I'm naked and on my knees as the steady stream of water hits my entire body head on, like Travis angled the shower head just right so none of me would be protected. Meanwhile, he's still in his jeans, standing behind me angling my head just right.

Water is beating down on me, the jets making it difficult to breathe, and still, he doesn't relent. I hold my breath, exhaling to avoid the water going up my nose, but I can only do this for a little while before I need to take in oxygen.

"Do you still feel dirty, Baby? Are you my good girl or bad girl right now?" I have no fucking idea what I want to be, except alive, maybe. And at this rate, with this shower on the verge of suffocating me, I'm not liking my odds.

"Bad girl it is, then." Fuck my life. Or better yet… yes!

Behind me, the unmistakable sound of a zipper sliding down the metal teeth wakes up every one of my nerve endings. I'm wide awake and ready for whatever it is he wants from me.

"Let me show you filthy, my favorite little slut, and then we'll see how accurate your description was earlier."

Warm liquid coats my spine, shoulders, and tits. At first, I think he's coming all over me and the thought brings me to the brink of orgasm. Then I see the transparent water on the shower floor slowly turn to yellow and I freeze.

He wouldn't.

There's no fucking way…

"Is this 'gross' enough for you?" Pulling my head back as far as it will go, I can see him upside down. Even from this position, the lust burning in his eyes is impossible to miss. I'm transfixed by it, mesmerized by the heat that lies behind those penetrating blue eyes of his. I know he's mentioned this before, that I okayed it, but I never thought that the upstanding Travis Kensington would actually do it.

"There is absolutely nothing gross about you. Or me. Or this." Bending at the waist, Travis takes my mouth in a fierce kiss as he continues to piss all over my tits. I guess he's happy with my answer. Only once he's finished does he release my mouth and help me to stand.

We don't speak as he grabs the body wash and loofah. No words are necessary as he uses gentle fingers to clean every curve and dip of my body, taking particular care of my nipples as he circles the hard buds before pinching and pulling hard enough to make me moan.

"Now that you're all cleaned up, I'm going to make you dirty all over again." Lifting the showerhead from the hook, Travis rains down the warm water over my head, gently washing away the shampoo, then moves to one shoulder and the other until all traces of soap are circling down the drain.

With two of his fingers under my chin, I meet his devilish gaze, my skin erupting in goosebumps at the grin that forms over his lips. He's got something planned, it's written in the glint of his eye and the way his teeth sink into his bottom lip like he's holding himself back.

"Stand." I don't hesitate, rising to my feet as quickly as I can without slipping and breaking a bone.

Shivers run down my spine as Travis wraps my hair around his fist and pulls my head back so his face is all I can see. I welcome the sting from the brute force of his action because with the pain always comes pleasure.

"This mouth?" He licks the water droplets off my lips and his moan makes my entire body tremble with need. "It's mine." In an instant, his kiss is the only thing that exists. It's as hard as it is thorough, with clashing teeth and exploring tongues, his fist holding my head at the exact angle that he needs. I don't need to think, I don't need to do anything because he's in complete control of this moment and it's exactly what I needed.

Travis swallows my yelp as his free hand finds my nipple and rough fingers pinch the hard nub before pulling far enough to elicit a full body shiver.

"These tits?" He bends at the waist and brings my nipple to his mouth, sucking and biting and laving it with his tongue. "They're fucking mine." I gasp when he bites the sensitive flesh, the juices gathering between my thighs is proof that pain is my gateway to pleasure.

Rising to his full height, he presses me against the tile wall, my head at an awkward angle as he whispers against my lips, "Now, suck my cock, my little slut, and make sure you swallow every fucking drop I give you."

It's then that I realize he's still in his jeans. I was so focused on his face and his eyes that the rest of him disappeared. The flaps to his jeans are open, his long, thick cock standing proud and eager as it taps against his navel.

My mouth waters, my skin heating at the thought of tasting him again.

Without prompting, I'm on my knees, grateful for the towel he's just reached for and placed on the shower floor.

No sooner am I in position than Travis places both his hands on either side of my face and feeds me his hard cock, a long, satisfied groan echoing around the Italian marble shower stall.

"Fuuuuck…" His pleasure fuels me, gives me the shot of adrenaline I need to bring him to his literal knees. Hovering over me with his palms resting on the tiled wall, he thrusts his hips at an unforgiving rhythm, forcing me to latch onto his ass cheeks and concentrate on not hurting him. His balls slap against my chin, the masculine scent of him like a drug to my libido.

I want more, need him deeper somehow.

Opening my throat as wide as it'll go, I press him to me, choking and gagging, saliva coating his cock and dripping down my chin. It's dirty and gritty and by the way his curses become louder and louder, he's loving every fucking second of it.

"That's it, my favorite little slut. Suck hard. Choke on me. Show me your appreciation." His words should make me blush, but they only make me hornier. My clit is throbbing, my pussy begging to be filled by anything at this point, but I have to wait. This is Travis's scene, his call. I agreed to play, now I must follow his rules.

"Goddammit!" He's close, it's evident in the way his entire body tightens, his knees locking and his groin grinding against my lips as the head of his cock blocks my airway. All he needs is a little push.

Sliding one hand from his ass cheek down to his balls, I hold them in my palm and roll them softly with one finger caressing that sensitive skin between his ball sack and his puckered hole.

"Fuck!" I'm pretty sure the entire state of New York now knows that Travis Kensington is about to come with a vengeance.

In an instant, his hands push off the wall and grab onto my head, eyes wild with lust, teeth bared as he reigns in the beast inside him right before I close my eyes and allow him to take complete control of the situation. My hands slide down to his thighs, hard and trembling from his efforts, as he pushes every single inch of his dick into my mouth and down my throat.

My nose is buried in his groin as he rubs against me, the air whooshing out from his chest as the first spurt of his cum coats my throat. Then another, followed by the filthy sounds he makes with every drop he feeds me.

I lick it all up, swallowing and silently begging for more.

More fucking and more cum.

He's right. I am his slut. I'm his own personal whore, and I wouldn't give it up for anything in the world.

As he pulls out from between my lips, careful not to hurt me or himself, a drop of his cum threatens to fall from the corner of my mouth.

My gaze meets his just as the lust in his eyes turns to something more sinister, but before he can rejoice in the fact that I didn't follow his orders by missing a drop, my tongue darts out and scoops it up. I swallow, making a show of it with an exaggerated moan as I close my eyes and let my head fall back. When I open my eyes again, I'm assaulted by the intensity of his stare, my pussy reminding me that my lust is still very much alive.

"On the bed, right fucking now." With nostrils flaring and his teeth bared, Travis is downright feral and it does something to me.

I'm the prey and he's the big bad wolf about to rip into me and devour every inch.

I don't wait another moment. Jumping to my feet, I surprise him with a kiss to his lips before I'm bolting out of the shower, dripping wet and sliding across the floors, throwing myself onto the soft comforter of his huge bed.

The unmistakable sound of wet denim hitting the floor

causes my tongue to wet my lips. Guess he's not the only one hungry for more.

I expect a good old-fashioned hard fucking, where Travis fucks me into the mattress with my body exhausted for a week after.

But of course, Travis never does what I expect. That would be too easy.

Waltzing into the bedroom like he has all the fucking time in the world, stroking his cock back to life, he paralyzes me with his penetrating stare.

"Show me how wet your pussy is, Briar." He barely ends his phrase and my legs are spread open, my core on fire with how much I need him inside me right now.

"That's my good girl. All willing and open, ready for my cock."

At the foot of the bed, he reaches down and slides a finger through my folds, circles my clit and, without ever taking his eyes off me, brings his finger to his mouth and sucks it clean.

It's erotic and romantic all at the same time, sending a zing of satisfaction throughout my entire nervous system.

Anticipation has my body primed for his touch but instead of lying on top of me and fucking me until I can't see, he takes a detour to the side of the bed, grabs one of the pillows, and removes it from the pillowcase.

"What the…?" This is not the time for chores. In fact, it seems wasteful to do the laundry before we get the sheets dirty.

"Good girls don't speak." With those words, I decide he's erring on the side of evil and maybe, just maybe, I'll punish him one day, too.

With the fabric in his hand, he walks around the bed and pulls the pillow from right under my head, taking the case before he palms the back of my head and slides the pillow back under.

"I think you've lost your mind." I didn't mean to say that out loud but... here we are.

"I think you've lost your speaking privileges." He bends to the floor and picks up my discarded panties from earlier and shoves them in my mouth.

That mothe—

Next, he winds the cases into a twisty snake and ties them around my wrists before securing it to the headboard.

"Now, you can neither touch nor speak. My perfect little slut, ready to take whatever I decide to give."

I would kick him in the shins if I weren't so fucking turned on, and judging from the self-satisfied grin on Travis's face, his fingers inside my pussy found me nice and drenched from his little stunt.

"Hmm, good girls don't need to beg. You get everything you want by doing everything I say." Punctuating his comment with his tongue thrusting inside my pussy, he nestles himself between my legs and sucks my folds into his mouth, licking my slit and biting my clit like he can't decide what he wants most. My body squirms from the onslaught of pleasure, my toes curling into the comforter and my fingers gripping the makeshift binds keeping me from touching this man. It's so fucking hot the way he moans into my pussy every time I clench my thighs and squeeze his head closer to me, exactly where I need him.

I may not be able to speak, but the noises coming from me are loud and it doesn't take a genius to know Travis wants more. Every time he glances up at me, his darkening pupils urge me to continue—as if I'd stop;. not while his tongue is doing that thing with the tip right over my clit.

My body humming and my skin tingling are clear signs that my impending orgasm is fighting to explode, but I'm not stupid. If I want more of them, I'm going to have to ask for permission. Except I can't with my fucking panties in my mouth. My first mistake is lifting my head in hopes of making eye contact with him. The sight below gives me sensory overload, with his head moving from side to side and up and down like he's french kissing my pussy, his hands holding my thighs and fingers indenting my flesh like he's two licks away from tearing me apart.

I try. I try really fucking hard not to come, but I can't tear my eyes away from the scene. I can't look anywhere but where his mouth is sucking on my clit, his tongue lapping up my juices like his thirst exists only for me.

Our eyes meet and I'm fucking begging. Pleading with him to give me this tiny little orgasm.

As though in slow motion, his eyes spark with mischief and

his mouth hovers just above my core with a growing grin that says he knows exactly what I need.

"Such a good little cunt, waiting for me to let her come." Two fingers thrust inside me and curl just at the right spot. Stars flash behind my closed lids, my pleasure so extreme it's turning into a hint of pain, and I revel in it. It's like nothing I've felt before and only Travis knows how to give it to me. "Now, come all over my face." With that, his mouth and fingers take their place back at my pussy.

His words crash open the dam and everything I ever knew about life and death are written in the pure ecstasy of this moment. I tremble, my wrists burning from how tightly I'm pulling on the binds, my legs kicking as my hips bounce off the mattress frantically searching out Travis's plunging fingers.

Just when I think he'll give me respite, I'm flipped over onto my stomach as Travis grabs onto my hips and raises my ass right where he wants it.

His cum-covered fingers slide into my ass in sync with his cock, now buried deep into my pussy.

"My dirty, dirty little slut. You love it when I fuck your holes, don't you, Baby?" I moan, my breaths harder and harder to catch with my panties obstructing my intake of air. It doesn't matter, though. Not when he's scissoring his fingers in my ass and his dick is hitting that greedy button deep in my core over and over again. Every thrust is a bull's eye, causing heat to creep up my spine and taking my breath away.

My mind is hazy, my brain fighting the post-orgasmic high, but the unmistakable sound of buzzing clears the fog and lights up every nerve ending in my body until my ass is primed for more play.

"Greedy little pussy and greedy little ass. Show me how much you want to get fucked, Briar." He knows I can't talk, but I can show him what I want and getting fucked in both holes will never be a pass for me.

Spreading my thighs wide, I press my ass into his pumping fingers, pushing harder and harder to let him know what I need. What I want. What my entire body is screaming for.

"That's my good girl." He positions the vibrating dildo at my puckered entrance and the cool gel coating my crack is the only warning I get before he plunges both his cock and the dildo into my body all at once.

Gentle went out the window as soon as we started this game, and Travis fucks me hard and rough, his hips slamming into me with enough force to move my entire body up the bed. Bruises are no doubt forming on my right hip where the pads of his fingers are digging deeper and deeper with every thrust. Alternating between my pussy and my ass, he fucks me like two men, and takes control of my body as though he were making up for the fact that the others aren't here.

We're both frantic in our movements, the control he usually keeps on a tight leash coming undone. The thump on the floor following the sudden emptiness in my ass tells me he's thrown the vibrating dildo away but I don't have time to miss the fullness. Pulling out of my pussy, Travis slides into my ass and reaches around my clit as his entire front presses against my back.

We grunt together every time he bottoms out, another orgasm building deep in my belly with every pinch of his fingers on my nub.

His hand releases my hip and slides up to my throat, pressing against my pulse point hard enough to cut off any air I was able to inhale through my nose.

"You may come again. Show me how much you love being my dirty, dirty good girl." Heat crawls up my spine, my extremities going numb, my head spinning with the overwhelming need to let it all go.

I come with a silent scream that he holds in the palm of his hand. Travis ruts into me, fucking my ass like he owns every inch of me. Circling my clit like he's the violinist and I'm his precious instrument.

The roar in my ear as Travis stills behind me sends me into a tailspin as yet another, less intense orgasm makes my body shake uncontrollably. We both still, our breaths heavy and erratic, right before Travis places a gentle kiss just below my ear and whispers, "You are the most beautiful thing in my life."

As gently as he can, he pulls out, unties me, and takes my panties out of my mouth before padding into the bathroom and opening the faucet.

A minute later, he's got a warm cloth at my pussy, then my ass, as his mouth rains kisses down my spine.

"Next time you feel gross, I'll remind you, again, that I love it when you're filthy."

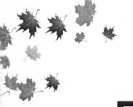

EIGHTEEN

BRIAR

Never did I ever think that Travis would be caught dead at the mall shopping for princess dresses… let alone all four of them in the store with wings and princess tiaras on.

This might be the best day ever.

Have I taken a million sneaky pictures? You bet your sweet ass I have, because there is no way I am not having proof of this day. Even if I just keep them for the days when the sadness tries to win, because it'll be a cold day in Hell when these pictures don't make me laugh.

The four of them are currently sitting at a small plastic table in our dining area while Katy stares at them intently, pouring fake tea. I'd have thought that, at nine–as of today anyway--

she'd be over this sort of stuff… but I'm also kind of beginning to think she's just fucking with them.

Which is kind of where I'm leaning too because she keeps smiling when she looks away from them in this almost crazy-ass psycho kind of way… it reminds me of that GIF of the creepy girl that smiles that's just kind of terrifying, but somehow, that makes it funnier.

I pull my focus back to my laptop and the dissertation I need to write to pass my psych class for this semester. Though, at this point, I feel like everything with my studies has slipped so much that I'm not sure what the point is in continuing with this semester… especially since I'm no longer in such a rush to get my degree finished. I feel like summer really can't come fast enough.

The giggling draws my attention again and I find my big, bad football player sipping from a plastic teacup, pinky pointed, and I can't contain my laughter any more. I've managed all day, but this is my tipping point.

Sawyer grins wide over at me while Travis rolls his eyes. Cole just continues like he doesn't have any fucks to give and thanks Katy for the delicious tea. My cackle is loud, but I just about manage to get myself under control.

"How is tea time, guys? Sorry I couldn't join, Katy. I really do need to get this finished."

"It's okay, Briar," Katy answers. "I just wanted the boys to play with me anyway." I'd have been mildly offended if she didn't give me an overdramatic wink. Instead, I press my lips together and nod at her.

Well played, kid.

Not only did she get the guys to skip classes yesterday and today, she also managed to get them to bend to her every whim. Not sure what they're teaching her at boarding school, but she definitely seems to have the world domination class aced.

Especially since we ended up at Chenzos last night.

Kid is an evil genius, and it just makes me like her more.

"Well, since I've finished my tea, does this mean it's time for birthday cake?" Asher asks as he puts his teacup back on the table.

Katy claps her hands and nods. "Yes, we still have birthday cake left, right? It was so good."

"We have birthday cake," Travis responds, and I nod while hiding my face behind my screen. I'm definitely down for cake, but I really, really do need to finish this freaking paper. I'm struggling because, well, the boy genius who helped me through classes last semester has basically fallen off the face of the Earth, and my attendance has gone to Hell in a handbasket the last several weeks. I feel like I've missed too much to even qualify this year, yet, I'm still here, trying to write despite having no idea what the Hell I'm talking about.

I let out a deep breath and slam the laptop closed. I need to research more before I try to finish this, which means I need a library. Everything might be on the internet, but there's something calming about researching in a library. Plus I find it easier to read an actual book rather than typeface when it comes to non-fiction. However, that means no cake for me. Dammit.

"You guys enjoy your cake, I need to head out for a bit," I say as I stand and slip my laptop into its case.

"Where you off to?" Asher asks, pushing his glasses back up his nose.

"Just the library," I tell him as I slip my Cons onto my feet. "Need to do some more research."

He stands and moves over to me, speaking quietly. "Are you sure that's a good idea? I know it's been quiet for a minute, but we still don't know who it is that's sending you these emails, who's killing these people. I'm not sure you should be going alone."

"Asher, it's the middle of the day. There will be literally thousands of people around, I'm sure it will be fine." I try to reassure him, but I honestly hadn't considered it. Call it me hitting my dumb bitch button, but things *have* been quiet. The worst I've had to deal with lately is Cole's mom and the stupid engagement party. I don't want to say I've been complacent, and it's not like I forgot that we have everything going on, but it's almost like I live in such a state of permanent stress and always have, that it just kind of slipped to the back of my mind where all the other bad shit lives.

"I don't like it, Briar." His insistence makes me feel a little uneasy, but at the same time, I don't want my life to be constantly under surveillance. I get the feeling that agreeing to marry Cole already means that my life is going to become a circus, so… for now, while I can, I want to hold on to the small semblance of normal I have.

"You don't have to like it," I tell him, trying not to be harsh, but still getting my point across. "I'll text Penn and meet her there like we used to. She doesn't have class this afternoon anyway. You guys should stay here and enjoy the time with Katy before she flies home tonight."

I watch as his internal thought process plays out on his face and bite the inside of my cheek when I know I've won so I don't smile.

"Fine, but turn on your location sharing. Don't think I hadn't noticed that you'd turned it off."

I roll my eyes and pull my phone from my pocket. "Fine," I say with an overdramatic huff. "There, see? On."

After he nods, I drop Penn a message to ask her to meet me at the library. When she responds instantly, I show him the message. "See? All good."

He rolls his eyes at me but nods. "Okay, but if anything happens, or you even feel a little uneasy…"

"I know, I know. I'll call. I promise. I'm careless, not stupid." I poke my tongue out at him and drag a small smile out of him.

"Thank you," he says, before kissing my cheek. "Should've inserted a tracker under your skin or something by now."

"Oh, don't tease me with a good time," I sass back with a wink before calling out my goodbyes to the others as I head for the door.

A pang of unease slithers through me as I climb into the Batmobile, but I push it back. I'm just going to the library, what's the worst that could happen?

"Can I just quit now?" Penn groans as she bangs her head on the desk in the library. We've been here for four hours and my essay is *almost* done, but she's having far less luck.

I shake my head at her and grin. "We're not quitting bitches, you know that."

"Oh I know, but I swear the text is swimming on the page. I could kill Connor for his MIA bullshit this semester. I had to agree to give up the dorm since he hasn't been home and the TA was threatening to report that I've been staying there so much, so after finals I have to find somewhere new to stay. On top of that, boy genius usually helps me break down the complicated stuff, and now I'm going to fail."

"He's still totally MIA with you too?" I ask, my concern for Connor growing. I've been the worst friend this semester, to them both, and while I know Penn forgives my crappiness, despite not knowing everything, she knows enough to have given me a pass since I'm still trying. But Connor? Yeah, I've dropped the ball there. Not helped by the fact that he's literally never around anymore.

She nods and closes the book she's been staring at. "Entirely. I spoke to my mom, and apparently his uncle extended his stay, so Connor has just been living at home while the uncle is around. I don't understand it. It's as if his uncle has entirely changed who Connor is as a person. It makes zero sense to me, but it's not like I can complain because he's stopped answering my calls and texts. I've been ghosted before, but this is like Olympic level. He's definitely not my boyfriend anymore and, at this point, I don't even know if he's still my friend."

I scrunch up my lips as I try to think of something to say, but I have nothing that will sound anything but patronizing.

"Maybe we should try to speak to him together?"

"Like an intervention?"

"Of sorts," I say to her with a nod. "He's our friend, even if he has been totally MIA. God knows I haven't been the best friend lately either. Maybe we shouldn't just give up on him?"

"Oh I'm not giving up on him as his friend… but as his girlfriend, I'm done. I've tried all semester to get through to him and I have been hung out to dry. I deserve better than this bullshit from someone who is supposed to be my freaking boyfriend. Not to be that toxic bitch, but if I'm too much, go find less, ya know?"

I nod, taking a sip of my now grossly-cold coffee. She laughs as I twist my face at the heinous taste.

"Plus, with everything I have going on with mom and Joey, this is just shit. He doesn't even know about any of that because he hasn't been here."

Jesus Christ, I am the worst. "I'm sorry. I haven't even asked how all of that is going. I just know that none of us were matches."

She shrugs and looks down at her books. "I wasn't a match either, so my mom, sorry, Erica, has shut me out again like I mean nothing to her, which I don't, but that doesn't make it suck any less."

"I'm sorry, Penn. I feel like a goddamn parrot. Is there anything I can do?"

She shakes her head and lets out a sigh. "There isn't anything anyone can do unless they find a donor. And I can't do anything because Erica won't let me anywhere near them. Not that I could do anything anyway, but I wouldn't feel so useless… which seems to be a recurring theme in my life right now with everything but my degree, so let's get back to studying. No quitting, even if that's what I beg for."

I press my lips together to stop the smile at her dramatics and nod. "We can do that."

Time skips by faster than I realize and by the time I'm finally shutting my laptop, it's dark outside. My stomach full-on growls at me as we stand and my cheeks heat when people at the next table look over at us. "We might've over done it," I say to Penn, who is too busy laughing at me to pay any attention to anyone else.

"Maybe. Come on, let's go grab tacos and margs'. I think we deserve them after today. And I know a place that will serve us, no questions asked."

"You do? Why haven't we been there before?" I ask, mock incredulity all over my face while she continues to laugh at me.

"Because my uncle can be a total douche canoe, but I know my aunt is running the place while he's out of town this week."

"Hold up, you guys *own* a Mexican restaurant? How did I not know this?"

She flicks her hair over her shoulder and grins at me. "I can't tell you *all* my secrets, B. Then what mystery would I have?"

I shake my head at her as I pull my bag onto my shoulder and we head out of the library. "To the Batmobile?"

"Hell yes, I don't want to drive. *But* margs means you probably shouldn't drive either."

"You're right. Let's drive to my place, and I'll get Sawyer to drive us!" I grin at the idea and she cackles.

"Oh, yeah. That boy is whipped. He'd probably even stay in the car while we ate."

"He would, but not because he's whipped. He's just lovely. I wouldn't make him do that anyway."

I pull my phone from my pocket and realize I have a dozen texts and missed calls. "Shit."

Showing her the screen, she grimaces and I unlock the car, climbing in before I call Travis back.

The line rings once before he's chastising me. "You were told to check in."

"Yes, Dad, I'm aware. But I was studying and lost track of time. You were tracking me anyway."

"Not the point, Briar," he growls, and I let out a sigh. "You need to come home. Now."

"Well, grouchy bear, I was actually already heading home. Are you going to tell me what the emergency is?" I roll my eyes while Penn snickers in the passenger seat as she pulls on her seatbelt.

"Just get home, Briar."

The line disconnects and I shake my head. "Pit stop?"

Penn smiles and nods. "The tacos will wait, let's go see why Travis has his panties in a twist."

We enter the house, laughing about a stupid meme that Dante sent to Penn, but pause when the door closes behind us.

I pause, frozen on the spot, when I see who is sitting with my guys. "Why is he here?"

"Briar—" Iris's dad says as he takes a step forward. Instinctively, I take a step backward.

This can *not* be happening.

This is a nightmare.

I fell asleep at the library.

Right?

I bump into Penn, who looks at me, confused, and I feel all the blood in my body pool in my feet as I go lightheaded.

"No. Get the fuck out."

"Briar." Connor's voice draws my attention and I focus on him. I hadn't even realized he was here.

"I am not who you think I am," Iris's dad says again, ripping that momentary relief away from me, and my knees give out.

"Shit, B!" Penn screeches as I drop to the ground, then Cole and Sawyer are in front of me, shielding me.

Why would they let him in here? They know what he did. Do they know who he is? They can't, right? That has to be why.

They wouldn't do this to me.

Would they?

My mind races as panic swallows me whole. My heart pounds so fast inside my chest that it's all I can feel around the fear, even as I register that my head bounced off the island as I fell. It's all I can do to pull myself into a ball before I freeze.

How could they let him in here?

I was supposed to be safe here.

I'll never be safe here again.

"I told you this was a bad fucking idea," Cole growls, but I'm not sure at who, because I'm bundled onto his lap and my face is buried in his chest while Sawyer strokes my hair.

"What in the ever loving fuck is going on?" Penn shouts, standing between me and the rest of the room.

God, I love her.

Because someone needed to ask, and I have nothing right now. I feel myself sinking down into that deep recess inside of me. The one where I'm safe. Where it's dark, and no one can get to me. I haven't been here in a long time, but I lived here a lot when *he* was in my life. I think he's the reason it exists at all.

It was my only escape.

My only refuge.

It's like an old friend, welcoming me back. A warm hug that protects me from what's happening around me. I can see, and I can hear, but I don't feel. Nothing can reach me here.

I'm safe in here.

He can't hurt me in here.

"She thinks I'm my brother. He's my twin, and he's dead, thank fuck. I just... I need to talk to her." I hear the words, but they don't actually register at first.

"So why are you here?" Penn asks while I try to gather myself.

"Me?" Connor answers. "This is my uncle."

"Wait, what?" Penn's screech pulls me back to the surface a little and I realize what the fuck everyone just said.

I take a deep breath and pull my face from where it's cradled in the crook of Cole's neck. "Will someone, not him, please explain to me what the Hell this is?"

My voice is quiet, but I know Cole hears because he tenses beneath me.

"Everyone shut up," he bellows at the rest of the room before looking down to face me. "This isn't the man you think it is. I wouldn't allow that. Ever."

He pauses, giving me a chance to speak, but I keep my mouth shut, nodding so he knows I've heard him, but I'm still not sure I believe it. Matty was able to lie to everyone. It's not hard for me to believe he's lying now.

"This is Thomas, not Matthew. They were identical twins. Matthew is dead." He speaks in short but firm sentences and, slowly, it starts to register properly. Not that the tightness of my chest loosens at all. "Thomas and Matthew are… were, Connor's uncles."

"So why are they here?" My voice breaks a little as I ask him the question and I see my pain reflected back at me in his eyes.

"Because," Cole starts before taking a deep breath. "Professor Crawford was also Connor's father."

"What in the ever loving fuck?" Penn shouts, and I hear Asher quiet her, and though I can't see her, I already know the look on her face. Normally, it would make me smile, but I don't have smiles right now.

"He's my brother?"

Connor steps forward, so he's separate from everyone else, on the other side of Sawyer so I can see him. He looks at me, and I can't quite read the expression on his face. "I'm not just your brother, Briar. I'm your twin."

LILY WILDHART

NINETEEN

BRIAR

"What did you just say?" Penn shouts while I sit in Cole's lap processing. All hell breaks loose as everyone starts talking over each other and I feel like I can't catch my breath.

"Everyone OUT!" Travis yells over the insanity, which just causes more shouting.

"Please, just stop," I call out and somehow, despite me not shouting, the room goes quiet. "This is all way too much. Why would you bombard me like this? Why would you bring him into my home without warning?"

"I don't understand—" Connor starts, looking over at Thomas like he's some lost little boy. "I've spent all semester trying to work out how to tell you this, and now you want to know why he's here?"

"He doesn't know," Thomas speaks up. "He only met Matty once."

"Doesn't know what?" Connor asks, exasperation filling his tone.

"That Matty raped me. Repeatedly. As a child." The words come out monotone but Connor takes a step back, as if every word is a blow to his chest.

"What? No... I don't—" Connor's words make no sense and I just look down into my lap.

"Can everyone please just get out?" My voice is small again, but I hear Penn's sad goodbye as she leaves, practically dragging Connor with her.

Thomas exits not far behind them after talking to Asher, though I don't really hear much of what they say. At least now that I know he's real I can stop thinking I'm crazy. I guess when I thought I saw Iris on campus, I was seeing his blond hair instead.

Once it's me left alone with my guys, I extract myself from Cole and wrap my arms around myself.

"Why would you let him in here? Why would you let me walk into this, knowing about my past already? I thought you were supposed to protect me. Love me. This wasn't love. This was... I don't even know. And you," I spit, turning to Travis. "I spoke to you, and you just told me to come home. You had the chance to warn me and you didn't. I don't know if I can forgive that."

Without another word, and ignoring their responses, I head up to my room and use the lock on the door for the first time since I moved in here.

I curl up in a ball on the bed, silent tears slipping down my face, wondering how it is we get past this. I don't even bother trying to deal with the whole twin brother thing. I'm not entirely sure I believe it. We look nothing alike. But that's not a right now problem.

My right now problem is figuring out if I can trust them again, and if not, how to escape?

"Briar?" The knock sounds at my door following my name, and I've lost count of how many times I've ignored their pleas for the last few days to just speak to them.

"Dammit, Briar. We're sorry. Please, just let me in." The growl underlining Travis's words pisses me off more. I throw the covers off of me and stalk to the door, yanking it open, chest heaving like I ran a marathon, but really I am just so freaking *angry.*

"You're sorry? You're sorry? Do you think I *care* that you're sorry, Travis? You let THAT MAN into our house. Into my safe space AND YOU DIDN'T WARN ME. You can take your sorry and shove it all the way up your fucking ass." The anger pours out of me like a raging river, and my panting somehow gets harder. "Get the hell away from me. Just give me some time to fucking *breathe*."

I take a step back and attempt to slam the door shut but he steps forward, stopping its movement with his shoulder. The thud as it hits him doesn't even make him wince, and that pisses me off more.

Stupid, hard-headed, asshole.

"Get out of my room, Travis." I huff as I stomp across the room before throwing myself back under my duvet just like a petulant toddler. I don't even care that I'm being a brat, he deserves it. I'm allowed to be angry dammit.

"Shutting us out isn't going to help anyone, Briar. Just hear me out."

Goddamn him for being right, but I'd still rather be angry at him than forgive him right now.

I fling the covers back off me and sit on the edge of the bed, arms crossed over my chest. Facing him while I'm this upset with him doesn't help me stay angry, but I refuse to yell at him from under the duvet. "I'm not ready to hear you out yet, Travis. I'm allowed to be angry."

"I didn't say you aren't allowed to be angry, but you took a lot of information on, and shutting us out with everything else, isn't going to help you. Let us in. Talk to us." His shoulders drop as he comes and kneels before me, cupping my cheek with his hand. "I know I should've warned you, but I thought if I told you, you wouldn't come home. For once, I didn't have the words… I couldn't fathom how to tell you and I also didn't think the news should come from me. Were you blindsided? Yes, of course you were, but we were going to be here to help with that. If I told you everything over the phone, while you were driving… I don't even want to think what could've happened…"

He trails off, and goddamn him all over again for being so freaking rational. He's right. Completely, logically sound. If I'd known who was here, I never would've come home. But that doesn't mean I don't get to be angry that I wasn't warned even a little.

"Just let us in, Briar. I can't imagine what's going through your head locked away up here. We just want to help."

I let out a sigh, and drop his gaze. Keeping these walls up probably isn't helping anyone, but just when I felt safe, it feels like I was thrown back out in the cold to the wolves. "I know you want to help, but I need some time to process. So please, just give me time."

He drops his hand onto his lap and I glance back up as he stands, but can't bring myself to meet his eyes. "We can give you time, but I won't give you much more, Briar. You need us, just like we need you. I need you."

Without another word he retreats from the room, the soft click of the door hitting me as hard as if he'd slammed it.

He might be right that I need them, hell, that I love them. But right now... Right now I'm not quite ready to forgive them.

TWENTY

BRIAR

After a week of groveling, I've decided that keeping up these walls isn't helping anyone. So after spending all day yesterday finally letting them know they're forgiven, after spending every other day holed up in my room, or in class, trying to work through my thoughts, ignoring my phone from everyone but Penn, tonight I want to go out.

Which is exactly what I announce as I bounce into the living room.

"You want to go out?" Travis asks, shock raising his brows since I've barely spoken to him all week. I forgave the others a little easier, just a smidge, but he had the chance to tell me what I was walking into the other day.

"That is what I said."

The four of them look at me with varied looks of disbelief.

"Like, out out?" Sawyer asks. and I nod.

I prop my hands on my hips, staring at each of them for a moment before moving to the next. I look far more powerful and confident than I feel right now, but fake it till you make it, right? "I want to go out and dance, and drink with our friends, and just not care. For one night I want to not be the broken girl with the crazy ass drama. College was meant to be about me getting a taste of normal, and I haven't had even the slightest morsel of normal. I want one night, then I'll deal with everything else."

"I guess we're going out!" Sawyer jumps to his feet, clapping his hands together. "C-dog, yeah, I'm testing it out, leave me alone. Anyway, you're in charge of the venue."

I clamp my lips together trying not to laugh at the whole 'C-dog' thing and turn my focus to Cole.

"Yeah I can do that," he says with a nod, pulling his phone from his pocket before looking over at Travis. "Want me to invite Carter and Denton?"

He turns to me before Travis answers and explains, "Limits the venues if they're coming, but it adds some security."

I shrug, because it doesn't bother me if they come, so long as they don't rain on my dance party. Otherwise, I'll... well, I don't know what I'll do. Carter seems like a pretty scary guy, but maybe I'll stomp on his toes or something equally as stupid. "Don't care, but I'm inviting Penn, which means inviting Dante, because since he was cleared, they've been attached at the hip."

No one bats an eyelid at the mention of Dante. Despite the initial suspicions, with him being cleared, and the fact that both Cole and I know him pretty well seems to have calmed any other reservations. Neither of us believed it could be him despite what the information said. Even if Cole was dubious for a hot minute.

"Not to question the elephant in the room, but if Penn is coming, is Connor?" Asher asks, and I glare at him.

"No, he's not. Penn hasn't spoken to him since that night either. I'll deal with Connor when I'm ready. Anymore questions to rain on my parade?"

He puts his hands up in surrender and shakes his head. "Nope, just curious."

"Yeah well, curiosity killed the cat," I deadpan, watching as he tries not to smile as he nods.

"That it did. I'm going to go and see what Sawyer is planning. Let me know when we're heading out." Cole nods and Asher heads upstairs after Sawyer.

"I'll call Carter now," Travis says, finally responding to Cole's original question. He pulls his phone from his pocket and stands before moving toward me. He puts an arm around my waist and kisses the top of my head. "Thank you," he murmurs, and I kiss his cheek chastely. He might have pissed me off spectacularly, but Travis seems to have a way of putting his foot in it then making up for it later.

And I'm positive he'll make up for it, outside of the

groveling he's already done.

I glance up at the news and my heart flip flops. "Turn it up."

Cole frowns when he sees what I saw, but does as I requested. "—a young man, known to the Serenity Falls community, a police officer, has been found dead in his apartment. More details have yet to be announced, but a source has told us that this is linked to the current string of murders, and pending further investigation. This is the first serial killer to have ever been in Serenity Falls—"

Travis walks in and turns the TV off, glaring at the screen. "No, not tonight. We're going out, remember."

I look at him and frown. "Should we be concerned?"

"I'm always concerned," he tells me firmly. "But we'll have Carter with us, which means his guys will be around to help keep an eye on you. We've had someone with eyes on the house since the last murder. No one is getting close to you."

I bite my lip, worrying over whether my supposedly great idea is still a great idea. The whole Connor thing seems minuscule in comparison to a serial killer who may or may not be trying to kill me. "If you say so."

"I do, now go get yourself ready while Cole and I plan. I'm thinking hotel." He slaps my ass and I let out a squeak before glancing at Cole, who nods, despite his furrowed brow.

"Okay, I'll call Penn and have her come here. Which means Dante will probably come over too."

"Fine by us," Cole says as Travis drops onto the sofa beside him.

I force a smile on my face and nod resolutely. Tonight is going to be a good night if it freaking kills me.

"You've been teasing us all night, pretty girl." Sawyer's standing behind me as the others invade the hotel room like it's their own private mansion. I can't ignore his desire for me, it's evident in his hard length sliding up and down the crack of my ass like we're not both still dressed, as though things like clothing are inconsequential when it comes to his need to fuck.

"It's not teasing if I plan on delivering." There it is, the growl I love to hear from my boys. When I look up, four pairs of eyes are on me and all of them are sporting tents behind their swanky slacks. "Well, it seems you're all on board with that."

Before I can take another step forward, Sawyer picks me up and throws me over his shoulder like he's my fireman and I'm a damsel in distress.

"Wait! Wait! I'm thirsty, I need sustenance before I work out." Cole bellows, his laugh unmistakable, while Asher smacks my ass and pulls me off his brother's shoulder, lacing his fingers in mine and walking me to the small fridge in the kitchen area. This suite is something else, which shouldn't be a surprise considering who I'm with, but still, it's fucking huge.

Bending at the waist, I make a whole show of it, making

sure my cocktail dress is riding up the back of my thighs and showing off the fact that I'm not wearing any panties.

"Fucking knew it," Sawyer mumbles behind me. "Should've fucked her in that hallway while those snot noses were sipping champagne and dreaming of ruling the country."

I grab five bottles of water, nice and fresh, and when I turn around, the boys are all in different states of undress. Sawyer's dress shirt is wide open, his black tie hanging loose around his neck, while Asher is just now unbuttoning his black shirt, his gaze on me through dark, thick lashes. Biting my lower lip, I snap my attention to Cole who's already bare chested and in the process of unzipping his slacks. God, his body is a work of art.

Travis is the only one still completely dressed—rolling up his sleeves to expose his mouth-watering forearms—which doesn't surprise me one bit. He'll be the last to lose his control and, as always, it'll be my pleasure to rile him up enough to make him roar like my proud lion.

"Grab the bag." I have no idea who Travis is addressing because his intense gaze is fixed on me, running a blazing path down my body like he's calculating the entire night and everything he plans for them to do to me. Tingles spread across my skin at all the possibilities and, without giving it another thought, I place my hand between my legs and collect the evidence of my arousal.

Asher drops the bag while Sawyer and Cole curse at my bold move. Four pairs of eyes watch me as I approach Travis and place my cum coated fingers at his mouth. Without hesitation, he sucks my fingers between his lips and licks my fingers clean with a growl escaping from deep down in his chest.

"This is what you do to me when you look at me like that." It's true for Travis, sure, but it's also true for the rest of my men. Sliding my fingers out of his mouth, I grin when he traps the tip between his teeth and frown when I hear a click around my wrist.

"What the fuck?" I gasp at the sight of the handcuff securely placed and locked around one of my wrists.

Travis leans in just as Sawyer comes up behind me, his large hands on my hips and his mouth at my ear. "Even if you deliver, it's still teasing."

"No more touching for you, Princess." Asher grins, winking at me.

"On the dining table. It's time for dinner." Travis' command is met with enthusiasm by all, including myself, even though I'm pretty sure I'm the dinner and the only meat I'll get will be shoved down my throat in punishing thrusts.

Holy fuck, the thought only makes me wetter by the second.

My sweet Asher undresses me, careful not to rip my dress off like any of the others would have done, and places soft kisses along the exposed skin. My bra is next, thrown over the sitting chair in the corner before he carries me to the table and sits me down on the cold wooden surface. He throws another pair of handcuffs to Travis, who catches them without a second thought and moving to my side.

It less than a blink, my other wrist is a prisoner too, the familiar click and pressure on my skin telling me everything I need to know. Movement beside me catches my attention and I frown as Sawyer somehow attaches a steel bar between the feet of the table.

"Trust us?" He raises a brow at me, daring me to deny that I would put my life in their hands. When I roll my eyes, he grins like a kid on Christmas morning, standing and bruising my lips with a scorching kiss that melts my brain a little.

"Enough. We're all hungry, brother." Asher runs the backs of his fingers along my stomach as Sawyer sighs, pecks me one more time, then pushes me down so my back is lying across the table, my head hanging off the side and my wide-open pussy on the other edge. Gentle hands position my arms out like I'm on a cross and, when curiosity gets the better of me, I watch—mouth agape—as Sawyer attaches the handcuffs to his homemade zip line.

"You're at our mercy now, my beautiful little cumslut." Travis is standing between my thighs, his lips moving against my mouth as he runs his fingers from my imprisoned wrists, across my arm and elbows until he reaches my nipples and tweaks them without an ounce of gentleness. "The only words we want to hear from you tonight, are 'yes, sir' and 'more please'. Anything else…" He pulls my bottom lip out with his teeth, the bite hard enough to make my entire torso arch from the table but through it all, I don't make a sound. "…and we'll have to gag you." At Sawyer's snort, Travis looks up and smirks.

"I'll gag her anyway… with my cock." It takes everything in me not to roll my eyes, mostly because I have zero doubts that he will.

With all the sexy foreplay, I almost miss the fact that they are all shirtless now, except, of course, for Travis, and as my eyes travel down the planes of each of their chests, I wonder how the fuck I got so damn lucky. But my musings are short lived when Asher brings the bag up onto the table and rummages through it until he finds what he's looking for.

"Here, got one for each of us." Asher distributes the small boxes to the others and they make quick work of opening them up.

"What are those?"

Travis cocks a brow at me like he's surprised I've already broken the no talking rule.

"We'll let it slide this time," Sawyer says, showing me his new toy. "Finger vibrators. And we've all got one. I think we could set a world record for orgasms in one night." It looks like an overgrown thimble—a silicone one—with two adjustable rings for their fingers. They've all got different colors and I watch, eyes wide and bright, as they all pop them on their fingers and a tiny orchestra of vibrations begin all around me.

"I think our dinner guest is intrigued." Cole passes around the lube, and each one doles out a generous amount on their finger. Sawyer and Asher are the first to test them. My nipples pucker at first contact, the wet vibrations stimulating my nerve endings. I have to bite down on my lip to keep from crying out, and just when I think I've got myself under control, Cole slides his toy down my stomach and onto my clit, rubbing light circles that make my entire body crave for more. Travis, always the overachiever, slides into my pussy and seeks out my G-spot, finding it on the first thrust. My groan is loud enough to alert the guests downstairs, I have no doubt.

"Easy, we don't want the staff calling the police on us." Travis's whispered words don't do anything to settle the lust that's growing deep inside my belly.

"For what? Premeditated orgasms?" Sawyer quips, and it makes me grin because, even in an intense moment like this, I can count on him to bring levity.

"Involuntary cuntslaughter."

"Analcide."

"Vibrating and entering." We all freeze at Travis's words, staring at him with mouths hanging open.

"Did you just make a joke?" Cole looks like he's trying to solve a calculus problem with half the formula missing.

"Shut the fuck up and concentrate on our girl." We all relax back into our positions once Travis returns to his normal self.

I don't have time to linger on the strange moment that just occurred before I've got four vibrating fingers stimulating me on various parts of my body, and when Sawyer gives me an upside-down Spiderman kiss, I forget everything in a flash. Only his mouth matters, the way his lips bruise mine, the way his tongue takes complete control and his teeth bump against my own.

Travis curls his vibrating finger just right, and I moan into Sawyer's face as Cole pinches my clit and Asher caresses the underside of my tit. It's too much already, my muscles tightening and my pussy squeezing around Travis's finger, I surrender to my first orgasm of the night. Without letting me go, Sawyer kisses me through my climax, swallowing my gasps and my moans until my body relaxes into a heap of jelly limbs.

"That's one, only one hundred and thirty-four to go within the hour if we want to beat the world record." My eyes fly open, my body tensing at Sawyer's words. I relax when I see the mirth dancing in his eyes. Fucker.

"Kudos for not yelling at me. I think you deserve a little reward." Sawyer looks up at Travis and with a quick, silent conversation they both move at the same time. Sawyer pulls me back toward him, my head now hanging from the side of the table, while Travis and Cole grab onto my calves and fold my legs until my feet are on the table, my toes curling at the spread out position they've put me in.

"Fuck, she's so wet." The sound of Cole's zipper follows his words and soon he's naked and stroking his cock as he watches my pussy beg for him.

"Open wide, Baby Girl." With a smile on my lips, I open my mouth as wide as I can and groan around Sawyer's hard length that fills me right to the back of my throat. In this position, he feels even bigger than usual, like he's taking up every inch of my mouth as he holds my head steady, gentle fingers caressing my skin in complete contrast with his rough lunges in and out of my mouth.

Travis adds another two fingers into my pussy, and I don't have to look to know that Cole is now sucking on my clit while Asher is laving at my nipples before placing them into a couple of nipple clamps. They are pulling out all the stops tonight and I'm not sure I'll survive their expectations.

The pleasure of sucking Sawyer's cock and having Cole's mouth spoiling my clit while Travis fucks my pussy with his fingers, almost gives way to the initial pain of the clamps. Besides, this is nothing compared to when they'll come off.

I pull against my handcuffs on instinct, my hands itching to touch Sawyer's ass and squeeze his cheeks apart so I can push a finger inside his ass. His libido knows no boundaries and it turns me the fuck on.

What I don't expect is the tight pinch on my clit and when my body stiffens from the sudden sting, I'm assaulted by the overwhelming stimulation from all angles.

"Relax, Baby Girl. Let the clamps work their magic." Fucking Hell, my nipple clamps are now attached to a clamp on my clit so every move I make sends tiny electric bolts across my entire body.

"Such a good little slut, taking everything we have to give."

Travis punctuates his words with a quick set of thrusts inside my pussy before he pulls out. A chair scrapes across the floor and then a wet heat is over my pussy, a tongue lapping up my juices and fingers digging into the softness of my thighs.

"Fuck, I need to pull out before I come down her throat." If I could move my hands, I'd latch onto Sawyer's ass and keep him in my mouth, the head of his cock bumping the back of my throat every few seconds. I love how he slides his hand off my neck, feeling the bulge of his dick as he pushes as far down as possible. My gag reflex, at this point, is a thing of the past, my breathing technique allowing my men to fuck me senseless without having to pull out.

Much too soon, Sawyer pulls out but I only get a few seconds respite before Asher takes his place and soon I'm getting a nice face fuck from his twin. My eyes are watering, tears falling from the corners and sliding down my temples as he uses a little more force than his brother.

"That's it, Baby Girl. Take my cock, all of it. Suck me dry." Asher's voice is strained, and I can only imagine his muscles taut, his jaw tight as he thrusts in and out of my mouth. Sawyer removes the clamps from my nipples before latching onto one them with his mouth, the warm feel of his mouth like soft velvet. Meanwhile, my pussy is getting a proper eating out, the slurping and sucking noises only amping up my lust and need for more.

"Give me some space." Travis is back, and with him is the lube that he's just leaked down my crack after lifting my legs and folding me, almost, in two. Asher is using my calves as leverage, his thrusts getting rough, the grinding of his groin a little longer, when my puckered hole is breached with what I'm guessing is a butt plug. That's when Cole removes the final clamp and sucks my clit into his mouth as he plunges three fingers into my pussy.

Without warning, my body begins to shake, my toes curling into nothingness as my fingers curl into fists in the confines of my cuffs. I shake and tremble, grunting around Asher's punishing face fuck.

"Yes, baby, give it to us." I'm a goner, my mouth goes slack and when Asher pulls out, he bends at the waist and bruises my mouth with a kiss that says everything I need to hear.

They've got me. They're here for me.

I can trust them.

"The bath is ready." In my post orgasmic haze, I hear Travis's words and try to smile with numb lips.

"I think our girl is liking the idea." Cole's low baritone vibrates through my body, or maybe that's just his finger working its magic inside my cunt.

I think I pass out for a minute because the next thing I know, gentle arms are holding me as we sink into the warm bathtub that fits all five of us like it was made specifically for us.

My lids flutter for a few seconds before I'm able to open them to find Asher staring down at me, holding me flush against his chest, the water all the way up to my jaw line.

"Hello, sleepy girl." Biting down on my bottom lip, I scan the tub and this time, we're all naked and wet. Travis is directly on the other side of me, his arms spread out on either side of him and his gaze so intense it makes the tiny hairs on the back of my neck stand straight up.

"Uh oh. Psycho Travis is in possessive mode and Asher is in his way." Sawyer is sitting right next to Travis, the head of his cock bobbing out of the water as he strokes it, languid but firm. My eyes darting from one to the other, I'm hit with a jolt of lust at the idea of watching them together again.

"I don't know what you're thinking about, Baby Girl, but whatever it is has your body heat skyrocketing and your juices flowing." My eyes are ping-ponging from Travis to Sawyer and from Sawyer back to Travis and it only takes them a minute to understand what I want.

Travis cocks a brow and Sawyer grins like the cat who drank the entire bowl of crème, positioning himself on his knees between Travis's legs.

"Is this what you want, you little cock slut?" Travis and his loving endearments.

I nod, "Yes, sir." They're the only words I've said so far and they're among those I'm allowed to say.

Pleased, Travis nods. "Such a good little whore, using your voice wisely." He places a rough hand on Sawyer's head as he gets himself comfortable. His eyes never leave mine, staring at me and watching every one of my reactions.

Cole slides over and Asher adjusts my position so I'm straddling him reverse-cowgirl style as his cock easily slides into my pussy. With the butt plug still inside my ass, he feels even thicker, more invading somehow. Kneeling between Asher's legs, Cole takes my nipples in his mouth—one at a time—and sucks until I'm sure I'll have bruises in the morning.

Meanwhile, Sawyer is sucking Travis' cock with hard pulls and loud grunts. His head is bobbing up and down with the help of Travis' imposing hand directing every single move he makes.

While Asher is fucking me and Sawyer is blowing Travis, I revel in this moment, this bond we all have. It's rare and it's perfect and with our lives being what they are, we need this outlet, this bubble of security.

"Enough!" Travis pulls Sawyer off of him and he turns back to face me. My gaze latches onto his tongue as it licks his swollen lips. I want to tell him to come to me but I'm not allowed to speak.

Thankfully, Travis reads me like an open book. "Our dirty girl wants to taste my cock on your lips." I don't have to wait for my wish to become reality. Cole moves out of the way as Sawyer grabs both sides of my face and forces his brother to stop pulling me up and down his cock.

"Brother, you're killing me here." But Sawyer doesn't give a shit. His lips are violent and soft all at the same time with Travis's scent wafting between us. It's so fucking erotic I almost come all over Asher's cock, and by the way he swells inside me,

I'm willing to bet he can feel the effect his twin is having on me.

"Hurry up, I need to fuck her tight little cunt and come inside her, right the fuck now." Sawyer has pity on his brother and takes a step back as Asher latches back onto my hips and fucks me with bruising speed and rough thrusts. My tits are bouncing so hard, the pain is almost unbearable.

"Fuck, she's perfect." I have no idea who said this, my thumping heartbeat too loud in my ears for me to understand anything else.

Sawyer palms my tits, pushing them together and thumbing my nipples in tight little circles. Cole slides his hand down my stomach and gives my clit some much needed attention as he pinches and flicks it with expert ease. I'm close, so fucking close, to another orgasm but something is missing.

Someone is missing.

My eyes snap open and there he is, sitting like a king, his eyes fixed solely on me, his right hand pumping his majestic cock in rhythm with Asher's thrusts, urging me to let go with just the uptick of his lips.

With his silent permission, I keep my gaze fixed on him as I let go once again, my hands clamping down on Sawyer's shoulders to hold me steady.

"Goddamn, fuck, yes!" Asher stills beneath me and the warm embrace of his arms as they entrap me against his chest, his groin grinding against my throbbing pussy, tells me he's coming inside me. In those few moments, everything turns quiet. The sloshing water calms, the groans and slapping wet bodies still. The only sounds I can decipher are the rapid breaths we're all desperately trying to take and the booming beat of my heart in my ears.

"I don't think I can take another orgasm." I'm pretty sure I'm slurring my words at this point. I feel drunk, like I'm floating on a cloud with divine angels lathering up my body and rinsing it off with warm water.

"You can, and you will. Let's go, Princess." Travis's voice is strained and I'm pretty sure he needs to come.

Fuck, I love watching him empty his balls inside me.

Next thing I know, I'm sprawled out on top of Sawyer, my swollen pussy lips sliding up and down on his wet dick, still hard and velvety and oh-so-fucking hot—like he's on fire.

All four of them are raining kisses down on my skin. The quick stings from their teeth and the deep sucking that will no doubt mark my skin keep me awake and aroused even though my body is screaming for me to take a break.

Except, the slow dance above Sawyer's cock is only awakening my libido all over again. How is this even possible?

As though he can read my mind, Travis wraps my hair around his fist and pulls my head back until my ear is at his mouth. "Because we own you. We own your pleasure and we own your pain. Every fucking orgasm is ours so if we want you to come again, you fucking will." He punctuates his declaration with a bite to my lobe before sucking the flesh into his mouth and kissing right below my ear. I don't know how he does it, how he can be so cruel and gentle in the breadth of a mere moment. It's his talent, I guess.

Sawyer spreads his thighs beneath me, giving Travis the room to kneel between them while Cole and Asher kneel on either side of my torso. My arms are holding me steady, my tits close enough to Sawyer's mouth that his tongue is teasing my nipples, round and round, then biting the sensitive buds until I moan, over and over again.

Travis places his hands on my hips and guides my pussy onto Sawyer's proud standing cock until I'm fully seated with him deep inside me. Turning my head to the side, I open my mouth nice and wide as Cole palms the side of my face and rubs my bottom lip, as gentle as can be, with the pad of his thumb. Our gazes lock and, in the depths of his dark orbs, I read his love and I feel his devotion deep in my soul.

Slow and steady, Travis sets the rhythm as Sawyer fucks me from below. In tandem, Cole feeds me his cock and every time my pussy is full, Cole's cock hits the back of my throat. Over and over until my eyes water and spit gathers at the corners of my mouth.

"You're beautiful like this, crying tears of orgasms for us. Suck harder, baby. Take all of me." And I do, I take every fucking inch on him until my breath is trapped in my lungs and my eyes can only see a blurry vision of my Cole. "Such a good girl. Asher's been patient, go give him a kiss on his dick."

Popping out of my mouth, I gasp when I feel added pressure at my pussy. My head whips around and over my shoulder, catching Travis's devilish grin as he bores his gaze down on me.

"Two for one, my little cumslut." Then he pushes, and even though he's coated me with lube down my crack and on his cock, the burning sensation at my opening cannot be ignored. Sawyer and Travis are fucking huge on their own but the two of them pushing inside my pussy isn't something I'll ever get used to, or will ever deny because once they're both seated inside me, my butt plug adding to the intense fullness, I feel like I'm flying high all over again.

Once they start their rhythm, I turn back to Asher and open my mouth, tongue hanging out and eyes wild with lust like I haven't just come three times. Cole palms my head and helps me to suck Asher off, guiding me as I lick and suck and lave the head of his cock while Travis and Sawyer fuck me into next week.

Asher's head falls back, his lips slightly parted, his nostrils flaring every time he bumps against the back of my throat.

"Cole, your turn." I'm riding so high that I don't question any of Travis's commands at this point. All I can do is feel.

Just as Cole kneels next to Travis, I'm left with only one cock inside my pussy but when the buttplug is pulled out and a generous amount of lube is pouring down my crack, I smile around Asher's devastating cock.

"I think our princess is happy to know what's about to

happen back there." Mirth dances in Asher's eyes as he angles my head just the way he needs it, fucking my face with forceful thrusts and holding my head with gentle hands.

I moan around his dick just as Cole pushes his cock inside my ass, pumping in time with Sawyer's easy pumps from below. Travis takes Cole's place at my side and Asher pulls out of my mouth, turning me to face Travis, whose cock is ready and waiting for my mouth.

"Taste yourself, take Sawyer fucking you." Fuck, his words make every cell in my body hum with unbidden need.

Where Cole and Asher were gentle but careful, Travis is neither. His hand wraps around my neck, his thumb pushing down on the bottom row of my teeth as he feeds me his impatient cock, soaked in my juices.

My lids fall closed as I taste myself on him, the compound savor of Sawyer's musk mixed with Travis's spicy scent all wrapped up in my cum gives me another bolt of adrenaline, my pussy riding Sawyer harder, my ass searching out Cole's dick as I push off my arms, harder and harder.

"Looks like she's loving that combo. Fuck, yeah, she's hot when she's high on lust." Sawyer's words barely register, I'm so consumed by this hunger that I want more. I need more.

More in my pussy, more in my ass, more in my mouth. I feel like I'm losing my mind every time Travis's cock pushes deep inside my throat, his palm pushing against the intrusion and cutting off my airway.

"Choke."

It's not difficult to obey him, he's doing all the work while Cole is gripping my hips and drilling my ass and Sawyer is using all his leg strength to fuck my pussy raw. Asher kisses my back, his lips trailing a hot path down my spine as he leaves my side and joins Cole behind me. Cole pulls out and Asher spreads my ass cheeks nice and wide and I can only imagine the gaping hole that they're greeted with. Asher spits into my hole and Cole goes back to fucking me, hard thrusts in and out before he pulls back out and Asher takes his place in my ass.

While the twins fuck me to within an inch of my life, Travis brings his free hand up and pinches my nose. My eyes grow wide as I watch the lust dancing in his eyes, knowing yet again he's in control of whether I live or die. He's the master of my next breath. He holds my fate in his hands as his thrusts in my mouth grow harder and faster and my tears fall freely, knowing I've only got a few more seconds before I pass out from lack of oxygen.

He knows this and it empowers him.

"I don't know what you're doing up there, man, but her pussy is fucking drenched." Sawyer confirms what Travis already knows and his grin says everything his words don't.

Stars blink at the periphery of my vision, blackness inching from the outside in until all I see is a narrow tunnel where Travis's stare traps me. I blink once, twice and just when I think I'm going under, he releases my nose and I gasp in air through my mouth and around his cock.

"Fuck, that's hot!" The awe in Asher's voice sets off an orgasm that gives me no warning. I shake and cry out just as Cole joins us on the bed again and Travis kisses my swollen lips, whispering against my mouth, "You're our girl, our very good, good girl." His tongue sweeps in and takes control of my senses before he's gone again.

I grab him by the side of the face before he's too far and bite my bottom lip, "I think Sawyer needs to get fucked, too." His pupils turn dark, his smirk growing wider.

"I take it back. You're our good, filthy girl with a kink for voyeurism."

I shrug because he's not wrong.

We adjust on the bed as Sawyer slides out from inside me and places me on my back. This time, I have the use of my hands and plan to take advantage of their generosity.

Sawyer straddles my chest, the head of his cock circling my lips like he's applying lipstick as his bright eyes thank me a thousand times for my request.

Travis settles right behind him, reaching around to tweak my nipples as Cole and Asher get settled between my wide-open thighs.

I wait while Travis preps Sawyer's ass, using lube and his fingers until he's satisfied that his cock won't rip him in half.

When he's ready, Sawyer pushes his dick inside my mouth, his balls slapping my chin with every push inside. I know the exact moment Travis pushes his cock inside Sawyer because his eyes roll to the back of his head and his cock slides impossibly deeper into my throat.

Below me, Cole lifts my ass so he can angle himself inside while Asher crouches over my hips and pushes his huge dick all the way to the root inside my hungry pussy.

Every one of my holes is filled and, in this moment, I am complete.

We fuck hard, a sacred rhythm in place as Asher pummels my pussy and Cole rips my ass apart with the skilled thrusts of his cock. Travis takes my hands in his as he fucks Sawyer's ass, giving him the right momentum to choke me from tip to root. Every one of their movements causes a butterfly effect and the vision before me is too much for me to take.

I have no idea how many times they've made me come and I can't understand how I could possibly feel the need to do so again, but when Asher pinches my clit and rolls it between his index and thumb, I lose my fucking mind.

My hips pump up, my fingers holding Travis's in a steel vice while my pussy and ass muscles squeeze the life out of Asher and Cole. As though choreographed, my reaction sets off a series of events.

Sawyer is the first to come, filling my mouth with his cum and forcing me to swallow every drop, pushing it back into my mouth as it begins to spill from the corners of my lips.

The visual sets Travis off inside Sawyer's ass and the look of pure ecstasy on Sawyer's face makes me want to take a picture for me to revisit every night.

It's Asher's turn to lose it next as he pumps in and out of my pussy, causing Cole's orgasm to set right off.

Within mere seconds, I'm full of cum. In my pussy, in my mouth, in my ass. I'm full of them.

Sawyer rolls off of me, panting and heaving as he takes one of my hands and squeezes his fingers around mine.

"I held back a little just for you." Travis aims his dick at my tits and with the last of his orgasm, spurts his cum all over my nipples, spreading it over my tits like he's slathering his very DNA into my skin.

We all collapse after that, into a melted heap of post-orgasmic bliss.

LILY WILDHART

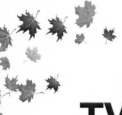

TWENTY ONE

BRIAR

Making plans to talk to Connor and his uncle—*our* uncle, I guess—seemed like such a good idea this morning. In my post orgasm haze, I was feeling light and happy and ready to face the world.

Then reality hit, and I found out that Jamie was the police officer killed yesterday. Another person linked to me. Except he was nothing but nice to me, so I don't understand it. The others were all people who had done *something* to me that was less than chill.

Whoever it was that was doing the killing seemed to be trying to protect me with the whole Crawford thing.

None of this makes any fucking sense to me. It's almost as if there are at least two people behind it all and they're not talking to each other.

My head aches just trying to piece it together. A detective I am not.

Taking a deep breath, I push open the door to the coffee shop by campus where I'd agreed to meet with Connor and Thomas and butterflies erupt in my stomach.

Why is this so hard?

Stupid question, I know. Thomas looks *exactly* like the man who was my literal living nightmare, that's why it's so hard. But facing Connor now that he knows about that, when he's supposed to be my family? How does any of this make sense?

I should have probably spoken to my mom already, but her lies are endless so I think I'd rather hear the story from them before I speak to her. If I speak to her at all.

Though maybe Connor wants to meet her.

Thoughts for later, Briar. Come on, big girl pants on.

Taking another breath, I search the cafe and find them sitting in the back left corner. It's dark back there, well, shadowed, and somehow that makes it scarier. My heart races when I see Thomas and, for a moment, I contemplate running the fuck away. He might say he's not Matty, but I never knew Matty had a twin.

What if this is just some elaborate lie?

What if *they're* the killers and that's why it seems like two people, because it freaking is.

Oh, God. Anxiety grips my chest and I can feel the attack coming.

Coming alone was a bad idea.

I should've brought one of the guys. Or Penn. Hell, anyone, just to be a buffer.

Yet I fought to come here alone—and oh man was it a fight—because I knew it was something I had to face on my own.

So freaking stupid.

"Briar!" Connor calls out, waving me down as if I hadn't seen him. Well dammit, now I can't even run away.

I will my legs to move and find myself moving toward them despite my entire body screaming at me to run away. They both stand as I approach the table and wait for me to slide into the booth before they sit down opposite me.

Yeah this isn't awkward at all.

"Thank you for agreeing to meet me," Thomas says, and I glance over at him before turning my focus to Connor because I can't look at him too much without wanting to climb under the table. "I know this must be hard for you, but I want to reassure you that I'm nothing like Matty was. He was troubled, from when we were small, and I should have done more. I'm sorry you went through what you did. I didn't know what happened to you until much later, after Iris's death."

"You knew I existed?" I ask quietly.

"I did," he says solemnly, and I just about manage to look at him squarely while he answers me. "I helped Connor be placed with my sister-in-law."

"I'm so confused," I sigh and he nods.

"Maybe you should start from the beginning," Connor suggests, and Thomas nods.

"Noah was my brother. He was the eldest, then there's my older brother Mike, Connor's adopted dad, then me and Matty. When your mom fell pregnant, she came to Noah and told him, and he... well, he was a pretty shitty human too. Anyway, I overheard their conversation and reached out to your mom, offering help if she ever needed it." He pauses as a server approaches us. We order a round of coffees, and once she disappears, Thomas begins to speak again. "I didn't hear from her again until after you were born. She hadn't been for regular checkups, she couldn't afford it, so she didn't know she was having twins until you were both born. Fraternal twins. She called me and told me that there were two of you. That she had no idea how to raise the boy, so either I looked after him, or she'd leave him at the hospital."

I bark a dry, sharp laugh. "That sounds like my mother." Pausing while the server brings our drinks over, I glance over at Connor, who looks as confused about all this as I feel. "You really didn't miss out by being adopted. Life was a freaking party."

"I'm sorry," Connor says quietly, and I shake my head.

"You've got nothing to be sorry about. I should probably

say sorry about my mom giving you up, but I stopped making myself feel responsible for her issues when I moved here." I pause before turning back to Thomas. "Sorry, I interrupted, please continue."

He nods, taking a sip of his drink before speaking again. "I wasn't in a place to look after a kid, and Noah was as likely to look after a child as Matty was, but Mike's wife couldn't have kids, so when I told them the situation, they jumped at the chance to have a child to raise as their own. I didn't know you were even here or friends with Connor until I came here a few months ago and saw you on campus. You look just like him. Noah, I mean. It was impossible not to see it. Well, for me anyway. I knew you existed, and you were the right age. So I started digging, and when I told Connor, well, you know he's been a little MIA lately."

I nod, glancing at Connor, who shrugs remorsefully. "I didn't mean to drop off the face of the Earth," Connor adds. "I was just trying to work through it all. I didn't even know I was adopted. It's been a rough few months."

"And yet you both still thought ambushing me was a great idea," I snark, rolling my eyes. I take a deep breath before speaking. "Sorry, anxious bitch mode is still in full swing."

"It's okay," Thomas says, smiling sadly. "I know this is a lot, but I came home to find out what happened to my brother and stumbled into all of this. I didn't want you to not know. Not now that you're here."

"Does my mother know you're in town? That you're telling me? That Connor knows?"

They both shake their heads. "I haven't worked up the balls to reach out yet," Connor says, hanging his head a little. "I didn't want her to think we were just after her money now that she's a Kensington."

"Fair point, she's exactly that human, so she probably would've accused you of it. But I can help, if you decide you want to meet her. Honestly, I wouldn't recommend it, you're not missing much, but also, I'm not you. And since our sperm donor doesn't seem like he was a stellar guy either, considering our conception, well—"

"What do you mean?" Connor asks, his gaze bouncing between me and Thomas.

"You didn't tell him?" I ask Thomas, who winces.

"Didn't know you knew," he answers with a shrug.

"Knew what?" Connor asks again.

I turn to face him and shake my head. "That our entire family are rapists."

He blanches and I can see as he puts all the dots together, then somehow goes paler.

"I need to go," he says, before standing quickly and running from the cafe.

Thomas stands, gaze chasing Connor's movements. "I should go after him. I'm sorry, again, for how all of this came about, but if you'd like to meet Mikey and his wife, who are much nicer humans than the two family members of mine you've met to this point, I know they'd love to meet you."

"I'll consider it," I tell him, and he nods before saying goodbye and going after Connor.

I stay in the booth, reeling. I probably shouldn't have told Connor like that, but this entire afternoon has been a bit of a shit show.

Finishing my coffee, I text the others and let them know I'll be home soon, trying to catch my breath after everything. Cole, Travis and Sawyer let me know they're still on campus–and remind me to have my location turned on since I'm alone–so they'll be home soon too, so I don't rush. Asher doesn't respond, but if he's in class, well, that's to be expected.

All I wanted after I moved here was to be normal… but I guess I must've killed an entire nation in a past life, because Karma is seriously kicking my ass.

I pause when I reach the top step on the porch as fear runs through me again.

Fuck this day.

The door is open, I can't hear the dogs, and if the door is open they could've gotten out. But why the fuck is the door open?

Somehow, I manage to override the stupid white-girl-in-a-horror-movie urge to enter the house and call Denton. The guys are in class, so there's no point calling them, and Denton carries a gun. I've seen it. If anyone should be checking the house, it's the guy with the gun.

"What's up, trouble?" he asks when he answers before it even has a chance to ring.

"Denton, the front door is open, I can't hear the dogs, and I don't want to go inside. Everyone's supposed to be in class, and I am freaking the fuck out after the murder over the weekend."

"Take a breath, Sweetheart. I'll be there in less than five. Go back out onto the sidewalk and wait for me. Do *not* go into that house. "

"Wasn't planning on it," I say, but the line is already dead. I swear I hear a noise in the house, and I know if someone is hurt, I should really go in, but I really don't want to get dead, and I know how much I'll get yelled at if I go in there.

But what if that noise was Asher? He didn't text back...

Fuck.

Before I get the chance to make the decision to go inside, a car screeches up by the Batmobile. Carter and Denton fly out of it and are at my side in seconds. I have no idea where they were or where they came from, but damn that was fast.

"Stay here," Carter all but growls as he pulls a gun from a holster hidden beneath his jacket. Denton does the same and they enter the house.

I swear the seconds feel like hours waiting for them. I'm

guessing they've dealt with stuff like this before, because they're fucking *silent.* When Denton reappears, I nearly shit my pants and jump out of my damn skin. "Coast is clear, Sweetheart, but we should call an ambulance."

"That doesn't sound like the coast is clear, Denton."

"Let's not waste time shall we?" he says sternly before pulling me in the house. I spot Asher lying on the floor, blood pooled beneath him, while Carter applies pressure to his stomach.

"Oh my God!" I gasp, my hands flying to my mouth. I knew I should've come inside dammit.

"Briar, ambulance. Now. He's losing consciousness," Denton snaps, pulling me from my panic, and I fumble for my phone, dialing 9-1-1.

I speak on autopilot when the call answers, telling them that he's bleeding and giving them the address while Denton calls who I assume is Travis.

The boys arrive at the same time as the ambulance, and everything happens around me in a blur. Sawyer goes with Asher to the hospital, but I have to stay here to give a statement since I came home to the house having been broken into.

By the time they've spoken to me, Carter, and Denton, I'm exhausted and I just want to know what's going on with Asher.

"Any news?" I ask Cole, who's been keeping in touch with Sawyer, once Carter and Denton leave along with the police.

"Not yet, he's in surgery. It was touch and go from the amount of blood loss, but Sawyer seems fairly positive. Hopefully we'll know more soon. Their parents are at the hospital now, so hopefully answers will come quicker."

"This is all my fault," I whisper as I crouch down, turning myself into a ball.

Travis slams his phone down on the counter after his call, pulling me from my minute of pity party. "Bentley is reviewing the security footage, but whoever it was must have known where our cameras are. Their face is turned away from all of them, but apparently it's a slim, tall person, whoever it is. Which, as far as information goes, is about as much fucking use as tastebuds on an asshole."

"Should we go to the hospital?" I ask them, but Cole shakes his head.

"I think it'd be best for everyone to let it be just them for now."

He smiles at me sadly and I nod. I hear what he doesn't say. That his family doesn't want me there. His parents already aren't exactly my number one fans, and now...

"You should pack a bag," Travis says, looking over at me. "We're not staying here tonight."

I nod, almost on autopilot. "Yeah, okay. Should I pack for the twins too?"

"Sure thing," Cole answers, like he's coddling me, but I'm not sad about it.

How the fuck is this our lives?

I head upstairs, and move without even thinking about it, shoving clothes for the twins into a bag I found in Asher's closet. Once I'm done, I drop the bag at the top of the stairs and head to my room to do the same.

I open my closet and freeze as I stare down the barrel of a gun.

"Oh, goodie. You're here."

TWENTY TWO

BRIAR

"**B**et you didn't see me coming, did you Little Miss Perfect Life? It was fun when I started all of this, it wasn't even about you. Then Noah found me, mostly because I saw him kill that girl in your dorm while I was hunting you… then we decided to team up." She cackles maniacally at me but I'm frozen, unable to look at anything but the gun pointed at my face. Her eye twitches and she licks her lips repeatedly, if her blown pupils weren't enough to tell me she's high, that would be a dead giveaway.

"He started fucking me, because he knew it'd get to you, and I let him. He paid me, of course. Why give out for free what you can be paid for? But then I realized what he was to you.

What he did. That he was going to kill you, and I didn't like it. I was going to kill him, but well… you beat me to it."

Emerson steps out of the closest and I take a step backward, pushed by the gun against my forehead, my blood like ice in my veins, despite the sweat dripping down my face.

"Emerson, I don't understand? Why… why are you here? Why do you have a gun?" My voice breaks as I ask the questions, barely able to even speak and she laughs.

She. Laughs.

I feel a tear slip down my face and realize that this is how I'm going to die. I've thought about how it would happen, but never, not once, did I imagine this.

"You never understand, and I just wanted you to see. All I ever wanted was for you to see. You were the sunlight… the joy. Even when you had bad days, you were still my sunshine. But then Iris died and you blamed me—"

"I didn't—" I start, but she waves the gun in my face and I close my mouth. I know I should shout for help, but Asher is already hurt and I have to assume that was her. I don't want anyone else to get hurt because of me, and if I shout… I know she'll hurt the others.

"You did! You blamed me because we went out that night. After that, you started pulling away. That's when I started killing, you know? Not people at first… no. That was too hard… but once I felt more confident, I moved to the junkies. No one ever looks that closely at an OD in the city, right? There's nothing quite like the thrill of watching the life drain from someone's eyes. Have you ever watched it? Who am I kidding, of course you have. Allison was me too. Did you know that? I did that, and you thought it was your fault she died!" She cackles, and I wince as she uses the barrel of the gun to rub my cheek. "That was the best kind of kill, the one where it was your fault really, because even though I did it, you were my reason for everything."

I blink at her, because I have no idea what to say. None of this makes any sense to me, and the Allison thing has me reeling. She held that over my head for *years*. It doesn't help that she's rambling like a crazy person, but also, my brain has gone into full freeze mode. I have no fight or flight in me. All I have is nothingness.

"Emerson, please, put the gun down. We can just talk about it."

"All you ever do is talk," she hisses at me, getting so in my face her saliva spatters my skin. "The time for talk is over. I tried to talk to you with the notes, and the emails, even with the people I killed. They needed to die. They were mean to you. They were awful. It's why I planted Crawford's DNA on them. He deserved to be blamed. But you wouldn't listen."

She starts pacing back and forth, brandishing the gun like it's just part of her hand. Using it to scratch at her face as she babbles to herself. I try to take a step toward the door, but her gaze whips to me as I try to move.

"I was going to gift you your mom. She was intended to

be my ultimate gift to you. So you could kill her with me. Free yourself from it all… but then you got comfortable here and I decided that wouldn't work anymore. I had to free you from everyone. The pretty emo boy was first. No, that's not right…" She pauses and tilts her head, watching me. "Jamie was first. He was on to me. He kept seeing me and I don't like it when they see me. Not *really* see me. They don't get to do that. They take enough, they don't get that too."

"I don't understand, Emerson." My words are more of a sob, tears streaming down my face.

Her face twists in anger and she stomps toward me, pointing the gun back at me. "You never understand, Briar!"

My hands shake as she pushes the gun into my chest. "On your knees. I'm going to make you understand."

"Briar? Is everything okay?" Cole's voice calls out, and Emerson's eyes light up. Panic floods me and I scream.

"Get out, Cole. She has a gun!" I try to push up to grapple with her, my hands around hers, but whatever she's on has made her crazy strong and I shriek as she hits me in the face, knocking me to the ground.

The door bursts open, the sound of wood splintering like it was kicked in, followed quickly by *pop pop*. In a blink, Cole is on the ground and my ears are ringing, but I feel the scream tear up my throat as I watch the blood bubble on his torso.

In a blink, Travis is in the doorway, and there's another *pop*. His eyes go wide before he looks down at the red pooling on his white t-shirt. I don't know how, but there's another *pop*. Then I see Bentley in the hall behind Travis and sound rushes back to me as I hear Emerson hit the ground with a *thud*.

The hole in her head tells me everything I need to know as my body starts to function again and the sounds start making sense.

Carter is there, Denton is there. Bentley is standing over me, and there are a whirr of sirens and voices, but all I can do is stare at the two men who came to save me, now lifeless on the ground.

I thought the rest of my life would be with them, even when I fought it... and now... now everything is over.

EPILOGUE

BRIAR

"**H**oly shit, did you hear?" Penn squeals as she runs up to me. She's practically bouncing on the spot. It's the first day of our third year, and there is no way she's this excited for class.

"Did I hear what?"

"Octavia freaking Royal is coming to Saints U!" She's shaking so hard that I think she might just combust.

"Are you kidding?"

She shakes her head with such vigor that I can't help but laugh.

"She's here. I saw her and her boyfriends climb from their car. That's when I started running here."

I pause, laughing for a beat, before I burst and continue again. "Penn, she's just a girl, like you and me. Her dad died last year and from what I've seen online, she's gone through Hell. She probably just wants to be normal and blend in."

"So what you're saying is, we shouldn't try to make her our new BFF?"

I shake my head and chuckle at her, looping my arm through hers and heading toward the new coffee shop on the edge of campus. "That's exactly what I'm saying. Fairly certain she has a BFF, and it's the girl the twins' mom tried to set them up with."

"Wait, the girl from last year with the bright hair?"

"That's the one."

"Holy shit, we have an in!"

"Penn," I say calmly. "Absolutely not. Leave the poor girl alone."

"But don't you want to be friends with the other girl on campus who knows what it was like to have multiple boyfriends? You can compare the insanity of juggling that much dick. I can't even hold *one* down, let alone four."

"Penn!"

She pulls back and stares at me before rolling her eyes. "Oh, bitch please. Don't try to tell me you don't love the juggling. Now come on, let's go get coffee and watch the chaos that ensues, cause you know her being here is going to cause carnage."

"Maybe we shouldn't watch?" I say, wincing. Having been in the media thanks to everything we've dealt with since the shooting… needless to say, I'm not a fan of being in the public eye. It has a way of tainting and twisting everything.

She lets out a deep sigh before relinking her arm with mine. "Fineeeee. But that means coffee is on you."

"That I can agree to." I grin at her, and my phone starts to buzz in my pocket. I pull it out and see Sawyer's name on the screen. "Why on Earth is he face-timing me?"

I answer and wait for the screen to load to find his very smiling face looking back at me. I am still thankful every day that he made it out of that day alive. It was an awful fucking day, one I'll never forget. But at least he survived. "Good morrrrninggggg, Sunnnnshiiiiiine."

"Have you been eating my chocolate covered coffee beans again?" I ask with a soft laugh, which just makes him grin wider.

"I have not, I learned my lesson last time. I'm calling because I got a call just now about someone who wants to come over to the house for dinner…" He trails off and I hear voices in the background. "Do not drop that TV!"

I guess the movers are there. More chaos added to my life.

"I've got that meeting this afternoon before I come to the new place, but who is the dinner guest?"

"You remember the girl my mom tried to hook me up with last year? Indi?"

"How could I forget?" I deadpan.

"Her and some friends are new to town, new to Saints U, and want to get away for a bit."

Penn lets out a squeal so high pitched beside me, I'm fairly certain she shatters my eardrum. Sawyer just laughs at me as I shake out my head while it still rings.

"I'm going to assume from Penn's reaction, I'm good to invite them, and that Penn needs a seat too?"

"Dante will want one too!" Penn says as she smushes up against me so she's on the screen.

"Done and done. See you later, Sunshine. I'll text you the details for dinner."

Just like that, the screen goes dark and when I look up, Penn is doing a happy dance in the middle of the sidewalk.

"I guess you get your wish after all."

She grins at me while continuing to dance and it takes everything I have not to laugh at her as she does. She flicks her hair over her shoulder in an 'I win' kind of way before doing a fist pump in the air. "My wish? This might just make my entire damn year!"

After calming Penn, I head to the coffee shop close to the campus main entrance to meet Connor. It should be weird that this has become our spot, but the last eighteen or so months we've really tried to work past all of the crazy that surrounds the fact that he's my twin.

We introduced him to Mom here, which was a whole lot

of fireworks all on its own... and it's where he met our little brother, Toby, for the first time too. Beyond those two moments, he hasn't seen Mom, and I don't blame him. Hell, I don't want to see her either and I wasn't the one she threw away.

Mostly, we try not to talk about Mom, or Crawford, or Matty, or even Thomas... We agreed to try and leave the past where it belongs and move forward.

To say that was hard at the beginning, especially after him and Penn 'officially' broke up, is an understatement, but they got there, which has made things *way* less awkward for me. Dealing with that alongside all of the revelations about Emerson and the whole investigation... well that was a mindfuck of its own.

Discovering that she had a whole network of men she was sleeping with that were somehow in love with her, and she'd deluded them into helping her with her quest to make me hers—which still freaks me out—explained how she managed to get the emails to lead to Dante... but seeing the pictures of the shrine she had of me in her apartment in the evidence file the Denton secured for us, *that* creeped me out beyond measure.

I push the door open to the coffee shop and spot Connor in our booth. Heading over to the counter, I wave at him before joining the line. Once I have my coffee in hand, I head over to see my big brother.

Big brother by like ninety seconds and *wowzers* has he not let me forget it. Once the weirdness cleared, he joined my protective bandwagon... along with Denton because after everything, he decided I needed him in my life on a semi-regular basis... obviously.

Insert audible eyeroll here.

"Sorry I'm late," I say as I slide into the booth. "It's been a day, and we're not even close to being done."

"No worries, I was just reading up to get ready for our paper that's due next week."

I groan and drop my head onto the table. "Don't. I haven't even started that yet."

He looks at me disapprovingly as he says my name. "You can't keep getting behind."

"Course I can," I shrug. "My brother is a genius and gives me his notes." He smirks at me and shakes his head before reaching into his bag and sliding me over flash cards.

"Yeah, I was already prepared. Little sisters are a pain in the ass."

"Maybe," I say with a smile and shrug. "But we're also awesome."

I take a sip of my peppermint mocha with extra whip and let out a contented sigh.

"You're going to have a heart attack if you keep drinking those daily."

I narrow my eyes at him and quirk my brow. "Do not start lecturing me on my caffeine or sugar intake again. After the last few years, I'm convinced it won't be my habits that kill me off. People around me just seem to die, and one day, it's going to be me instead."

He winces at my blasé statement, but nods. He can't exactly argue it. All you have to do is look at the last few years and see the truth in my words. "You doing okay with everything? Still seeing the therapist?"

I roll my eyes at him but nod. "Yes, still going weekly. Don't worry, I'm being a good girl. Sawyer crawls up my ass every time I so much as hint at stopping."

"One, good. Two, I don't want to know about what your boyfriend does to your ass."

I cackle at him, and catch up on the last few weeks since I've been out of town mostly dealing with stuff for the homeless charity I work with. It's been one of the few things that's helped me stay focused since the shooting with Emerson.

I swear I still see the hole in her head every time I close my eyes. Even with everything she did, all the loss she caused, her face still haunts my very frequent nightmares.

"Briar?" I refocus and find Connor staring at me, concern obvious in his furrowed brow. "You okay?"

"I'm fine," I say, waving him off, catching sight of my watch as I do. "I do, however, need to get going otherwise I'm going to be late. It's moving day."

"I did wonder if that was today," he says with a nod. "Let me know if you need any help, okay?"

"I will," I say, giving him the warmest smile I can muster. "I'll see you in class on Monday?"

"You will," he says with a nod. I finish the dregs of my now cold coffee before giving him a quick hug and beelining for the door.

This day is going to be chaos and it's barely even half way done.

I walk into the new house, knowing the guys are around here somewhere. The place is already fully unpacked because God forbid any of these guys pack or unpack their own stuff. Not that I'm complaining that much, because well, unpacking sucks. Plus, most of this stuff was delivered from various stores and arranged by some woman Travis hired.

This might be my new home for the foreseeable future, but God only knows I didn't want to deal with furnishing this monstrosity. I mean, it's beautiful, and I know there are a lot of us, but it's still huge.

Apparently a six bedroom mansion comes with more square footage than I ever thought, and a price tag I don't want to think about. Travis bought the place, and as much as I hate the amount of money it cost, it's nice having a space that's ours. Especially after everything that happened the last two years...

My Converse squeak on the shiny floors and I wince as it echoes through the huge entrance... yeah, can't call this an entrance *hall*, but space, I guess.

"You coming up?" Sawyer calls down from the mezzanine, and I grin as I tilt my head back to look up at him.

"I don't know, what's up there?"

He wags his brows at me and I laugh. Throughout everything, he hasn't changed one iota. He's still the guy who can make me laugh without fail and I hope that never changes. "The best kind of things."

I shake my head but walk toward the staircase anyway. Exploring can wait. "I need to change before you guys have anything in mind."

"Oh, Sunshine, you think you're going to need clothes for what we have planned?"

I laugh again, my shoulders shaking as I crest the top of the stairs. "I'm guessing not?"

"Ding ding ding. We have a winner." He holds a hand out for me and I take it, letting him lead me down the hall toward the master suite. Our shared room. I pause at the threshold and take in the sight before me. The wall of glass with summer sunshine spilling through, the door that leads to the giant balcony area with a hot tub.

The huge California king bed in the middle of the far back wall, which Cole and Asher are currently sitting on the end of.

The sofa opposite the bed that Travis is sitting on, a TV hanging above it.

All done in forest greens, browns, and natural colors. It's just so… calm.

Which is good after this day, but I get the feeling what's about to happen is going to be anything but calm and I am *so* here for it.

"Oh, good. You're here," Travis says, standing and running his hands down his shirt. "But you're still dressed. Why are you still dressed?"

He quirks a brow at me, and I feel Sawyer leave my side as I stay captured in Travis' view.

"Because I'm waiting on instructions?" I mean, we literally just got here, I thought I'd get a minute to explore but apparently not.

"Is that a question or a statement?" Travis takes one step closer and I feel like a gazelle frozen in the stare of the lion.

"A statement?" *Fuck.*

"Briar." I clear my throat, stopping myself from fidgeting, then take a deep breath. "I'm waiting on instructions." I keep my shoulders back, my gaze steady and strong, knowing I've got four pairs of eyes just waiting for the green light to tear me apart in all the best of ways.

"Good girl. Now strip and show me how wet your cunt is for us." I don't hesitate. Travis's words are like a gun being fired at the races and my arms rip off my top right over my head then push my jeans down as I wiggle my way out of them, only to get caught by my shoes.

I growl, frustration growing with every added second that I'm not at their mercy.

Travis just stands there, that infuriating smirk firmly planted on his delectable lips, while Sawyer reaches back and pulls his shirt off, momentarily blinding me with his delicious abs.

"Tick tock, little whore. The longer you take to follow orders, the longer you'll wait to come." With narrowed eyes aimed straight at Travis, I get back to work on stripping, doing my best not to talk back.

"Well, if Sawyer would stop trying to distract me, then maybe I would obey." I said 'doing my best', never said I'd succeed.

"Did you hear that, Sawyer? Our little slut here is blaming you for not being efficient in her undressing." Travis speaks to Sawyer, but his eyes are staring straight at me and they are not indulgent. In fact, I'm pretty sure I'm about to get punished.

The thought makes my thighs clench and my heart rate accelerate.

Sawyer brings his hand to his chest, right above his heart, and faux pouts. "I'm crushed."

Asshole.

"Here, this should take care of that problem. No sight, no distractions." Cole throws a satin sash at Travis, who catches it without even putting in an effort, all the while grinning at me like this whole fucking thing was planned.

Holy shit.

I look at Asher, who's lying back on his elbows, his jeans opened at a V and his cock peeking out and resting on his belly.

"You planned it like this?" I can barely hear my voice, that's how impressed I am with their bullshit. Am I that fucking predictable?

"You know I don't like leaving anything to chance, baby, especially when it comes to your orgasms. Now, on your knees, thighs spread, hands behind your back." I don't even think, I just act. Once in position, Travis walks to my front and the heat against my back tells me Sawyer is standing barely an inch away. From the corner of my eye, I see Cole and Asher stand and make their way to me and before I can register what's going on, I am the eye of their perfect storm as they surround me on all sides.

"Your punishment for sassing, m'lady." Sawyer swipes the scarf from Travis's outstretched hand and kisses the top of my head before immersing me into total darkness. My wrists at the small of my back are fastened with what feels like silk ropes and my lips are pushed apart with what I'm guessing is another silk scarf tightly tied behind my head and pressing down on my tongue. Drool gathers at the corners of my mouth as a pair of lips slide across and down my outer ear.

"The gag comes off only when we fuck your face, do you understand?" It's the low baritone of Cole's voice in my ear and it does crazy things to my insides, my juices pooling then sliding down my thighs. When it takes me too long to answer, a quick sting at the back of my head is all the warning I get of their impatience.

I nod, over and over, until Asher's words cover me like a balm to sunburnt skin.

"Good girl. Now, spread your thighs." I push my legs out as far as they'll go until I feel one, then two fingers in my pussy, spreading my wetness around like lube before a good ass fucking.

"This is going to be fun, guys. She's so wet we could DP her without prepping." Travis sounds proud, like he's the reason I'm so soaked for him.

Well, he is—they all are—but still, a little humility never killed anyone.

A large hand clamps down on my hair and fingers curl around my loose strands, yanking my head back and exposing my neck. All I see is black, but that only means my other senses are on high alert. Their unique scents dance around my nostrils and with every breath I can taste them on my tongue.

Two fingers start at my lips, pushing inside my mouth and pressing the scarf down until they're tickling my gag reflex. Seconds before I start coughing, they pull out and light a burning trail down my chin, neck, and between my breasts.

I'm already panting, the anticipation of what they'll do to me working its intended magic.

"I think I'll start by fucking your tits." If I could, I'd lick my lips but, dammit, it's physically impossible to do so. "Set her up."

Behind my black silk scarf, I blink at Travis' words, studying the noises and movements around me to try and guess what's going to happen next.

Except, they're distracting with their hands on my tits and fingers pumping inside my pussy. It's hard to listen when your heart beat is thrumming in your ears.

"She's perfect." I'd recognize Asher's even tone anywhere, always the gentle one, the considerate one. And yet oh-so-fucking filthy.

"What's better than perfect? Because that's what she's going to be on our Sacred Bed of Fucks." I frown. *Our what now?* Sawyer chuckles, so I'm guessing he can see my confusion. "This is the bed where we'll use you and abuse you and then love you. Our Sacred Bed of Fucks. Because we do give fucks. Lots and lots of them."

I don't have time to think about his silliness because I'm whisked away in strong arms, and by the smell and size, I'm guessing it's Cole, his murmured, "I've got you," only confirming it.

I'm placed standing on the mattress, legs spread wide and arms raised in a V. My head turns with every sound around me, the clicking of metal, the sliding of wires, the soft give of the mattress as one or two of them stand beside me.

I'm handcuffed, how, I have no fucking clue, but it feels like a pulley system with a little bit of give. Next, my ankles are cuffed to what feels like a steel bar, keeping me from closing my legs and making me completely vulnerable to all kinds of dirty pleasures.

Wetness slides down my thighs and I smile around my gag. No matter what they try to do to me, my body always responds with a resounding yes.

"Fuck, look at that." Sawyer's voice sounds in awe just as a tongue licks a path from just above my knee, up my inner thigh, and straight to my pussy. I whimper, the hot tongue welcome at my center, the sucking on my needy clit like a godsend. "And delicious as always."

Sawyer places himself between my legs, his hands on my thighs holding me steady while two others, Asher and Cole, I think, stand beside me licking my tits and biting my nipples then alternating with their fingers as they pinch and roll my nipples between their index and thumbs. My head falls back onto a chest and I sigh at the feel of Travis behind me. I don't feel a stitch of clothing on any of them, which gives me hope that they're all naked.

Suddenly, my head is snapped back with one hand in my hair and another at my throat, fingers digging at my pulse points, cutting off my air.

"Have you ever been fucked and licked at the same time, my little whore?" Travis knows the answer to this, yet he sounds angry, like he's jealous of some kind of alternate world where this could have happened to me.

I shake my head and he pulls my head back even further until my face is parallel to the ceiling and his tongue is licking around my lips and delving inside my gagged mouth.

"That's right. You haven't. And do you know why? Because we haven't. Because you're ours to abuse and to fuck like the perfect little whore you are. And to reward you for that, you're going to experience it. Isn't she, Sawyer?"

Below, Sawyer just mumbles as his tongue fucks my pussy like a cock would, in and out and then sliding up and teasing my clit before plunging back inside. Then, I feel a hand at my entrance and from behind, Travis slides his cock between my legs and Sawyer helps him to push inside me. I've got hands and tongues and a very talented cock in my pussy while Cole and Asher lavish me with their tongues on my tits and neck.

In my mind, I can see it all. I can imagine them worshipping my body while I stand there like their toy, accepting whatever the fuck they want to do to me. Mostly, I wish I could see Sawyer licking my cunt and Travis' cock at the same time. His tongue is everywhere, his hand guiding Travis' dick as he licks my juices every time Travis pulls out and Sawyer bites my clit every time Travis thrusts back inside me.

My knees begin to buckle, the clear picture in my mind almost as erotic as what I've always imagined the scene to be. Me all tied up and helpless and four men giving me everything I need.

Travis still has my head pulled back, his lips on mine, whispering filthy things, spitting inside my gagged mouth as my own spit gathers at the corners and trails down my chin and chest. It's hard to swallow in this position but when two fingers plunge down my throat, tears sting the back of my lids as I fight the urge to gag.

"Through your nose. Don't you fucking dare throw up on me." God, that would ruin the scene, wouldn't it?

I concentrate on breathing through my nose, in and out, and settle my baser urges.

"That's my good little slut, taking everything I give you like a good little girl." Fuck, why do I love his praises so much? Why do I need them?

His hips are thrusting harder, Sawyer's lips sucking my clit deep into his mouth as Asher and Cole bite me so hard I know I'll have marks in the morning.

"Come all over my dick, right the fuck now." At Travis' words, two fingers delve into my ass and I gasp, a gurgle of spit and saliva making a sound that is not fucking sexy but holy shit, my body begins to tremble and my thighs can't seem to hold me up. I know that if Sawyer weren't holding me, I'd be putting all of my weight on my arms.

"That's it, fuck yeah, give us your cum." Sawyer is licking me up like a fucking lollypop, sucking on Travis' cock then eating my pussy like it's a five star Michelin feast. My orgasm washes over me from head to toe until all I have is nothingness. I'm numb, feeling light as a feather and heavy all at once.

I may have blacked out for a second because I'm lying on my back now, the scarf gone and the gag removed. I still have the bar between my legs and when Asher positions himself at the back of my head and Cole is teasing my pussy with his cock, I silently thank them for giving me my eyesight back. They're so fucking hot that it pains me to look at them. The ridiculous waves of muscles at their abs, the pulsing veins at the forearms when they strain, trying their best to hold back their orgasms. The ecstasy on their faces when they finally succumb and spill themselves inside my holes.

On either side of me, Sawyer and Travis are looking down at me with matching smirks that have a sudden effect on my cunt all over again. I just came, how is their mere presence making me horny so quickly?

Kneeling at my side, Sawyer gets on all fours, his body like a bridge over mine until his mouth is on Travis, licking the tip of his cock, licking me off his cock.

"Can you see how fucking delicious you are? Watch him clean your cum off my dick." And I do, my eyes on Sawyer's mouth just as Cole thrusts inside my pussy from tip to root as he holds my legs straight up by the bar, using it as a lever. Asher lifts my head until I'm leaning against his stomach, offering me a better view, all the while his hard as fuck cock is sliding up and down my neck. I want to suck it into my mouth but if I do, I won't see the show.

"It's okay, beautiful, enjoy it, I'll fuck your mouth in just a second," Asher murmurs from above, his gorgeous face hovering just above mine.

Sawyer engulfs Travis's cock all the way down his throat, his nose tickling the pubes at his groin before he hums and makes Travis groan a couple of obscenities. That's when Travis begins to fuck in earnest. His hips thrusting ruthlessly in and out of Sawyer's mouth, Cole fucking my pussy at the exact same rhythm and it feels like I'm getting fucked by them both. It's surreal how my mind and body sync together.

My orgasm takes me by surprise just as Travis pushes Sawyer away and straddles my chest. Pushing my tits together, he makes a perfect tunnel for his dick to fuck me as Asher pushes my head down and forces my mouth open.

"Tongue out." I obey Travis right away just as the tip of his cock bumps against my tongue. Cole adjusts his thrusts to Travis's and together they push in and out at the same time. When Asher sticks two fingers inside my mouth and Sawyer two fingers inside my ass, I lose the little control I had, coming all over Cole's cock and feeling him empty his sack inside my pussy with a long, drawn out grunt. Sawyer and Asher take themselves in hand and the sound of them jacking themselves off is like fucking music to my ears, extending my orgasm, making my skin tingle, my toes curl, gasping for air. It sounds and smells like sex as Sawyer spurts his cum over my pussy and Asher comes all over my mouth, nose, and chin. Travis marks my tits with his seed, long strands of cum landing over my nipples and between my globes.

I'm covered in semen, and I've never felt better in my entire life.

Cole releases the bar between my legs and gently pulls them down, kissing the inside of my thigh. He catches me watching and throws me a sultry grin. "You're a sight, Baby. Let's get you cleaned up."

Travis and Sawyer go down to the kitchen to get us some food while Asher and Cole take me to the shower. Asher kisses me, probably tasting his own cum on my lips, while Cole gets the shower set up, testing the water.

"S'all good." Cole's baritone hits me right in the clit, his cum sliding down my thighs. If it weren't so damn sticky, I'd opt to keep their mark on me all night long.

With Asher at my back and Cole at my front, I let them take control of the shower. Cole has the body wash and shampoo, lathering me up before passing the bottle to Asher and running his hands all over my front. Pinching my nipples and fucking my pussy with his fingers, he does a very thorough job as Asher mimics his movements behind me. Once I'm clean, he pushes the middle of my back until I'm eye level with Cole's cock and Asher's dick is thrusting inside my pussy.

"Goddamn, I needed this." As Asher's words soothe my soul, I take Cole's cock in my mouth and revel in the fact that he's already hard for me. They both are. The water is beating down on my back as I'm spit roasted in the shower, loving the feel of Asher's hands on my hips, keeping me steady while he pummels my pussy like it's like the last time he'll get a chance to fuck me.

"It's ready!" Sawyer walks into the bathroom and whistles at the sight in front of him. "Fuck yeah, looking good, Baby. Damn, that's hot." I don't get a chance to make them come again as Asher pulls out, kissing between my shoulder blades and Cole pulls my head away from his cock, rinsing me under the shower head and kissing my lips with tender touches of his tongue.

"Let's get you fed, Beautiful. You're gonna need it."

I get fussed over and padded down with a fluffy teal towel that could wrap around two of me, interspersed with rogue kisses and squeezing fingers on my flesh. When they're done, Asher sweeps me up like a bride and carries me down to the kitchen where Sawyer and Travis are whispering and plotting. Didn't realize that making snacks was such a covert operation.

"What are you two knuckleheads conspiring about?" Cole sprints down the stairs and swipes a carrot off the tray, only to be slapped on the back of the head by Sawyer, who steals the carrot back and takes a big bite into it. Travis punches him in the arm and mumbles something that sounds like my name.

"I know it was for Briar, dude, fucking chill." When our eyes meet, Sawyer grins and makes a big show of cracking the carrot and chewing like an obnoxious child.

"I live with fucking children." Travis sounds like an old man who never wanted kids.

"After what we just did upstairs, that's kinda gross." At my words, Travis freezes. His back to me and his hand still on the handle of the fridge, he slowly turns his head to look at me over his left shoulder. The glint in his eyes gives a jolt to my heart, causing it to almost beat out of my chest. It's like what I said was a challenge or something.

"Eat. Now." He closes the door after taking out a platter of cold meats and a bottle of electrolytes. Holy shit, he's not fucking around.

"Oh, Baby Girl, you're in trouble now." Cole whispers in my ear as he hands me a sandwich. "Better hurry up and eat, we have plans." I blink up at him. We're both sitting on stools at the center island in the kitchen when Travis rolls out a velvet mat on the counter like he's about to play Texas Hold 'Em. Except, he's not placing cards, he's placing toys. And those toys aren't plastic or glass or even silicone.

"Time for dessert." Asher's cheek is next to mine as we both look at Travis's neatly placed items. A mango, two kiwis, a knife big enough to carve up a pig… but before I can see what else he plans on using, Asher distracts me with his soft lips and hungry tongue. My sandwich is forgotten as I turn fully into him and run my hands into the silky strands of his hair. We moan, my body arching toward his as he gets closer and closer. They're all in their boxers, while I'm only wrapped in a towel, hair still wet and body turning to molten lava after only a few minutes of foreplay.

"Up she goes." Cole taps the counter and seconds later I'm

lying on the cold, unforgiving surface of the marble island.

Once I'm on my back, my head turns toward Travis and Sawyer—who are at the stove doing God knows what—I notice the height of my mouth and, consequently, my pussy is perfectly aligned with their crotches. Huh, neat.

"We had it custom built. You like?" I turn to Asher, eyes wide and mouth gaping.

"You had a whole island built for the sole purpose of fucking me?" These guys are fucking nuts.

"Humility, Princess. It's also great for cooking and eating." Travis gives me the side eye but his dilated pupils and the smirk at the corner of his mouth tell a whole different story.

"Yeah, eating your pussy." I meet Sawyer's gaze and we both laugh because, of fucking course they did.

"We also had hooks installed on every side with a steel wire that runs all around." Cole grins and I prop myself up on an elbow to see that they did, in fact, have that done.

"Did you hide handcuffs all over the kitchen, too?" I'm guessing we'll be using this place a lot in the future.

"Nah, we left them in plain sight. Didn't see the need in hiding them." Sawyer shrugs, answering me with a straight face.

"Enough. I'm hungry." Travis places two white creamers behind my head and opens my towel like I'm some kind of wrapped dessert, leaving it hanging down the sides. He tweaks my already-hard nipples and pinches them enough to make me jolt, my back arching toward his touch.

"If you're a good girl, we won't tie you up or blindfold you. But you sass us, all bets are off." Travis is looking straight at me as he speaks, his hand going behind me and taking the first creamer. Keeping it high above me, he tilts it just enough for a thin line of cream, or maybe condensed milk, to overflow and coat my nipple. It's warm as it hits my skin, the consistency reminding me of their cum from earlier. With that vision in my mind, I have to grip the side of the counter to keep myself from reaching out and sinking my hands into Travis's hair as his mouth connects with my skin and his teeth bite down on my cream-covered tit. It stings, the electric sensation running throughout my entire body. He repeats this on my other nipple where Cole is right there licking and biting and sucking on the cream and my nipple.

"Delicious." I watch him as he circles my flesh with his tongue, his dark eyes fixed on only me.

Taking the knife, Travis slices both kiwis into two even parts, giving one half to each of the guys. Cole and Asher trade places and as soon as Asher is at my side, he takes his half of the kiwi and places the soft fruit on my tit, twisting and turning until the juices are running down, all around the globes of my breasts. Then his mouth is there, licking up every drop and sucking on my skin hard enough to leave marks. Travis repeats the same thing on my other tit and my head leans back as my chest rises and falls with their erotic ministrations. Above me, Cole takes his kiwi and squeezes it right above my mouth, the juices and pieces of the fruit falling onto my lips and open mouth. I chew and drink and lick my lips, seeking out more of the sweetness until my breath is taken away from me.

Legs spread wide, Sawyer is crushing his half in the palm of his hand, licking up my pussy as the kiwi's juice falls on my mound. He takes turns licking my slit and lapping up the kiwi.

I feel like a goddess being worshiped by mere mortals who need my flesh to survive. It's fucking heady and I really need a dick in me right now.

"Relax. In due time, little whore." Travis's words are almost cruel but his tone is reverent and that combination only makes me want it more.

Rising to his full height, Sawyer pushes his boxers down and, although I can't see him very well, I know he's stroking his cock right now as he looks at my cunt.

"Asher, come taste this, brother."

Asher rounds the table and dives in like a starved man, his tongue fucking me, his face rubbing against my wet pussy as his fingers dig into the flesh of my thighs. Cole and Travis hold me down as I moan and grunt with every swipe of his tongue over my clit. I'm bucking, not to push him off but to beg him to fuck me. Always deeper, always more.

Cole jumps on the counter and straddles me, his dick at my mouth, and without even thinking, I grab his shaft and bring his cock straight to my lips, swallowing him whole right down my throat. He's fucking me with quick thrusts, out and in, staying buried in my mouth a little longer each time. Tears fall from the outer corners of my eyes, sliding down my temple and landing in my hairline or ear. Saliva is pooling at the corners of my mouth every time he goes deeper. When he places one hand on my throat, applying enough pressure to make me see stars, I swallow around the head of his cock, making him grit his teeth.

"Fuck, that's so fucking good." Then he pulls out and jumps off me, replacing Asher at my pussy as he takes his fill, eating me out like I'm his own personal buffet. Sawyer jumps up on the counter next. Travis hands him the second creamer and it turns out it's not condensed milk, it's melted chocolate. Like Travis, he places it high up, except this time it's not above my tit but his cock instead. I watch, rapt, as he coats his dick with creamy deliciousness, rubbing it all over his shaft before he positions himself, just like Cole had earlier, and in slow, practiced moves, pushes his dick into my mouth. His musky scent mixed with the sweet and earthy smell of chocolate make me hungry for him. For his dick. Mixed with the fact that Cole is going to town on my cunt, I'm about to lose my fucking mind.

"Take it, Princess. Swallow me whole. Fucking take it all." I relax my throat and let him seat himself completely until my nose is tickled by the groomed patch of hairs on his groin.

"That's our little whore, sucking our cocks like a good girl." Travis croons just as he joins Sawyer on the counter and pours the condensed milk on his own cock.

They alternate fucking my face while Cole is bringing me

closer and closer to the edge of another orgasm. I'm sucking Sawyer, then Travis and my body is reacting to Cole, then Asher who pushes two fingers inside my ass, turning and scissoring and driving me fucking crazy.

"Clean them, little cock slut. Lick them nice and dry." I do as I'm told, my tongue eager to please them, my mouth hungry for them.

They both jump off and it's Asher's turn to feed me his cock while Sawyer and Travis clean their cocks at the kitchen sink. Cole is now fucking my pussy with his fingers, one, then two, then three, stretching me impossibly wider until Sawyer and Travis replace him.

"Hmm, I think she's ready, don't you?" Travis's words are dotted with dark undertones and I know he's about to give me a little pain with my pleasure.

I gasp around Asher's cock—his is flavored with mango juice—as he feeds me the sweet concoction, which tastes fantastic after the chocolate. I want to concentrate on him but I've got what feels like two heads pushing into my pussy, the burning as they demand entrance is almost too much. The pain with the pleasure of sucking Asher's cock is the perfect balance.

I gasp again when they each take a thigh and force their way in, opening my cunt wider than I ever thought possible. I heave around Asher's cock, trying really fucking hard to breathe, when Cole begins rubbing soothing circles around my nipples and clit, massaging me and giving me the pleasure I need to counterbalance the cock invasion inside my pussy.

"You look so beautiful with three dicks inside you. So fucking perfect." Cole's mouth is now on my tit, sucking and licking and lavishing it with attention.

Soon, I'm being fucked in an alternating rhythm. Asher thrusts inside my mouth just as one dick pushes in and the other pulls out, over and over again, as Cole rubs perfect little circles over my clit.

Just as Asher pulls out, I heave in a deep breath, incapable of holding my orgasm back. I come all over their dicks, my hips seeking them out, my toes curling around the edge of the counter, my hands flying above my head and knocking off all of their props, followed by a loud clanking and shattering on the kitchen floor. No one cares, though, because I'm crying out at the top of my lungs as my entire body trembles with this mind-blowing orgasm.

"Fuck, I have to pull out or else I'm going to come. Carry her to the couch and be careful not to step on the broken shards." I hear Travis speaking but it's like I'm in a tunnel, my vision barely there.

I have no idea who's carrying me as strong arms envelop me in the towel and take me to the huge three-tier couch big enough for all five of us to lie down.

"Lie down on me, Baby Doll." At this point, I'm just following orders and taking everything they're giving me. With my back to Asher's chest, I spread my thighs over his bent legs as Sawyer and Travis position themselves at my entrance once more. Below me, Asher's cock is being lubed up like a fucking champ as Travis pours half a bottle over my pussy and ass, rubbing the thickness over my puckered hole and probing it with two, then three fingers.

Slowly, Asher pushes his cock inside my ass and I help guide him, taking him in as deep as I can. The burning sensation is forgotten with Travis and Sawyer, who return to double fucking my cunt. Biting down on my lip, I close my eyes and imagine how filthy I look with three cocks fucking me. My body relaxes as the vision gets me wetter and wetter.

"Fucking Hell, I don't know what you're thinking about but it's coating our cocks like natural lube." Sawyer's voice is reverent, urging me to take them even deeper.

Once I'm relaxed and ready to go, Cole straddles my chest, his hands on either side of Asher's head, he pushes his cock into my mouth, effectively cutting off anything I might say.

With four cocks fucking me, I decide I'm the luckiest bitch in the world.

As much pleasure as I'm getting out of this, the bite of pain is what heats my body and prompts my libido into yet another orgasm.

Sawyer and Travis alternating their drives with Asher who is trying not to pop out of my ass, using only shallow thrusts in and out of me. Cole is fucking my face like it's a competition, making me gag around his girth. He brings one hand around my throat and cuts off my air, choking me with how deep he goes, always so close to my gag reflex.

"Goddammit!" Asher is the first to come. He pulses inside my ass, his head thrown back and his eyes closed, mouth slightly open as he tells me how perfect I am for him.

As he slides out of me, Sawyer and Travis accelerate their alternating plunges and fuck me like it's the last time they'll get their dicks wet. I'd cry out their names but I can't with a mouthful of cock, so I moan, hoping the vibrations will travel all through Cole's body.

I'm rewarded with Cole's cum spurting down my throat, on my tongue, over my lips and running down my chin. I lap it up as my pussy gets pummeled.

Cole kisses me softly on the lips after I've licked his cum right up and heads to the bathroom when twin roars echo throughout the new house.

Sawyer and Travis come together and their faces prompt my own orgasm. Electric bolts of lightning fire off every one of my nerve endings as both my men mark me from the inside, coming long and deep, mixed with my own juices.

My head is swimming, stars dancing at the edges of my sight, and when they both pull out, I drop back and let out a happy sigh.

If this is how the rest of my life is going to go, I'm not going to complain at all.

The End

Miss Serenity Falls already?

Make sure to join my newsletter on www.lilywildhart.com for news on when we head back with Carter & Denton.

ACKNOWLEDGMENTS

Well we're here, the end… well for now anyway. We will be back in this universe with Carter and Denton, so keep an eye out for that in my newsletter!

This series has carried me through one of the hardest times in my life, and the struggle has been reflected in the constant mindset shifts of Briar and her guys. She was my therapy book, and I'm not sure if she loves me or hates me for that… but since she's the voice in my head, well, she can just deal aha.

That said, this series wouldn't be here without a ton of amazing people. Sarah, Eva, Jenna & KC, you guys rock my socks every damn day. Thank you for being my biggest cheerleaders, for sitting with me on zoom through various meltdowns and just generally helping me cross the finish line.

Megan, Nicole, Zoe, Lisa & Keira, thank you for loving these guys and yelling at me for more every time you got a chapter. Your encouragement got this series done, and I love you for it.

To everyone in The Society - You guys do so freaking much for me, and I am eternally grateful. I'd name you all here, but PAGES of names aha!

Finally, thank you to you guys for taking a risk on a new series. It's only my second contemporary series, and I know that not everyone will pick up a new author, so there aren't words to truly express how thankful I am. But all I have is this, so thank you.

ABOUT THE AUTHOR

Lily is a writer, dreamer, fur mom and serial killer, crime documentary addict.

She loves to write dark, reverse harem romance and characters who will shatter your heart. Characters who enjoy stomping on the pieces and then laugh before putting you back together again. And she definitely doesn't enjoy readers tears. Nope. Not even a little.

If you want to keep up to date with all things Lily, including where her next book is out, please find join her newsletter at www.lilywildhart.com/subscribe.

ALSO BY LILY WILDHART

THE KNIGHTS OF ECHOES COVE

(Dark, Bully, High School Why Choose Romance)

Tormented Royal

Lost Royal

Caged Royal

Forever Royal

THE SAINTS OF SERENTIY FALLS

(Dark, Bully, Step Brother, College, Why Choose Romance)

A Burn so Deep

A Revenge so Sweet

A Taste of Forever